Winner of the BNLF 2019 Award in recognition for Community Service.

LORNAMARIE

The Lawyer's Dilemma

To the prosecutor it is murder
The Defence call it suicide
"A gripping legal thriller, Suspense. Drama. Twisty. Gasping"
Crime fiction lover

The Lawyer's Dilemma

By

LORNAMARIE

This is a work of fiction. Names, characters, places, and incidents are either the product of the author's imagination or are used fictitiously, and any resemblance to actual persons, living or dead, or to actual events or locales is entirely coincidental.

A CIP catalogue record for this book is available from the British Library.

ISBN: 978-1-71692-170-4 (Hardcover
ISBN: 978-1-71692-389-0 (Paperback)
eISBN: 978-1-71686-673-9

Praise and plaudits for *The Lawyer's Dilemma*

"Lornamarie delivered a great story and this is a brilliant page turner. Initially when I received my hard copy of The Lawyer's Dilemma, I turned to the author's note at the back of the book to read it, 'I liked her style of overviewing the story in her notes at the end of the book. She did same thing in her first thriller book The Plea on Oath. I find this book to be well researched and well written. She reminds me of Agatha Christie's novels."

— *Albert Henshaw*

"Lornamarie narrated an absorbing story with all the twists and turns that one came to expect from her. It is a moral tale of the plight of a prosecutor in dilemma between his career and family, the story lead you into the plot and it is full of surprises. I just couldn't put it down. It is the first time that I would read a sentencing remarks in a crime fiction. She brought me to tears."

— *Sabina Swanhild*

"Natural story builder with incident flowing ready to inform, too. I couldn't be more impressed; the story moves the plot along in the second half of the story. You won't be disappointed: just read it to the end."

— *Magdalen Bellecote*

"A gripping combination of courtroom drama, locked-room mystery, suspense to the end on how Steve died: I could not put it down until the end. If you like legal novels then this is certainly worth a read. Well done on another stunning achievement for Lornamarie; and I personally hope to be reading many more of her novels to come."

— *Viviane Holland*

"A classic thriller by Lorna Marie with her unique style debut touching the reader's heart on the dangers of kidnapping and abduction in some countries and it's adverse consequences on the victims of such crime.

— *Simon Odukoya*

"A legal masterpiece illustrating the injustices in some legal system and how justice can rely abortively on the location or flaw of an investigation, trial, and sentencing. Why didn't the investigators

discover CCTV footage during the first trial? Perhaps if they did, there wouldn't have been need for a retrial. I shall say no more of the plot and outcome for fear of spoiling any readers enjoyment. No one will regret time spent reading The Lawyer's Dilemma. A thought-provoking crime fiction.''

— Jordan Draper

''The author narrated many seemingly insurmountable problems, surprises and side issues along the way. I find discussing Keith's paternity in the book very interesting as talking about paternity is a sensitive or private matter, for the author to bring it into the story is a clever thing to do. The descriptions of processes are enlightening and always interesting. This book is another cleverly constructed legal thriller by Lornamarie.''

— Alice Griffin

"Rich storylines brimming, gripping, full of zest. A good and solid legal mystery and I find it informative as well on topics like drug abuse, mental health disorder, adoption, suicide and depressive disorder during criminal trial. This author thinks out of the box and very knowledgeable about what people go through, she has a lovely voice, she knows her community and the challenges faced by people generally."

— Evelyn De Lorris

"I read Lornamarie's first legal fiction thriller The Plea on Oath and I really loved it and now she's cleverly constructed The Lawyer's Dilemma, I can't wait to see more of Lorna Marie's exceptional talent evolving. I have said it before and I am saying it again.''

— Tioluwalase Adisa

Dedication

As always this book is dedicated to my husband Tayo and the boys Ibitayo and Olugbenro.

Acknowledgement and Dedication

I give glory, honour, adoration, and thanks to the almighty God, the all-knowing God, the repository of the seed of knowledge and in whom lies the mystery of wisdom, knowledge, and understanding.

As always, this book is dedicated to my husband Tayo and the boys, Ibitayo and Olugbenro.

A big thank you to my wider family, friends, readers, booksellers, libraries, and those who have spent time reviewing this book. Thank you all very much. I could not have done it without you all.

I am grateful to all the editors for their patience, support, and expert advice with dedication throughout this work and for making this fiction the best that it could be.

I dedicate ***'The Lawyer's Dilemma'*** to the commemoration of 30 years of my post call to bar as barrister and solicitor of the Supreme Court of Nigeria.

Lorna Betty Ibidun Marjorie Adekaiyaoja LL.B (Hons). BL. MCLIP. BIALL (nee Ademokun). Lorna Adekaiyaoja is the Winner of the BNLF 2019 Award in recognition for Community Service.

Acknowledgement and Dedication

[illegible]

Contents

Chapter 1

London August 11th, 2011, 13:45 Hours

‘‘Tom, come let us go out in to the street – everyone is out getting things free.’’

‘‘What do you mean they are getting things for free?’’ replied Mark.

‘‘Gary just messaged me, all the guys are out – and I mean everyone – is out on London streets, (see pictures), Gary has got himself a free Nokia phone and even free jumpers from the shops.’’

‘‘But where is he going to get that kind of money? he does not work, he's been inside for fifteen months and just come out – unless you mean he nicked it. I'm not into that kind of stuff. I need to enjoy my holiday from College and, I don't want to get into any form of trouble. I'm not coming with you.” Mark said.
Tom pulled his Blackberry phone out of his pocket the second time it vibrated. It was Gary again with a video recording the London riots. Gary was in Croydon with his mate Connor when they came off the trams at Reeves corner – they saw so many people running up and down, down and up like a yoyo. The furniture shop on the corner at Reeves had been set on fire, carbon monoxide was emitted in the air. The riot was all around London. The buses were at a standstill, there was chaos everywhere, from Tottenham to Brixton, Brixton to Croydon, no one could ever forget the London riots of 2011.
‘‘Well if you are not coming with me I'm going to join in the free take away, there is no way that I'm going to be missing out on this. Gary and Connor have got their hands full with cloths, phones, pants, kickers, canvass, designer trainers and T shirts from high street brand names. All free. Come let's join them, Mark.’’

"No I'm not coming with you, what if the cops come after yah?"
"No one is being nicked by the cops….. it's all free on the high street – you can trust me on this.'' Tom said.
"If it is free why is everyone running away then?, They are all doing something wrong – that is why they are running away like criminals'' Mark remarked.''
''I'll see you later Mark.''
''Yeah, see you later Tom, I'm staying home. My A level results will be out next week the 17th August and if I make the grades I'll be in University before you know it.''
Tom left Mark's house to go and join Gary and Connor on the High street where they met up with other youths in the August 2011 London riots.

On his way he met his mate Neil. Neil too had his hands full of things he picked up from the supermarket. He was hungry after his night shift job and as he was getting back he saw so many youths breaking the windows of various shops on the High street and helping themselves to goods and items on the shop floor, so Neil grabbed himself some sandwich – and just one diet coke from an already looted local shop on his way home.

"Neil, what is the cause of all of this riots?'' asked Tom.

''Well it all began when a guy who was arrested by the Police in North London who was accidentally gunned down and died. The youths went mad and attempted to attack the Police as they tried to restrain them from looting and violence. The chaos and riots then spread from Tottenham, down to central London and then Brixton in South West London, – it all spread very quickly, – then it got to Croydon in Surrey, Greater London and that was when Reeves Corner was set on fire during the incident.'' Neil explained to Tom.
"I'm going to look for Gary, he said he is on the bus to South Norwood from Croydon, would you like to come with me?"

"No not really I've not slept all night I've been at work, and I'm heading straight home now to rest my eyes and body in sleep."
"Ok then, I better let you go, where did you get the sandwich from?"
"One of the supermarkets left its doors open. People went in to get food so I did the same."
"You mean the shop down the road?"
"Yeah that one that is down the road."
"Ok then I'll go and grab something to eat before going to meet Gary."
"See yah."
"Yeah see yah."
Neil walked down straight home. The food that he nicked off the supermarket was enough and was going home. Tom went ahead to join Gary as the play roles in the riots along with other youths.
The London Metropolitan Police had hit the streets to bring back some peace and quiet. All roads of London were patrolled for safety, security alert was heightened, arrests were made. Footage of lootings and violence were recorded on road cameras and CCTV video cameras owned by the Local Authority. Neil, Gary and Tom were all caught on CCTV in the acts of senseless rebellion and debauchery.

It was not the first time that Tom would get into trouble, he was well known to the police for being in and out of jail cells for offences ranging from rape, theft and grievous bodily harm.

Chapter 2

After the riots, 11:45 Hours, 12th August 2011

The Police made some arrests alongside using other means to protect The High street shops from looters. There was confusion everywhere – violence, theft, arson and some other misdemeanour offences. It was the school summer holidays with lots of youth involved.
Gary and Tom were arrested for some incidences that they've been involved in…the two boys were known to Police for always getting into trouble. Gary's is a 22 year old ex-convict, a thin man with a dark complexion, hair, and eyes, and easily forgettable features. He prefers trouble to peace.

Gary, until six months ago lived in the United States of America. He's lived in Sugar Land, Texas, for most of his life. He moved to the UK six months ago, NYPD know him well too. He was always in and out of jail cell. His grand Uncle is British and they've decided to relocate him from US to UK to help him with his addiction to narcotics, he was addicted to heroin and these habits have had their toll on him.
"You do not have to say anything ...anything you do or say can be used against you in the court of law."
His hands were handcuffed along with other youths as they were arrested. Tom was caught along – side with Gary as they looted one of the high street shops. The boys were in possession of all manner of things that they had stolen from the shops on 11 August. The Police put them in the Police van after their arrest along with other people who were also arrested.
"Do you understand the caution?"
"Damn it, I have heard it so many times nothing is new."
"I need you to answer the question that you are being asked."
"Yes sir."
''I asked you if you understand the caution or would you like me to repeat what I have just said?''

''I would like a repeat.''
Inspector Kelvin repeated himself ''You have the right to remain silent. Anything you do or say can be used against you in court. You have the right to a lawyer. If you can't afford one, the state will furnish one. Any questions?''
''Can I call my half-brother?, his name is Steve. He did not come out with us cos he is in University.'' Tom asked.
''I don't have a problem with you doing that but it is time for you to go ''inside'' again young man''. Kelvin lifted him up, and pulled him upwards lowering his knees into his back. He slapped the handcuffs into place and Tom was dragged out of the door, across the pavement and thrown into the back of the Police car where he found Gary was already sitting with handcuffs on his wrists.''

The disgraceful news that Tom, Gary and Neil had been arrested after the London riots was soon to spread very quickly.

The three young adults were convicted and found guilty of theft and other offences. The defence lawyers managed to negotiate a plea bargain to get a reduced sentence. Tom, Neil and Gary pleaded guilty; their images were caught on public CCTV with the stolen items in their hands. The defence lawyers argued that the goods stolen was worth less than £200, for low-value shoplifting under s176 of the Anti-Social Behaviour, Crime and Policing Act. The Magistrate sentenced the three men to six months in prison.

Chapter 3

The Release, 13:00 Hours, 1st March 2012

Tom was released from prison and the local authorities helped with his placement into a temporary accommodation. The hostel was located in London. Gary was also placed in the same hostel accommodation. Neil returned to his fostered parent family.

Tom's heart was far from repentant, he remained fragile like a sensitive plant. He would often shrink into himself, living in the same hostel as Gary did not help. Tom was ready to make a new start. Gary was stuck to the past.
The two young men met in the hostel lounge where there were comfortable sofas, a plasma tv, stereo and table tennis for anyone who would like to play. The room adjacent to the lounge is an office where the residential housing support team stayed. They helped the residents with various needs like going back to education, employment, vocational training and travel trips to the countryside and was organised by the chaplaincy for the residents. Several rooms were located on all the floors of the nine story building. There was a professional kitchen on the ground floor with breakfast, lunch and dinner served to the residents. A social worker manager lived on site to deal with emergency queries.
''Good morning young man…how are you today?'' asked Fredrick.
''Good morning…Fredrick.'' replied Tom, his greeting was a nod and a blink, almost befitting someone who'd stepped out of the shadows.
''What are your plans for today?''

''I am planning to complete some training application forms online.''
''That is wonderful, what training do you have in mind?''

''Maybe training to become a mechanic or work as an apprentice in a factory or something like that.''
''All you have to do is to work on your mind set and that is what you are doing right now'' he remarked. ''I was looking at your record, you mentioned something about having a half-brother somewhere is that correct?''
''Yes his name is Steve – that much I know, I tried calling him when I was about to be arrested but he did not answer his phone or reply to my call.''
''Why would he do that to you?''
''Well we really don't know one another very well, I stumbled upon him one year ago.''
''How do you mean?''
''I was involved in a motor car accident when I went out with Neil, we were out in London when the accident occurred; and the car rolled on to its side when one of the tyres burst at full speed – I was lucky to be alive. All I could remember was that I woke up in St Thomas Hospital in London with a man by my side. He introduced himself to me as Steve. He said his fiancée was admitted into the same hospital at the time. He saw the medical team discussing the man on the stretcher – me – who had no family to sign a document on his behalf as it was an emergency. That was when he asked for my name and he was told my name was Tom Blackstone. He stepped in as if he was the only family that I had. When my medical records were retrieved from the central National Health Service (NHS) system he discovered Blackstone was my adopted name and that Bradford was my biological parent's surname. He became curious because his grand mum had told him that he had a half-brother whose name was Tom. To cut the long story short fate brought us together to meet. We are brothers born by the same mother. He grew up in America but came to study in England. He is a qualified chartered accountant.''

''It would be good for you to reconnect with him.''
''I am not sure if he would like to have anything to do with a low life like me.''
''Why do you say that?''

''Well when the Police were about to nick me after the London riots, I called his number and he never picked it up.''
''And have you tried to call him since then?''
''No, not really.''
''Give him a call, you never know. Family is important.''
''Yeah I know, but like I said, fate brought us to meet – we really did not grow up together.''
''Try to give him a call.''
''Yeah I suppose I should.''

Chapter 4

The Re-union, 19:00 Hours, 30th March 2015

For some reason I could sum up the courage to contact Steve, I guess I was not sure whether I am ready to be ignored again, so I decided not to call him again. After my release from prison, I saw a missed call from a number that I was not familiar with, and I did not pick up my phone. My instinct told me that it could have been Steve, but I ignored it all.
I was lucky to get an apprentice training at a local factory where some goods were manufactured. Gary was involved in another incident that got him into yet more trouble with the Police but he was not jailed this time. I tried to avoid him as much as I could. I think Steve too must be wondering where I was and maybe he was in a better frame of mind to get in touch with me. I don't know. But my phone rang on a weekend and the number was not a familiar one, but I picked my phone up and it was Steve. Tom thought.

''Hi Tom…is that Tom?'' Steve asked.
''Yeah this is me, sorry I don't recognise this number…''
''Yeah I changed my number long time ago.''
''Really?''
''Yeah, how have you been?''
''I'm ok...yeah I tried to call around September last year but you did not pick up your phone. I thought you did not want to have anything to do with me.''
''No – why would I do such a thing?''
''What are you doing at 7pm next weekend?, we should go out for a drink or two?''
''That would be great.''
''Where would you like us to go to?''
''Is West End ok?''
''Yeah sounds good to me.''
Steve likes the traditional pubs in the city, he had one particular pub in mind, they have basic menu and sport on TV,

plus a large beer garden and a kid's play area. The glitz and glamour to explore the dark side of London's most popular relaxing destination. It was bubbling, exuberant, expensive and an exhilarating area. After all, anyone who knows London tends to think of the West End as a pleasure ground for the masses. The colossal shops of Oxford Street and Regent Street. The glitzy restaurants of Soho and Covent Garden. The tourist magnet that is Leicester Square. And, of course, the gorgeous theatres of St Martin's Lane and Shaftesbury Avenue. Can we say it is a place teeming with criminals? Like any other city in the world there is corruption, injustice, violence and inequality of urban life to make it a fearful place. Steve put all the difficult questions behind him. He can't be bothered. All he's really looking forward to is to meet his half-brother again and he is hoping that Tom will make the journey down to London from Croydon.

Tom arrived in time at West End. Steve was already at the station waiting for him. They hugged each other.

"How are we going to settle the bills cause you know I only do apprenticeship in a factory, I can't even afford to get here by train. I am five years older than you and I am the one begging here."
"Of course you are not begging, I asked that we hang out. I will foot the bill."
"Oh thanks…I have been worrying about that while in the train." he said with a grin on his face.
"Come let's go in and sit down, what would you like to drink or eat?"
"Anything…"
They went close to the bar to order their drinks. Both men ordered Gin and Tonics one after the other, they then went to the far corner where they sat down relaxing.
"What happened on the night that you were trying to get hold of me?"

''Forget that now it is past and long gone. Nothing to worry about. I was with the wrong guys and we got nicked for the London riots.''
''Was that last year?''
''Yeah.''
''Oh gosh.''
''Yeah.''
''Sorry to hear that.''
''There is nothing you could have done anyway even if I spoke to you on the phone.''
''Yeah but at least I could have come to visit you in detention or something?''
''Never mind that is long gone now.''
''You said you had something to tell me about our grand-parents.''
''Grandad died in Pennsylvania and I had to travel for the funeral, you remember when you recovered from the hospital, we travelled to see Matthew and Phoebe.''
''Yeah, they could hardly recognise me. It was interesting that they still have my pictures with mum when I was a baby. You are very lucky to have them bring you up after mum died.''
''You can say that again.''
''I have been meaning to ask you; did you ever see mum after you were adopted?''
''No. Life has been cruel to me, when dad walked out on mum, she was vulnerable and the social services took me into care. I have been in social care all my life until you found me in that ghastly motor accident.''

''Your survival is a miracle and how we met remains a mystery to me as well.''
They soon finished their drinks and went to the bar for another two glasses of gin and tonic. Tom said he was hungry so they ordered some chips and Lasagne served with salad. When they finished their meal, Steve ordered another glass of gin and tonic for two.

Before parting Steve promised Tom that he will help with financing his training to become a mechanic. He gave him some money to buy stuff that he needed. Tom wept as they hugged one another before they walked to the train station.
''Listen bruv, thank you for all that you have spent tonight I really appreciate it from the bottom of my heart. I am happy that you are doing well after your University training. I really wish you well. I should be the one looking after you and looking out for you.''

''No, don't say that. I may be doing that today. Who knows what tomorrow holds? Just let us appreciate the moment we have to be there for one another and to be together. We cannot do anything about the past, but we certainly can make the future better.''

''Yeah…yeah…you are right in saying that ... I appreciate you bro, just keep on doing what you do best is all I can say.''
''Let us make sure we always keep in touch.''
''Yeah we should'' And they waived before getting on different train platforms.

Chapter 5

April 2015

My mother died when I was only two years old. I cannot remember my dad walking away from his marriage. I was too young to remember when the local authority social service took me away from my mum. I was also too young to remember my arrival at the home of my first foster carers.
At the age of thirteen years of age I had moved around to five separate carers. I met Gary in one of the hostels that I lived in. At the age of ten years old I was out on the street to shoplift and I was prosecuted in the juvenile court. I was known by the youth offending teams and probation officers.
I was told that my mother was a heroin addict when she was alive. Her licence to practice as a nurse was taken away from her due to her addiction to drugs. I grew up to become emotionally unstable like my mother was. I was not fortunate to see my mum suffer the consequences of addiction, perhaps that would have deterred me from most of the problems that I got myself into at an early age. My biological father was nowhere to be found. I watched various role models picking up their bad habits along the way as I had to live with different types of families. So my knowledge of drugs at that age was pretty poor. I knew you shouldn't do them, in the way that you shouldn't really smoke, if you want to take care of yourself. I have heard that if you took too much of heroin that it could kill you, but I had no idea that dope, coke, acid, ecstasy, and speed – glue even – were all potential killers as well. It was not uncommon for me to see pimps and prostitutes take drugs, as did gangsters and low-lifes.
Gary introduced me to cocaine. We were out together in the evenings, we went out to Brixton, I saw how people did drugs in fancy night clubs, on council estates because there was nothing else to do. The family I lived with had family friends who visited us, they smoked marijuana. Gary had seen people use cocaine, he as a kid had experimented with smoking

marijuana, he was into dope sometimes at parties, I only feel comfortable joining in drinking if there were no adults around, some of our street friends would have a drink.
But everything changed in an instant the night that I took my first line of cocaine. I was out for the evening with Gary at a pub in Croydon. I did not tell my foster parents where I was going but I guess they thought it was fine because I was with Gary. We would be meeting up with another friend Neil, who was then twenty and working in the City. My parents knew that I would be OK. I was always looking older than my age, so there were no problems getting in. We had been to local bars in Wimbledon before and my age had never been an issue with the door men. I didn't set out that night planning to take drugs. I don't think anyone does the first time they do them. I still don't know how I got myself into my first proper sniff. The whole idea of taking cocaine was completely alien to me. I just wanted to go out and have a fun time with my friends. To dance with the girls, have few drinks. But it did not turn out that way. Neil and his girlfriend worked in the City. He was tall and dark with piercing chocolate brown eyes. To me he was a role model. Someone you could look up to and copy – Neil placed in front of his girlfriend a paper wrap on a nearby table, and carefully opened it up. It was filled with a fine white powder.
''Do you want one?'' As he lifted his shoulder in a half shrug, his words were more of a statement than a question – as if what he was doing was a thing of fashion that we were being invited to join him in doing. Gary and I did not hesitate to join in. I had seen cocaine before on television, I kind of knew what the substance was in the package that Neil was holding. I always assumed that it was a drug that the big guys in the City Rich and famous people took, not Gary and I from down town Brixton and Croydon. Neil would not mislead us, I thought, he was someone that we looked up to. He works in the City so I thought it best not to make a fuss. Gary and I did not want to lose face with Neil. We wanted him to continue to like us enough to take us out. He cannot harm us. He and his

girlfriend are doing it and it looks fashionable and fine to me, or so I thought.
"Yeah, I'll have one." I inclined my head. Neil gave Gary and I two paper wraps, we opened it up in our hands while he emptied a small amount of the powder on to the surface. He then brought out from his wallet a card, and spread the powder around the plastic surface before cutting it into two lines about three centimetres long and a millimetre thick. Neil and his girlfriend sniffed and took their first line first. He brought out a £10 note from his wallet and he rolled it up, talking to us as he did so. Gary and I watched Neil as he raised his left hand to his face, pressed a finger against his left nostril and snorted the cocaine up his right one through the bank note. Neil inhaled deeply, and as he finished he put his head back and breathed in and then out, as if to get the full thrust of the hit. Gary and I did the same. It was my first time. As I snorted the cocaine my nostril tingled slightly. My face glistened with sweat as I rolled my eyes, I felt a horribly bitter sensation, the taste slide down the back of my throat. Being my first time I felt it was choking me and it was disgusting. After few minutes of taking the drug I began to feel its effect on me. The drug took hold of my body, it was like I was on top of the world with a feeling of exhilarating experience I had ever had. I experienced right there and then a surge of a bursting energy. I felt high and I liked the way I felt. I liked it a lot.

Gary was on the same level as Neil and his girlfriend. It obviously is not their own first time taking cocaine. It was me that got initiated into drug life. An experience that was going to shape my life forever. After about thirty minutes I was flying all over the place, going up and down like a yoyo. It was a case of a dead person that now became alive. I felt I could do anything and became courageous all of a sudden.
"Come let us go into the pub to get some drinks," Neil said with a smile tugging at his lips. My face was lit up as if to say I was ready for anything.
"What will you have?" he said with a beam.

"I'll have vodka and lemonade," I replied with a smile tugging at my lips.
"Same," Gary said without hesitation with his mouth curved into a smile.
I did not like alcohol but don't know where the courage to request for it had come from. I love my sweet drinks, but I just wanted to fit into this social life in front of me. I have never liked the smell of alcohol either, but after that night out with Neil, his girlfriend and Gary, I became a drug addict. The lemonade inside my vodka help to disguise the taste of vodka to help me cope with the bitterness. Gary and I asked for another glass of drinks when we finished our first. We were offered cigarettes - Marlborough and Benson and Hedges from the pub's vending machine.

As we smoked and chatted the music came on and I couldn't stop dancing. I felt so wonderful and on top of the world, adrenaline pumped through my body. I felt cocaine is not as bad as they say it is, it made me feel good, I thought. I had another glass of vodka but this time with orange. The cocaine had counteracted the effects of the alcohol so I did not feel drunk as such. I smoked one fag after another. It all made me feel great. I have just had one of the best nights of my life with excitement and fun with Gary and Neil. With my first attempt at the Class A drug cocaine, my life was changed forever. A cab dropped me at my foster parent's place before it proceeded in taking Gary home too. When I got home, I went straight to bed and as soon as my head hit my pillow I fell asleep, and when I woke up in the morning I felt ok. I just could not see anything wrong with the Class A drug cocaine that I had just taken. Last night was great and I would do it again if the chance came my way. I thought. I soon became a regular. I accepted any offer of a line without hesitation when Gary and I went out to private parties, it became more regular for someone to offer me cocaine and I would accept it.

I got a job in a chemist and loved it very much. I learned new things. Each time I snorted cocaine I feel am able to do more

and more work. It didn't do me any harm the first time I took it. I was not sick. I felt better about myself and there was this high feeling with esteem that made me feel really good.
Once I began to earn money from my chemist job, I was able to afford to purchase cocaine on a night out or just when I crave for it. A gram of coke cost as much as £60 or even more. With my salary I could now buy all the cocaine I wanted.

Chapter 6

December 2015, 14:35 Hours

It is now eight months since my first snorting of cocaine. I could not stop myself. My addiction had now reached the point where it had become an actual physical sickness and by that I mean I felt ill without it. I needed to snort not only for a great time or to get a kick. I could not do anything without me feeling shaky, nervous and lacking in energy. I used it to keep me alive at this point. I believe that I needed it to survive. I could not function without it, or so I thought. I now admit that I have a problem.

I was adopted by a lovely family. My 'new' parents did all they could for me to get rehabilitated. I was registered for counselling and guidance sessions with experts. I attended meetings organised for other people struggling and battling with drug use. My parents James and Rebecca Blackstone helped me through the difficult process of trying to quit my addiction. I suffered from incessant depression, low self-esteem, self-harm, anxiety, panic attacks. I walked the path of a dark and lonely place. All of these conditions were because of my addiction to cocaine.
It was a miracle that I was able to keep my job at the chemist. My employers knew that I had issues with drug use. My colleagues were understanding whenever I was at work, my lunch time breaks, tea breaks would take longer than expected. I literally became dependent to snorting. I became a slave to heroine.

And even though my biological parents parted ways through divorce when I was only eighteen months old, not knowing both of them personally was also an underlying problem that I have had to deal with in my life. James and Rebecca played a good role in getting me into rehabilitation at the Priory Hospital in Roehampton here in the United Kingdom, a leading centre for the treatment of a range of conditions. I was allocated a specialist psychotherapist for my addiction to drug abuse, as well a depression, anxiety, stress and self-harm. I was admitted into rehab the second time in two years. Three years before now I had been admitted into Nightingale Hospital to help treat my mental health disorder. I was in the hospital undergoing a treatment programme that lasted 30 days and I really wanted it to work for me.

The breakdown in the marriage of my biological parents had its effect on me psychologically, if my mother was alive she would not deny the fact that my addiction to cocaine had anything to do with her divorce to my father, who is currently is nowhere to be found. I suffered the consequences of my parents' divorce. My addiction and behaviour was a constant source of worry and concern for my adoptive parents James and Rebecca and though they treated me as their own child they dealt with my problem in very different ways. They were united in their shared sense of hurt, disappointment, shame and fear. Personally, I had no one to blame for my problems but myself, my adoptive parents did not see it that way, I guess it is quite natural for parents to lay the blame on themselves when the children in their care go off the rails, and I know that there were times when my mother and father visited me in the rehab and thought: 'where did we go wrong or what have we done wrong?,' I simply cannot fathom why they would feel so, they had only provided me with a home to live in and in any case there is only so much you can do as a parent to protect your kids from other bad kids they would have to meet in the world that they live in. There is peer pressure that parents do not have control over. But James and Rebecca just couldn't help blaming themselves. I brought my personal problems into the home of the very hands that fed me. I forced them to live on the edge. I caused them countless sleepless nights. I created tension in their marriage. I don't believe that the tension I caused was in their marriage before they took me into their home. It got to an extent that my parents would lie awake in bed waiting for that call to say that I was in trouble, trouble became my second name, they ever feared that the police may call them to tell them that I was dead. It was that bad. They only know peace when I was in the hospital, at least I am in the hands of experts. They showered me with love, I bore their surname ''Blackstone'' which was obviously different from my biological father's name. Tom thought.

At 15:45 hours the doorbell rang. My dad went to the door and it was the Police at the door.
''Good afternoon officer.'' with a line etched between his brows as he wondered why the police could be knocking at his door.
''Good afternoon sir, we are here to see one Tommy or Tom Blackstone'' as his forehead creased.
''Sorry, what has he done this time?''
''My name is Inspector Kelvin Armstrong, I understand that he was the last person to see a young gentleman who is now deceased, he was a middle aged man and they were last seen together having drink in a pub in London. Can I please come in to ask few questions if he is in the house please?'' he then sneered as he brought out his ID badge to show James.
''Yes he is at home, please come in.'' James replied.
The Inspector was led into the living room where he sat down. James went into the bedroom to call out Tom.
''Inspector Kelvin Armstrong is here looking for you, what have you done this time Tom?''
''Me, nothing, I have done nothing. I have not been out lately''
''I thought so too.''
As Tom entered the living room the Inspector stood up to his feet to give him a handshake before asking him to sit down for some questions.
''Good afternoon Tom I wonder if you could help us to resolve a mystery, my name is Inspector Kelvin Armstrong?''
''Good afternoon sir, how can I help you?''
''Do you know a gentleman named Steve Claxton?''
His eyes glanced up at the ceiling as he replied. ''Yeah I know Steve Claxton''

''What do you know about him on the night of 30th March 2015 at 19:00 Hours.''

''We went out to London – we had not seen each other in a long time so he came down to pick me up from the hostel and we went out to have some fun.''

''How long ago did you last see Steve?''

''About two to three years before we met again in March 2015.''

''So would you say that you were happy to see one another?''

''Yes we were happy to see each other again, he bought the drinks we had on that night.''

''Did you see him feel unwell after you both had drinks on that night?'' asked Inspector Kelvin Armstrong.

''No, nothing like that, we also had some chips and Lasagne to eat on that night and we were both fine. Please tell me that Steve is ok, what's happened?''

''We are investigating the cause of the death of Mr Steve Claxton, so any information on what happened on the night he died will be helpful to us Mr Tom Blackstone?''

''The cause of Steve Claxton's death?! Surely you must be joking – is he dead?!''

''We wouldn't make something like this up, Mr Tom,'' the inspector sighed. Steve Claxton slummed inside the train that he boarded at the station''

''Oh my God!'' I shouted as my eyes flooded with tears and glistened.

''That is why I am here to see if there is anything you can do to help us about what you know about on the night that Steve was with you, Mr Tom Blackstone.''

''I am in shocked that Steve has died. What then could have killed him?''

''We do not know at this stage, a thorough investigation is going on about what actually killed him and the coroner is involved too. Do you know whether anyone else was with the two of you on the night, or whether he left the pub with anyone else before he boarded his train?''

''No. I did not see anyone with him as he boarded the train, I only waved good bye and we parted.''

''Well thank you Mr Tom Blackstone for the information that you have given me this afternoon. If we have any cause to ask you further questions, then we would return to invite you to the station for further questioning.''
James' eyes shot sparks as he looked at the Inspector Kelvin Armstrong.
''What would you like us to do now?''
''Absolutely nothing at this stage, please there is nothing for you to worry about. We are only making preliminary investigation and the main reason why we've come to see Tom is because he was one of the people that Steve Claxton met on the day that he died. So he is a viable witness to give us information on Steve when he was still alive. Obviously Steve is now dead and it is difficult for him to give an account of what had happened to him. But as many people as we are able to gather useful information from is important to us at this stage.''
''Ok. Inspector Kelvin Armstrong.''
''Yes like I said, we will be back if we need further information. But there is nothing for you to worry about at this point.'' he said as he walked towards the front door where he came through into the house.
After the Inspector had walked out of the house, James again asked me some questions about what was going on.
''Are you very sure that you know nothing about what this Inspector Police officer is asking questions about concerning the death of Steve?''
''I swear, I know nothing about what he is talking about, I am in shock and I hope they get to the bottom of it.''
''Ok. I take your word for it.''
''You can trust me on this, dad – even if you have never trusted me on anything else. Yes I am a drug addict and I have issues that I am dealing with, I won't kill an insect, I am petrified of spiders and I can't stand looking at someone bleeding let alone kill anyone.''
''I take your word for it again, we'll leave it there.''

Chapter 7

1st January 1990

Steve's mother went into labour at 11:45, fifteen minutes before midnight; her labour began in the early hours of New Year's Eve. Teresa was a single mother who had divorced four years ago and so when she met Steve's dad at the local pub she felt it was time to let go of the past and start afresh. She'd too much to drink on the night she met Brian Claxton, it was a fling that got her pregnant with Steve. Brian was never ready for a serious relationship, besides – Teresa was seriously battling with a drug addiction. As at two days before giving birth to Steve she attended a meeting of Alcoholics or Narcotics Anonymous in Arizona. During the second half of her pregnancy she spent twelve days at Cottonwood. Brian dropped her there because there was nothing anyone could do anymore for Teresa, it was obvious that her addiction was the demon in her life.

On the night she arrived at Cottonwood, she woke up in the middle of the night at 'bout four or five in the morning. She was feeling very hot and she couldn't breathe, she was heavily pregnant, she couldn't breathe. She got out of bed and went outside onto the veranda and lit a cigarette. She had smoked throughout the pregnancy. She liked the peace and serenity that surrounds her in Arizona. She would sit down in the dark and watched the Phoenix Lights which was one of her favourite things to do there. Every now and again she would listen to the sound of the coyotes, gaze, and at the stars, and watch the colour of the sky change from deep black to golden blue. For the past four years she'd never seen the dawn like this. All she did was take drugs. Teresa found herself in the middle of something really beautiful with the Phoenix Lights. The peace, it was spectacular. She loved seeing the noon sun burning brightly and also illuminating her light, goldish red hair.

"I think it is too late bringing me here Brian, I am an addict, and I will be till the day I die."

"You cannot give up on yourself Teresa." he said focussing his eyes on her with his cocky Northeast accent somewhat tempered with sometime in the South.

"Why do you say that?" she asked with her hands thrust deep into the pockets of faded, starched, well-fitting jeans. The noon sun was burning brightly and blinded her as she looked up in Brian's direction.

"The whole idea of bringing you to Arizona is to save you and the baby, so that you can get well, There are people here to look after you: the nurses, the psychiatrist and the nutritionist, they will see to your wellbeing. There is also a team of counsellors on hand round the clock to talk to the patients."

"Yes I know that even if it was three in the morning, there would be someone here to talk to."

"That is great!" He replied with closed eyes and a deep touch of concern edged through his icy words that made her feel better hearing his warm voice.

Brian left Teresa and went back home. Matthew and Phoebe were Teresa's parents who lived in Pennsylvania and were excited that their daughter was about to give birth to their second grand-child. They travelled down to LA were they were supposed to be meeting their flight to Arizona to visit Teresa at Cottonwood.
The ambulance was called by the nurses when Teresa went into labour at 11:45 on New Year's Eve, she was taken to the maternity hospital and there she was taken into the labour room where she laboured for over 16 hours. Teresa had planned to have a natural birth but the baby finished up in the breech position, so in the end at 14:50 hours on New Year's

Day Steve was birthed by an emergency caesarean. Teresa had been told by the Doctors that the baby would be fine even though breech, but it still preyed on her mind that all hadn't been well with her during the pregnancy; there might be something wrong with her baby given that she was four months pregnant when she overdosed. Despite all the odds the baby boy came out miraculously not been affected by Teresa's drug abuse and when he was delivered he came out crying like a little fighter, weighing in at a very respectable 6Ib 14oz.

Mathew, Phoebe and Brian were all at the hospital and were sitting outside in the waiting area: A six foot tall medical doctor with stethoscope around his neck came out to see Teresa's family in the waiting area. Usually if all was well it is the midwife that came out to share the good news that mum and baby are well, but this was different. The Surgeon came out to see the family.

''Congratulations Brian, Mathew and Phoebe. Teresa gave birth to a bouncing baby. The baby is well, but I am afraid I have to …''

''Afraid?, of what?'' Phoebe said nervously.

''Let the Doctor talk please Phoebe...'' Mathew said putting on a brave face.

''We did all that we possibly could but we lost Teresa. She did not make it, I am sorry. She did not come around. We did all we could medically but it was not meant to be.''
Phoebe broke down in tears, she sobbed like a child, she cried bitterly for her lost daughter.
''Ahh but Teresa cannot be dead. No…!. She can't go anywhere!. Can someone tell me that this can't be true? Oh my God, why is this happening to us Mathew?'' Phoebe broke down and sobbed bitterly.

''Just like that!'' Brian said looking at Mathew for an affirmation so to say.
''This is a kind of joke or movie on television, how can life be this transient, I need someone to tell me.''

With his soft Southern accent Dr Luke Smith announced:
''Well a full autopsy is going to be carried out on Teresa's corpse and a report is going to be given on the circumstance surrounding her death. You will need to let them know at Cottonwood, that she will not be coming back.'' Obviously sensing their confusion. Dr Smith elaborated what steps needed to be taken next, since Teresa's parents were in a state of confusion and sadness.'' He had practiced medicine for 15 years originally from New York, and was long in the tooth but good at his job. He was Six foot tall with short brown hair and of medium build.

Phoebe took her second grandson home to Pennsylvania later that afternoon of 2nd January. Mathew gave her all the support that he could. The couple were in their mid-sixties when they lost their only daughter and only child Teresa. Teresa had a son in her first marriage, his name was Tom. Tom was taken into care by Social services due to Teresa's drug addiction after her first marriage to Keith Bradford broke down at the time. She was not able to look after Tom. Tom was fostered by a family in the United Kingdom. Mathew and Phoebe up until Teresa's demise were not told the details of Tom's whereabouts only the Local authority social services knew the details of Tom's whereabouts, and who his foster parents were. After living with several foster carers, Tom was finally adopted by an English family, it was at this point that his surname was changed from Bradford to another name.

Chapter 8

11th September 2001, 13:00 Hours

It is going to be eleven years in December since the loss of my daughter Teresa. Mathew and I have nurtured Steve Claxton since the 2nd January 1990 after the demise of his mother at child birth. It was the right thing for us to do. We are now both in our seventies. We decided to look for Brian to get him to start playing a father role to Steve. We heard that he had remarried and settled down with a wife and three children. He had not been in touch with us since Teresa's passing.

''Do you think it is wise for us to look for Brian Claxton?''

''Yes I do think it is the right thing to do.'' replied Phoebe.

''If he wanted to have anything to do with his son why has he not been in touch with us?, He just eloped after the mother of his son died, and I can imagine he will live with the guilt for the rest of his life.''

''Well Steve needs to know who his biological father is.''

''And what happens after that?''

''After what?''

''After, … he knows his biological dad, – what difference is that going to make in his life.''

''A boy need to settle that score in his head I am afraid, Besides we are not getting any younger.''

''So suddenly we are looking for Brian to take over from where we stop or what?''

''No. I am not saying anything is going to happen to us but we need to let the boy know that he is not an orphan don't you think so?''

''Yeah now that he is just starting high school there will be a lot of questions going through his mind…I think we should try and reach Brian.'' Phoebe replied.

''The last time he contacted us was when he came for a conference on behalf of the accounting firm that he was working for at the time, He came all the way from New York to Pennsylvania to see us. Steve was only five years going to six years at the time. I am not sure whether he can remember Brian being introduced to him as his Dad.''

''Did you not scribble his number somewhere in your diary?''

''Yes I actually did.'' Mathew remarked. ''I have to go and look for my old diary then''

''What is on the news?'' Phoebe switched on the television and as soon as she did all hell had broken loose as the breaking news of the World Trade Centre tragedy on September 11 reaching the news desk and studios and was being announced as it unfolded.

''What is going on?'' Matthew exclaimed.

''I really don't know Mathew, is this all happening in reality or is Hollywood at it again?'' Phoebe was anxious and fretful at the news headlines: It felt like a movie was on the TV, seeing air planes lowered, launching into the World Trade Centre complex, including the 47 story 7 World Trade Centre tower as well as significant damage to ten other large surrounding structures.

It was a day of sorrow as the country witnessed a series of attacks that shook the world with a wakeup call on the wickedness of the wicked. The 9/11 disaster witnessed a series of four coordinated terrorist attacks by the Islamic terrorist group against the United States.

The astonishment was beyond what any human mind could comprehend: Mathew and Phoebe were both pensioners who woke up on that morning to the most horrific news that they have ever listened to on the American news. It was a Tuesday morning and four passenger airliners operated by two major U.S. passenger air carriers (United Airlines and American Airlines)—all of which departed from airports in the north eastern part of the United States bound for California—were hijacked by 19 al-Qaeda terrorists. Two of the planes, American Airlines Flight 11 and United Airlines Flight 175, were crashed into the North and South towers, respectively, and the World Trade Centre complex in Lower Manhattan. Within an hour and 42 minutes, both 110-story towers collapsed. Debris and the resulting fires caused a partial or complete collapse of all other buildings in the World Trade Centre complex, A third plane, American Airlines Flight 77, was crashed into the Pentagon (the headquarters of the U.S. Department of Defence) in Arlington County, Virginia, which led to a partial collapse of the building's west side. The fourth plane, United Airlines Flight 93, was initially flown toward Washington, D.C., but crashed into a field in Stonycreek Township near Shanksville, Pennsylvania, after its passengers thwarted the hijackers. 9/11 is the single deadliest terrorist attack in human history and the single deadliest incident for firefighters and law enforcement officers in the history of the United States, with 343 and 72 killed, respectively.

The attacks killed 2,996 people, injured over 6,000 others, and caused at least $10 billion in infrastructure and property damage. Additional people died of 9/11-related cancer and respiratory diseases in the months and years following the attacks.

There was a repeat of the incident over and over again throughout the day until Mathew and Phoebe got sick and nauseated listening to the news.
Phoebe had enough of seeing humans flying out of their office windows out of the tower buildings, they were jumping into further complications. It was hell that broke loose on that day. This single incident changed the world forever.

Chapter 9

Wednesday 12 September 2001, 11:45 Hours

I remembered that Brian always spoke about someone he knew at Cottonwood in Arizona. That was when he referred the late Teresa to meet someone he knew who worked there at the time. It was clear that Teresa needed rehabilitation. He did say that the lady was his cousin. She helped him to see to it that Teresa was in good hands and well looked after at the rehab.

''Mathew can you remember the name of the lady that Brian said was his cousin at Arizona?''

''That was almost eleven years ago, do you think she will still be working there?''

''Well you never know, perhaps someone there may know where she's moved on to if she no longer works there.''

''You are right, should we give Cottonwood a phone call to make enquiries first before going there, that is if she still works there.''

''Good idea – I will give them a call tomorrow.'' Mathew promised.

When Matthew and I called Cottonwood we were told that the lady's name is Patricia and she still worked there. We felt a huge relief hearing that there was someone who could tell us about Brian whom we had not seen for six odd years. Patricia was his cousin and that makes it even easier for us to think that she would know Brian's whereabouts.

The outcome of our conversation with Patricia revealed that she would need to see us face to face to tell us about Brian.

That was not a good sign for Matthew and me because if it was good news why would she just not spill the beans, why would she want to see us to break good news. Something must be amiss. I thought.

My husband and I then arranged to travel to Arizona to see Patricia before the end of the week. Steve was scheduled to commence his high school in September and we thought it would be a good idea for him to meet his dad again to settle the score. A second chance opportunity for him to bond with his biological father. We are his grand-parents and even though we have tried our best to bring him up to this stage, we were not getting any younger in doing so to the best of our abilities.

We arrived at Cottonwood nice and early in the morning. Patricia was already waiting for us in her office. She is a professional Psychiatrist and she's worked in Cottonwood for over fifteen years.

We sat down in the reception area just by the foyer that led to Patricia's office. Her administrator led us into Patricia's office. Her office was big and behind her table was a heavy duty, rotating executive chair. I studied her very closely, not having seen her in a long time. Her navy blue well ironed professionally fashioned long sleeve shirt was neat and nicely pressed. Her thick, curly wavy long hair fell perfectly on her shoulders.

''Good morning, Mathew and Phoebe. I have not seen you for such a long time. I guess eleven years ago when we had your late daughter stay with us here in Cottonwood for recovery. I am once again sorry that she did not make it through childbirth.''. She held our hands firmly, mine first then my husband's.

''Thank you for having us Patricia,'' I replied.

''Nice to see you again. What can I do for you?''
''We are looking for Brian your cousin, as you know he is Steve's dad. Steve was the child Teresa had through caesarean operation at birth before she died. The last time we saw Brian was when he came for a conference in Pennsylvania. He popped round to see Steve, but we have not seen him since then.''

''Oh what a shame. Do you know where Brian works?''

''Well the last time we saw him he said he worked in New York, he gave us his phone number. We tried the phone and he was not picking up our calls. That makes me wonder what is going on.''

'' I am sorry to be the bearer of bad news to both of you Phoebe and Mathew. I know this would come to you both as a surprise, more so as you have not seen or heard from Brian in such a long time. The tragic incident that occurred few days ago has changed all our lives forever, as I speak to you we think Brian is one of the victims of the 9/11. Deceased worked in one of the buildings at the World Trade Centre complex in Lower Manhattan. I would like to think that he would be one of the survivors, our family had not given up hope on his survival or whether he could still be found alive in the rubble or debris, we are hoping to see him again alive. But as I speak to you, the last time his wife saw him was when he left home for work on the morning of that 9/11. I am sorry to let you know that when he left home on Tuesday he went to his work place on that fateful day and his office is on one of the tower blocks I'm afraid.''

''Oh my God! What did, Do you mean we left coming here to find Brian too late?''

''I am sorry, the incident that occurred on that Tuesday morning is bound to touch all our lives in one way or the other. The security officials are all still counting the number of casualties with hope to save more lives, but who knows. It is sad and painful. Isn't it just?''

''Oh dear! What are we going to tell Steve about his dad, the dad that we were hoping that he would meet soon?''

''Well you may have to wait for him to grow a little older before spilling the beans I'm afraid. He is too young to understand what happened to his dad at the tender age of eleven.''

''You are right, it is a shame that this visit has turned out to be what it is. If only we'd arranged a visit earlier perhaps things would not have turned out this way.'' Matthew explained looking stuffy after the news.

''But you cannot blame what has happened on yourself; what will be will be, what is going to be is going to be no matter what.''
''Brian was a clean – cut family man, he was a workaholic, devout Presbyterian, he was an occasional drinker, and smoked cheap cigars to fit into social life. He met Teresa at the pub on one of his nights out and they developed their relationship from there when he found out that she got pregnant with his child. He truly really tried to help Teresa with her drug addiction. He was a well-paid accountant and I could remember him paying the cost of Teresa's staying at Cottonwood. He paid £3,000 a week as this kind of treatment that we give here does not come cheap. He was all out to help her recover from drug addiction. She agreed to come here, she was determined to fight her demon, and were glad to be able to meet her at the point of her need. Many people who come into rehab make the mistake of thinking that after a five-week boot camp in Arizona they will be cured from their addiction for good, but it doesn't really work like that. We often make it clear to people who come here that there is no miracle cure for addiction, it is a daily, ongoing battle. It is possible to live without drugs and to have another life.'' Patricia explained.

Brian was kind to Teresa and her death came as a shock to him and to everyone. I am not sure whether he would have married her with her baggage of problems of addiction at the time he met her. But one thing was clear. He was determined to help her get through her addiction. May their souls rest in peace. I prayed.

Chapter 10

August 2007, Through Teenage Years

Steve was aged eleven years old when his dad Brian Claxton died in 2001. He is now sixteen going on seventeen. Matthew and I were in our sixties when we lost our daughter as she was giving birth to her second son, we have brought up our grand-son for seventeen years. I turned seventy-eight this year. Matthew is eighty-three and he is getting frail. This is one of the reasons why we went out looking for Brian six years ago with the hope that he would start to bond with his son and give him some role model father figure but that was not destined to be. Steve has been a good boy so far. He is good at school and bright and talented. It does not surprise us that even with the fact that he was being looked after by aged grand-parents he was in line with good training. Around the age of six we made sure that Steve began elementary school also known as primary school in some parts. He then proceeded to secondary school in Pennsylvania. He completed middle school and went on to the second program for his high school. At the end of his high school, he obtained a diploma upon graduation from high school. His 12th grade school examination results were good which makes him eligible for admission into a good College or even University to proceed into higher education. Steve performed excellently in his twelfth grade with high percentages that were converted into letter grades. On his return from school I met him by the door, gave him a hug and a pat on his back before asking him for what he would like to do next.

''Steve so which University or College would you like to go to?''

''Nan, I will now have to submit my academic transcripts as part of my application for admission to University, my

transcripts are copies of my academic work bearing all my grade point average GPA.''
''Oh I see that is very good, so what step would you like to take now?''

''My tutor and I have gone through the measurements of my academic achievement and performance and I meet the criteria to get into a good University in the United Kingdom. I want to study outside the United States. I have done some research into Universities that are in London and most of the schools there are very good.''

''So what would you like to study at University?''

''Accountancy and Financial Management.''

''Wow! That is the same line of work like your late dad did. I won't call that a coincidence. Would you?''

''I can't say cause I don't even know him.''

''He was a kind man to your late mother. He visited you when you were six years old. I doubt if you can remember even that now.''

''Yeah vaguely somewhere as a visitor, but I didn't register him as my dad. Grandpa is the only dad I have known all my life.''

''Well you are right in saying that.''

''As far as I am concerned I was brought up by my grand–parents because I am an orphan sadly.''
''You can say that but see the good side of things, you are turning out to be a responsible young man about to go to the university''

''I suppose you are right nan.'' Steve paused.

''There is one problem though, if I go and study in London I will be regarded as an international student and I have to pay tuition fees for my University education which means we can't really afford the College fees.''

''Why do you think that?''

''Because I feel I should be looking after you and grand–dad at your age and not you looking after me by worrying over paying my University tuition fees''

''You don't worry about us, all you have to do for now is to worry about yourself.''

''I may have to pay my way through my education by working in the grocery stores or something like that.''

''Mathew and I are happy to pay for your flight ticket to England when you are ready to travel there to study. What you may need to consider is to seek employment for a year to save up some money for your University and then travel to England.''

''Yeah I can defer my admission to London School of Economics until the next academic year, giving me the time to work and save up for my University education.''

''Clever boy, that is smart of you. That also gives you time to grow up to age eighteen which is the age criteria for admission into the London School of…what do you call the name of that school again?''

''Nan it is a very popular school in London and it is London School of Economics.''

''Oh I see, London School of Economics. I will explain all we have chatted about to your grandad when he returns from the doctor's, he's gone to get his blood and urine tested, you know he is suffering from diabetes, we are both getting older by the day.''

''Thank you Nan, you are the only mother that I have ever known in my life and you've have done even more than a mother would probably have done. You are the best.''

''Well you can say that, but what I want you to do for me is to continue in your wise ways and don't join those nasty gangs out there who have no respect for law and order. Even their parents cannot talk to them.''

''I'm sure I will not disappoint you Nan, trust me I won't.''

''I'll take your word. By the way when your grandad gets better with his hospital treatment, he will discuss some important matters with you about this property where we live. As you know your mother, Teresa was the only child and daughter that we ever had before we came and so when we were in our fifties we got a lawyer and made our 'Will and The Last Testament'. At that time, you were not yet born and so we bequeathed all that we had to our only child. She was the sole beneficiary. Since her death we have had to make changes to our Will. Mathew and I will talk to you about some things that you now need to know as you are getting close to your eighteenth birthday next year. You need to know before you go to University in England.''
''Oh I see. Ok nan. I remember you said that my late mum was previously married for four years before she later got divorced. Is that correct?''

''Yes that is true. Your late mother got divorced in her first marriage. Unfortunately her marriage broke down to this English man she met in New York, he was a Federal Attorney at the time he met your late mother. They got married here in Pennsylvania for 'bout five years before you were born. They then relocated to England after having their first child here in the US. According to what Teresa told us, Keith continued to practice his law career when they returned to England and he was successful.''

''Are you saying that I have a brother somewhere in another part of the world?''

''Yes you do have a half-brother from your mother's first marriage. He will be about four to five years older than you. When your mother went into depression after her marriage broke down irretrievably, she had your half-brother to look after because her husband walked out on her which was when she stopped her nursing career because her license was taken away from her as she could no longer cope with any form of pressure. She started to take cocaine, heroin and it was when she took an overdose at work that she was reported to her professional body and her practising license was revoked. She became unemployed unfortunately. That led her into recurrent depression, with low self-esteem and slight mental health problems. She battled with panic attacks, anxiety in her dark and lonely place. She began to compare herself to others and her smoking graduated to addiction of heroin and substance abuse with drugs.''

''Nan you have had to live with this sad story all your life haven't you?''

''Yes your gran-dad and I have not found it easy since your mum travelled to England, that is why I am a bit worried about your going there to study''

''But Bill Clinton and some other American President all went to study in Oxford and Cambridge Universities in England and they all came back to the US to become positive role models.''

''You can say that and you are right, anyone will believe you for saying so.''

''What happened to mum's first child then, cause going by the story he should be 'bout twenty-one to twenty-two years old now. Do you know where he is now?''

''Obviously not. Due to your late mum's trauma, we asked her to return to US so that we could monitor her health and look after her. She refused us for years. Things got worse when the Social services forcefully took her son away from her because she could not look after him properly due to her addiction to drugs.''

''Nan what is his name?''

''You mean your half-brother and his dad?''

''Yeah.''

''His name is Tom. Tom Bradford. His father's name is Keith Bradford… Attorney Keith Bradford … if my memory serves me right.''

''So you are not sure?''

''I am pretty sure of those names. From what I can remember from what your mum told me. Tom was fostered by a family for about three to four years after which he was adopted by a family. He's surname was changed after the adoption.''
''Nan do you know what his new surname is?''
''No, not on top of my head right now, but I can find out for you, it will be in your mother's diary somewhere.''
''You said you and grand-dad asked my late mum to come over from England to US so that you could both look after her, but that she refused to do so. You also said something along the lines of some Social services taking her first child away from her because of her drug abuse, is that right?''
''Absolutely correct. It was when the Social services took her son away that she suffered from panic attacks and anxiety to a great extent. You would feel sorry for her in her state of

health. She refused to come over to the US and she drifted away for many years. When your grand–dad and I went to look for her in the UK she had changed her address without telling us. She was not answering her phone when we called her. She isolated herself from her parents and became estranged sadly.''

''Oh dear, poor mum. Do you know why her marriage ended in divorce? What actually happened?''

''Well, they lived in England, Keith and Teresa, like I said they got married in USA. They started well. He was a Prosecuting Attorney and she was practising nursing. Tom came along not long after they got married. When your mum began to battle with drug addiction, she did not get enough support from her husband. He walked away from the marriage at the nearest opportunity. He should at least have looked back on saving his only son from being taken by the Department of Social Security, but he never did. He just walked away. Teresa could not handle it after they separated.''
''Oh dear!''
''Yeah it was a shame.''

''Did she at any point in time become suicidal?''

''She must have been because when she finally came over to Cottonwood Arizona for rehab, I found some strange marks on her arms and thighs, she told me that she attempted self-harm and became suicidal when things really got bad and that was when her only child at the time was taken away from her by the Social services.''

''When did she meet my Dad?''

''Your mum met your dad during a night out, it was a fling, she said it was not a serious relationship, but she later found out that she was pregnant, according to what she told us, when she broke the news to your dad, he asked her to keep it. He was nice to her and made her feel like a woman again. It was your dad Brian that encouraged your mum to return to US and not to live but to receive treatment at Cottonwood in Arizona.''

''I see. Oh dear. I am glad that you opened up these stories to me Nan. I would never have known the full story.''

''You are most welcome. That is why we are here.''

Chapter 11

November 2007, 6:45am

My nan had told me a lot of stories that I needed to know during our conversation after we both rejoiced over my excellent twelfth grade examination results in July. I worked very hard trying to look for work. I needed to find a job that will be regular so that I can start to save up money for my University. I have already been admitted, I deferred my admission so that I can work hard to save up for my tuition and accommodation. My nan and grandad have promised to sponsor my travel ticket.

On the morning of 20th November at 6:45am I set out to attend my first job interview at a shoe factory, it was meant to be a fixed term contract for one year. The shoe factory was located on an industrial estate and was about forty-five minutes on the train from where we lived. That was a journey that I think I could cope with. My interview was scheduled for 9:00pm. I set out nice and early just 'bout seven fifteen giving myself a good almost two hours to get to the factory.

When I got to the street where the factory was located it was a typical industrial area. I was punctual for my first job interview at the shoe factory; it is one of the oldest children's shoe manufacturer, the company takes pride in offering "good shoes" for children. They produced classic and cute shoes.

It was my first interview and I got the job. I was put on minimum wage, but that did not matter to me as long as I went home with my pay cheque to save up for going to England to study at the University.

I was able to save up a reasonable amount of money because I did not pay rent. Living with my grandparents made that possible. After about eight months in my new job I had saved

enough money to buy myself a travel ticket to England and some money to pay for my tuition.
It was Friday night, I came home very tired and could not join my nan and granddad at the table for dinner, so I went straight to bed at eight pm. My grandad woke me up at eleven pm asking not to go to sleep on an empty stomach. When I got to the kitchen, nan had covered my food with a microwave cover and left it in the fridge. I warmed it up in the microwave and ate it before going to bed.

On Saturday morning my granddad knocked on the door to my bedroom. I was already awake, just resting after a busy week.

''Can I come in for a chat?'' he asked.
''Of cause you can gran-dad.'' I replied. I was taken by surprise because usually he would have nan with him when it comes to serious discussions, but this time he is asking me for a chat alone with him, I thought it must be an important matter to discuss, so I sat up straight on my bed, expecting him to sit down next to me or on the small sofa I had in my room.

''Steve, I know you have your mind set to travel to England for your University education and your nan and I are so very proud of you for having your eyes set on something constructive being a young man. You are following in your father's footsteps, he was a very clever man and he helped our daughter Teresa as much as he could when he was alive. What I am about to tell you is very important. You must keep it to yourself and not tell anyone at this stage. Phoebe and I bought this house before your mother was even born. We worked very hard to pay mortgage on it. Your mother was the only child that we had so she was the sole beneficiary to this property until she died. Phoebe and I are now retired. We have agreed to make you a beneficiary of this property when we pass on. Like Phoebe already told you, your mother had a son from her first marriage whom she lost contact with when the Social services took him away from her as a result of her addiction. His name is Tom. At the time he was taken away for fostering,

he bore the surname of his father which was Bradford, after he got adopted his surname changed and we do not know what his adoptive parent's surname is. We have included Tom as the second beneficiary in our Will and The Last Testament. If he happens to show up one day then the lawyers will let him know, but should he never look for us then ALL we have will be yours.''
I remained speechless for few minutes...I don't know what to say to these grandparents of mine. I wish my mother was alive to see this here and now.

''Thank you grand pa but you have already done a lot for me since my mother died and now this'.' I replied.

''Well family is everything and you are now the only family that we have. It is important that you know this information before you travel to England.''

''Ok. You and nan are going to need a support worker to come in to help you to do the chores at least a couple of days of the week when I am not around. You need good care as you are now getting older.''

''You don't need to worry about us, we will be fine. What you are doing about getting yourself educated to tertiary level is a good tonic for us. We are proud of you.''
''Thank you grand-dad.'' I replied.

After our discussion we decided to go out to the garden centre to buy some flower seeds to plant in our garden.

Chapter 12

September 2010, London School of Economics

I arrived in England to commence my tertiary education at London School of Economics where I have been admitted to study Accounting, Banking and Finance.
The accommodation and student hall of residence is comfortable.
It was 9am in the morning as I set out for lectures I meet a young lady trying to do the same. Our eyes met as I crossed the pelican crossing. She was driving a small Ford escort car. Her car was going along the road leading to our faculty building. I continued walking down the road until I arrived at my destination. When I entered the lecture room this lady had already arrived in the lecture hall. There were other students in the hall. I chose to sit down about 2 rows away from where the lady sat. She was beautiful, her hair was braided into two plates, and was about 5'8 tall, light skinned, brown eyes, with very little makeup on her face. She was wearing a pink blouse over black trousers, with average heeled shoes. She sat down quietly as we all waited for the lecturer to walk into the lecture room.
At the end of our first lecture, I walked to where she sat to chat her up.
''Hey my name is Steve, Did you find the lecture impactful?''
''Hi Steve, yes I did and thank you for asking, How about you?''
''Yeah good lecture notes, the lecturer was articulate with his dictating. Interesting topic too.''
''True'' she replied, as we both walked out of the lecture room along with other students in our class.
I did not want our conversation to end and even though I knew that she drove a car to campus, I asked how she was intending to get to her hostel.
"I parked in the car park.''
"Do you mind if I walk you to where you parked?"

“You can if you wish, you have a strong American accent, you obviously are American. You’ve come all the way from the US to study Accountancy, Banking and Finance here in London.” She noted.
“My mother lived in England for many years before returning to the US when she was alive.”
“Sorry about your loss. How long ago was that?"
“I lost my mum when she was giving birth to me."
“Oh dear. So sorry to hear that. My name is Evelyn it’s nice to meet you."
By this time we had reached the car park and our eyes met again before we bid each other good bye. I then walked back to the faculty to read all the notices on the student board. I then went to the Library to check some references in my first lecture notes.
The name Evelyn echoed again and again. She had a chronic British accent. Her personality is distinctive. She is inexplicable; she makes me feel really good just by being around her and yet brings such great sadness when she’s gone. Evelyn had a slim svelte figure, her body was saplin thin and her lips were ripe.
My eyes behold her waist like a bumble bee, I could not keep my eyes off her berry-red lips. Her skin was glowing an apricot hue, a pigment perfect tincture. Almost flawless and impeccable skin with an ochrous hue. Hers was an unblemished skin, and had plucked eyebrows of midnight brown black, a symmetrical eyebrows. Her lashes were silky over her acorn shaped eyes.
To me her ears were elfin ears with half-moon cheekbones.
She had a pointy nose above her blush pink lips, her orchid pink lips glowed just like a film star.
Evelyn’s teeth were gleaming, breach-white and a cherubic smile.
Her fingernails were stiletto shaped with coracle-perfect.
Evelyn’s hair was midnight black and it flowed over her shoulders. The locks and braided chestnut brown hair nicely curtailed her oval face.

She had effervescent, champagne brown eyes, Her lips looked blossom soft.
We've only just met but I could feel a cheerful character, a bubbly outlook with lady–like temperament with genteel persona and a winning disposition.
She had a songbird sweet voice and her hair blazed in the sun. Her pink blouse and black thin trousers were in and out of jitter fashion.
For once I thought she's one of the reasons why fate brought me to London. I was hoping to travel round the world after my degree, I would like to travel to Asia, Africa and the Caribbean Island. I really would like to tour Europe, it is my dream to visit France, Germany, Italy, Spain, Iceland, and then New Zealand and Australia. In Africa I would like to touch on Uganda, Ghana, Nigeria and South Africa. All I need to do right now is to focus on my degree and get it done.
If things work out between Evelyn and I, then we may be touring the world together when our degree hurdle is over. Evelyn has got everything that I would like to see in a woman.

Chapter 13

December 2010

It is now four months since I met Evelyn Blackstone, but it felt like we have actually known each other for longer than that. I remember William Shakespeare said, ''The course of true love never did run smooth.'' She is the one person who can see right through me. I find that amazing about her. She doesn't want to admit that she's actually falling in love with me. There is an underlying problem that I can perceive from her; like a post-traumatic stress or some other terrible experience she's had in the past and I really hope she would open up to me what this ''thing'' eating her up inside is. I feel she is somehow distant from me even though we are close. On the first day we met, when I walked her back to where she parked her car, I told her that my mother died at my birth and that my grandparents raised me up in Pennsylvania. I could feel her empathy. I know we have some culture clash. She is British and big city girl while I am a small-town boy from America or whatever you like to call it back home in Pennsylvania. But we have a lot in common, we are both studying Accountancy, Banking and Finance at the London School of Economics.

On the 10 December I bought two tickets for us to watch a movie in the cinema, it was a cold Saturday night. We both love live shows but it was too costly for our student budget.

On Sunday we went out for lunch at a restaurant in Soho – it is the gloriously grubby beating heart of London and has a killer range of restaurants to satisfy anyone's culinary craving, at any price. Evelyn knows the best joints for outings in London.

A small, unshowy restaurant that's made a name for itself with a short but perfectly formed menu and an easy-going conviviality. Dishes are seasonal and it's good value for

money. Tables are closely packed and in the evening it can get noisy, but otherwise it's hard to fault the place. Adept, friendly staff are a further plus. We can't handle the no-booking policy at dinner, so we settled for booking our table for two which was accepted for lunch.
We took our coats off and checked them into the cloak room at reception before settling down at our reserved seats located is a far corner where the table is just for two, it was a tucked in private corner. It was literally not possible for anyone to hear our conversation in the secluded corner we were, it was nicely sheltered and private just for two.

''It is nice and cosy here.'' I said.
''You wait until they serve us our meal.''
''You mean they are really good.''
''Yeah their food is nice and so is the price.''
''Wow.''
''You don't look too cheerful today, what is up?'' she observed.
''I'm ok, just that this is the first time I am spending December away from Pennsylvania and my grand parents''
''Sorry to hear that, but I think you will have a lovely Christmas here in London'' she said with her songbird sweet voice which gave it away that she had fallen head over heels in love with me. By this time the waitress had served up our starter and we started eating.
''Evelyn.''
''Yes?''
''You will tell me if anything was bothering you, won't you?''
''Of course I will.''
''Ok, you remember yesterday at the cinema, remember in the film, the guy who was convicted for indecent assault with his secretary…you started to shed tears when she was being cross examined during the trial, then you said you knew where she was coming from.''
''Yes I said so.''
''What made you say so?''
''I'll rather us not talk about it…''

''Why?''
''It is a long story…'' she then broke down in tears, and instantly I knew there was deep pain being bottled up inside Evelyn's mind, I wanted her to open up the cankerworm that has been eating her up inside, and I wish she would spit it all out for me to hear. The question is, am I able to handle it, the same way she coped with the story of my mum dying at my birth and so on. May–be I can use this opportunity to open up to her that my mum was a heroin addict as well.
''I have learnt from the past that talking through whatever is bothering us is a good therapy, sharing past and present painful experience helps us to rise above it and to move on in life. Don't you think?''

'That is true, well I hope that after you've heard my story, it will not 'break us', but that it would 'make us'. My last relationship ended after my boyfriend heard my story, it was too much for him to handle, being a mummy's boy that he was. So maybe if I tell you early enough in our relationship, you can make up your mind whether you would like to proceed or break off''

''I hope you're comfortable enough to share your story with me – I'll be able to handle it.''

''I am the only child of my parents. When I was nine years old my parents decided to adopt a child. At the time he was adopted he was eleven year old while I was nine year old. We were a happy family and I felt I had a brother. We bore the same surname which is Blackstone, so most people assume that we were biological siblings.''
''Then what happened?''
''Five years after he was adopted, he was sixteen years old while I was fourteen years old. On a cold winter Saturday afternoon, I was not feeling too well, my parents had gone out to do some shopping and to get some medication for me at the pharmacy leaving me in the house with my 'brother'. I was in my bedroom sleeping when I heard a knock on the door. I

actually thought it was my mum knocking, the next thing I saw was my 'brother' walking into my bedroom''
Evelyn again broke down in tears…she sobbed bitterly.
''What else happened…?''
''He said he came to check on me and I told him that he should have waited to be asked into the room before he just walked in without an answer to his knock…he ignored what I said but instead walked swiftly towards my bed…, I was sexually assaulted…He was taller and bigger. All my efforts to escape from him pining me down was to no avail… I was in shock as he initially moved close to my face to kiss me…then he touched me. I shouted no the first time… and then repeated no again. He ignored me, he then said yes, giving me a dirty slap, I then shouted you son of a bitch after which he hit me three times each, each one landed on my cheek and it got harder as it increased. He became a wild beast that was a complete stranger to me, his eyes became wild, crazy, he was stronger than me, he then pinned me down… and put his hand lower down to pull down my panties…he used his fingers…..pried my legs apart…I then began to fight him…'trying to push him away off the top of me… Fought him but he was too strong…he was bigger than me…..he then forcefully pushed himself into me…I shouted and cried in pain….I shouted son of a bitch….he ignored me as he began to breathe heavily and groaning…, I cried and cried.''
''Then what happened?''
''The pain that he made me go through would never go away. He stole my innocence away from me. By the time my parent returned I had already been raped. My mother was devastated when I summoned courage to relay what happened to her. She passed the sad news to my dad and that was when they decided to involve the social services in the matter, the young man was taken into a youth residential home. My father asked the state to prosecute the young man for the offence of rape and the matter went through the Family Juvenile court. This experience left me emotionally destabilized for many years, I could not trust anybody in trousers except my dad.''

''Sorry to hear about this experience, you are brave just by sharing the trauma and ordeal you went through.''
''The most painful part of the story for my parents to hear is that they genuinely intended to help Tommy have a family environment to grow up in, his mother was deserted by his dad when he was less than two years old, since then he's been fostered by three separate families. At the age of nine he was on addictive substance abuse and going through rehabilitation.''
''I now understand why you burst into tears while we were at the movie yesterday''
''Yeah I had gone through a similar ordeal to the girl who was being cross examined in that film we watched.''
''Oh dear!''
By this time we were on our main course meal and I decided to share with Evelyn how my own mother had suffered and battled heroine addiction that cost her dearly before she met her own death.
''Well my history is similar to yours, my mother did not live to raise me up, she died during rehabilitation for drug abuse.''
''Was that in the United States?''
''Actually it was both in the US and UK.''
''How do you mean?''
''My mother got married to my dad in the US before they both travelled to UK where they lived before they divorced, my dad walked out because of my late mum's addiction.''
''Sorry to hear that. Did she remarry after their split?''
''Yes she met my own dad and that was when they went out for a while before she got pregnant of me. According to my grand-parents, she was going through rehabilitation when she lost her life during child birth''
''Did she die in the US?''
''Yes she did travel from the UK to the US where she was receiving treatment in rehabilitation during pregnancy.''
''That means you are a living miracle yourself then.''
''Yeah that is why I said we have common grounds with our past.''
''Where is this boy who did that to you?''

''I never heard of him since then, my parents said he was in and out of prison cells, and became a notorious criminal.''
''What was his name?''
''Tommy.''
''What are your parent's names?
''My parents have biblical names: Rebecca and James… why do you ask?''
''Just curious. Is your dad Italian?''
''No, it is the other way round, my mum is Italian and my dad is English.''
The waitress brought our delicious pudding. We ordered coffee after our pudding before we left the restaurant.
I never wanted the evening to end. The story that Evelyn had just shared with me was emotional. I could relate with the pain and anguish that she had been through at such an early age. I made sure that I walked Evelyn to her door before making my journey back to the halls of residence. We both needed to spend the evening in our respective hostels preparing for another academic week on Monday which was just few hours away from Sunday night.

Chapter 14

At the Tea Table, 12 February 2016

Three men sat at a small square shiny mahogany table.
Keith Bradford became the lead prosecutor in his department at the prosecution service. Chief Inspector Kelvin Armstrong had received some useful information about the case he was investigating on the sudden death of Steve Claxton. Kelvin interviewed Tom in December 2015 at his parent's home, but he could not be linked to the death of Steve Claxton going by the interview that Kelvin had with Tom.

Colonel Peter Blacksmith along with Keith and Kelvin were drinking black tea, - rich in tannin. Peter was drinking an English café's idea, but he endured it for the sake of being on equal terms to the other two men's conference.

Kelvin was shaking his head with his hands buried in his hair… ''Honestly, if you ask me what I am thinking about'' dropping several lumps of brown sugar into his black brew and then stirring it, ''I doubt if we would ever get to the bottom of the truth about Steve's murder, this case will never be brought to trial. We'll never have enough evidence.''

Peter shook his head and took an approving sip of his tea. Keith did not share the same view.

''The burden of proof is Onus probandi and it is on us the prosecutors to prove our case beyond all reasonable doubt, we have to see to it that this is done.'' Keith threw his head back.
''But how are we going to do this when there is no clue leading us to the crime, needless to mention the scene of crime?'' Kelvin lowered his head regrettably.
''I was reading the coroner's report on Steve's death, the inquest found two letters in the pocket of the trousers that

Steve Claxton was wearing.'' Keith gave a lead as he stroke his beard.
'' What was the letter about?'' Peter flashed a peace sign.
''Before we go to the content of the letter, tell me Kelvin– what was that boy Tom or Tommy like when you interviewed him briefly at his parents?''
''He was the last person to see Steve Claxton after they met up to have a drink.''
''How would you describe him?'' asked Keith.
''He is about your height, same description of your face coincidentally, the only difference with this young man and yourself is that he is half your age…'' Kelvin replied.
''Does he have a history of crime?''
''Oh yes he's been in trouble so many times with Police. He's got a history of arrests. I think he was adopted by the parents he lived with at the time of my visit and interview.'' Kelvin explained with his eyes welled up, Keith gave Peter and Kelvin a frosty look, but a part of his face was glistened with sweat.
''We need to ask Tom more questions and here is the reason why we need to do so …'' He put his briefcase on the shiny mahogany tea table, flipped the briefcase opened, then thrust his hand into the side and drew out crumpled-up two folded pieces of papers, both were letters. The briefcase clicked shut afterwards.

The first letter was written by Mathew who was Steve Claxton's grand-parent, the second letter was written by Steve's mother, Teresa, but she did not live long enough to hand the letter to Steve because she unfortunately died at Steve's birth, so the letter was given to Steve by his grand-mum Phoebe, who had kept the letter for all these years. Mathew had written the letter before he became old and frail following on his second stroke at the age of '82. Then a heart attack, followed by two more major strokes and several small ones. His days were numbered, and he had long since accepted the fact that he would most likely catch the big one and die. Before Mathew died, he gave the letter he wrote to Phoebe with instructions to hand it on to Steve Caxton. It was when

Steve attended Mathew's funeral in Pennsylvania that Phoebe handed the letter to him.
''This is getting very interesting, why would Steve Claxton take these two personal letters along with him to see Tom on the night of his death?'' Peter asked as he stuck his nose in the air.

''Keith you are taking this case to another level, lead prosecutor please read on...'' Chief Inspector Kelvin Armstrong said with his nostrils flared.

''Our dearest Steve, it is very likely that by the time you are reading this letter, I may no longer be around to see you, but there is nothing in this letter that I have not already told you in my conversation with you before you left Pennsylvania for England for your University education. As you already know, Phoebe and I are not getting any younger, we are now getting old, we have looked after you since your mother died well over two decades ago, Like we explained to you she was a lovely daughter but, sadly, she was not lucky to live to see you after your birth. She was the only child that we had and as she is no longer with us, you are the beneficiary of our assets. Pennsylvania will always be your home. All our real estate and savings will pass to you on our demise.

Your mother gave birth to a son before she met your father, I hope fate would bring you to meet your half-brother, I hope you do find him. I pray he turns out to be a nice man like you, and that you would both get on, that is something that Teresa, your mother would love. Phoebe and I do not have control over that, we have instructed our lawyers on what he should do if you eventually find him. We do not know him very well because he was taken away from your mother when he was very young by the social services in England. I think I should also let you know that your mother in her first marriage owned a property which she manages through an estate agent. It is a four bedroom house which she decided not to sell. It was the property she bought with her first husband who was an attorney when she herself practiced as a nurse in England before she started to battle with drug abuse. Upon her demise the ownership of the property passes to you, however, in the event of you finding your half-brother, you could mention it to him so that you both could decide on what you would like to do with the property. My lawyer will be able to help you both with that.

Grand-son, I wish you all the very best in all your endeavours and I pray you find a good wife to marry and that your marriage will be blessed with good children. Phoebe and I are pleased that our great-grandchildren will come through you. I don't know how long I have to live from the time of my writing you this letter; I am getting more and more tired and frail by the day. I can only leave you in the hands of God.
Hope to see you soon.
As always,
Grand-dad
(Mathew and Phoebe)''
The letter broke off.
Kelvin stood up motionless, staring down at the piece of paper. ''There is so much to gather from the information in that letter, but why would Steve Claxton take letter along with him to the meeting he had with Tom at the pub?''

The second letter was a letter where Steve Claxton's late mum asked her parents (Phoebe and Mathew) to help her get back to the United States, when Brian her husband at the time helped her to settle down in a rehabilitation centre at Arizona.

''Dear Mum and Dad, thank you for always being there for me. This is a trying time in my life and I am happy that you are by my side to see me through coming clean and getting my life back on track after birth. Brian has been very supportive and I cannot explain how very lucky I have been since I met him, we are both happy with the child I am carrying.
I am sorry that I will not be able to live with you in Pennsylvania initially when I arrive in the States, Brian has

booked me into the rehab in Arizona, where I am receiving treatment. Don't worry, I am going to be ok. I promise that this is it for me and after all the treatment I will be fine this time.

See you in two weeks' time.

All of me,
Teresa''

''Is that all?'' Peter asked.
''Yes, that is it'' he said as he fought back tears.
''What is going on here?. Why are you getting emotional?, we have to be professional here, these letters are evidence that could help us to link Tom to the crime, we only need to figure it out.'' Kelvin said as his brows snapped together, but Keith's eyes were already narrowed and tears shone in his eyes.
With his forehead furrowed, ''But I don't get it.'' Kelvin said.
''Well gentlemen, I can only fear the worst after reading the first letter……..I think Mathew's letter to Steve is a big clue to me, could it be that Steve met Tom his half-brother whom his grand-dad mentioned in his letter?. The big question is what the coroner's report found out which was that Steve Claxton died from poison. If the last person he saw was Tom, and the last drink he drank was in the pub with Tom, then Tom could be the one we have been looking for and he should be arrested. The only reason why I think Steve Claxton took that letter with him was to show Tom; we could assume that Tom is the half-brother that his granddad referred to. He found him in England.''
''But what is the motive behind the killing?'' asked Kelvin.
''Why would Tom poison Steve Claxton with Cyanide poison?'' asked Peter.
''And Keith why are you getting so emotional about a case where you don't even know the parties concerned?'' asked Kelvin.

"That is where my fear come in...if my greatest fear is confirmed to be true, then I cannot be involved in prosecuting in this case" he sniffed.
"But why Keith…what is going on here?"
"I will explain to you in detail when I have found out more about Tom…" Keith said.

"It is not what I am thinking…please….you mean Tom could be your son or family?"
"Yeah and I don't want to be seen to pervert the cause of justice."
"Oh dear...he looks so much like you….that boy looks so much like you…tell me what happened exactly, he can't be your biological son because his surname is not Bradford, his surname is Blackstone."

"But you just said earlier on that he was adopted by the parents he lived with. Well about twenty-eight years ago I married to a woman called Teresa, she gave birth to a son, but she battled drug abuse and we divorced after few years, Tom was only eighteen months old, my heart bleeds right now, I need to have DNA done to confirm if he was the same child Teresa and I shared."

With his jaw dropping, "And where is Teresa?" Kelvin asked.

"From the first letter she's dead, that is why Steve was brought up by Mathew and Phoebe."

With a corner of his mouth lifted, "I don't think that Tom is yours, you can't just assume so, you have not even met him yet." Peter said.

"So what should we do next?" asked Kelvin.

"You take the coroner's report home with you and study it, let us find out how the murder was carried out before we make any arrests."

''Good idea Keith, I agree, let's all read through the inquest notes and then we can meet here tomorrow afternoon to discuss our next line of action.'' Kelvin affirmed and Peter pursed his lips.

Chapter 15

The Arrest, 12 noon on 13 February 2016

Four men reconvened at twelve o'clock noon on 13th February. They have read and digested the inquest and coroner's report. A lot of details were mentioned about how Steve Claxton had suffered a violent death, it was a clear case of murder. There were 101 questions to ask and answer regarding the case. Inspector Jasper Willard joined Colonel Peter Blacksmith along with Keith Bradford and Kelvin Armstrong who were drinking cups of very strong coffee, rich in caffeine. The four men had a lot to discuss before making any arrests. Keith was not allowed to pull out of the prosecuting team yet until it's been ascertained that Tom was his blood, his gut instinct told him to start thinking of negotiating a plea bargain with the defence team and to find them wherever they were for his only son. But it had not come to that yet. They needed to establish that Tom's arrest should be made today and Keith couldn't wait to set his eyes on this young man called Tom. Who was he? Is he his biological long lost son or not?

''The inquest report is robust: a post-mortem examination and autopsy had been carried out on Steve's body following his death. X-rays, photographs, images of his body organs during the post-mortem examination. The pathologist expert's investigation found out the cause of death. The results of examination were in the Coroner's report. Steve's body cells was prevented from being able to use oxygen, his body enzymes was inhibited in the mitochondria of cell from doing it's vital job of capturing oxygen and transforming it into cells. After his drink was poisoned, the report showed that Steve's body suffered a violent attack showing symptoms of cyanide poisoning with general weakness, shortness of breath, confusion, headache, dizziness, excessive sleepiness and bizarre sudden behaviour as his body responded and reacted to sudden consumption of silver nitrate and sodium chloride.

According to the eye-witness who saw him last on the train, Steve suffered symptoms that progressed to seizure with a convulsed face before he slumped to the ground and went into a coma and his eventual death. Cyanide had been dropped inside the drink that he drank either in a gas, liquid or solid form. The investigation team think he may have even been made to smell certain scents without him knowing that it was poisonous.
Inspector Jasper Willard was a Police officer with thirty-years' experience with the Crown prosecution service and his experience would be very relevant to the Prosecuting team in this case.

''We have to find the motive for this murder gentlemen.'' Jasper said as his forehead puckered.

''Going by the content of that letter Keith read out yesterday, we can assume that Steve went to meet his half-brother Tom, we need to investigate what type of wine the two men drank and who the waitress was?'' Colonel Peter Blacksmith explained.

''Are you saying that Steve went to meet his half-brother Tom, that Tom's motive for murdering Steve was to maybe to claim insurance money or to inherit the estate of their grand-parents?'' Keith said his eyes taking on haunted look.
''Yes I agree with that, could it also be that he was a brother who felt very inferior to Steve looking at his crime history, we could presume that murder makes him feel powerful and important.'' Inspector Kelvin Armstrong pointed out.
''Yes you could be right'' replied Jasper.
''Looking at Tom's work history, he's worked in a chemical producing company before, so he is not ignorant of how chemicals work, he was an apprentice there, he did not work there long enough to be an expert though'' Peter said.

''That leaves us with the fact that Steve was so happy to see his half-brother and to even go out for drinks with him but did

Steve really know what Tom is capable of, I mean as in - does he know about Tom's past life?''

''I don't think he had an iota of idea on who Tom really is'' Jasper replied.

''I think we have enough evidence so far to issue a warrant of arrest for Tom. Let's get him into the Police station for interview gentlemen.'' Keith directed.

''Keith, are you going to lead the prosecution team in this case, that is if we proceed with charging Tom for the alleged crime?'' Kelvin asked as he stroke his beard.

''I don't know what is going to happen to my involvement with this case yet, I would have to withdraw from the prosecution team if it is confirmed that I am related to the accused person, gentlemen we have to wait and see, but this arrest must be done and justice must be done in this case'' Keith answered Kelvin as he let out a harsh breath.

''The alleged offence here is a capital murder indictment, the jury at trial can find the defendant guilty of manslaughter, which carries twenty years, or capital murder, which carries life as determined by the jury, And the jury can find the defendant not guilty'' Jasper explained.
''Again, you're assuming he'll be indicted.'' Keith lifted his chin.

All four senior ranked Police officers and Keith who was an Attorney at Law arrived in the Police van, they pulled the van to the side of the road, alighted and walked to the front door of Mr and Mrs Blackstone; Rebecca and James were at home, it was now 16:45 hours and as the doorbell rang. Someone came down-stairs to open the door.

''Good afternoon officers, how can I help you?''

''We've come to see Rebecca and James regarding a young man known as Tom also known as Tommy, I believe we have come to the right address?''

''Yes of cause you can, do come right in...'' replied Rebecca as she flashed a peace sign.

''Thank you'' chorused the Police officers as they stepped into the house.

''Tommy!' Rebecca called out and within a minute Tommy came down the stairs to the living room where the officers were already sitting down.

''Hello young man…we have met before - can you remember my last visit about Steve, your half-brother.'' Kelvin greeted.

''Yeah, I can remember- that was in December 2015 last year.'' replied Tom.

''You have a very good memory Tom.'' replied Kelvin.

''Why are you here again?'' Tom queried.

''I know you told me when I last visited you that you do not know anything about the death of Steve, your half-brother. But there has been some recent evidence on the case which means we are here with a warrant of arrest to take you with us to the Police Station for an interview and questioning. You have the right to remain silent. Anything you say will be used against you in court. You have the right to a lawyer. If you can't afford one, the state will furnish you with one. Any questions?''

Tom shrugged, he lifted his shoulder in a half shrug then said: ''Mum, what can I do now?''
''This is what you get when you do not stay out of trouble, I asked you if you have anything to do with Steve's death and

you said you don't.'' Rebecca said as a muscle in her jaw twitched.

''But I don't, I swear I don't know why these guys are here again''

''You must know something that we don't know.'' replied Rebecca.

'Yeah, please what time is it?'' He said looking directly at Keith as if he saw something absurd.

''Young man it is time to go to the police station with us.'' replied Kelvin.
Colonel Peter Blacksmith brought out handcuffs, slipped them onto Tom's wrists and slapped it into place, From there Kelvin led him out of the house followed by the other officers where he was thrown into the back seat of the van. The Police van was driven with the full siren on all the way to the Police Station. Rebecca decided to call their family solicitor after discussing what had happened with James.

When they arrived at the Police Station, Chief Inspector Kelvin Armstrong led Tom down the hall to his office in the front section of the Interview room; he removed the handcuffs and seated him in a wooden chair in the centre of the room. Colonel Peter Blacksmith looked at Keith and then looked at Tom, he nodded and flashed a peace sign towards Keith.
Keith sat in a big chair across the desk and looked down at the defendant with a gut instinct as he stretched out his legs in front of him.

Kelvin looked in Tom's direction across the table where he sat and introduced him to the team. ''Mr Tom Blackstone, this here is Colonel Peter Blacksmith from Scotland Yard, Over here is Inspector Jasper Willard from the Crown Prosecution service, and this here is Attorney Keith Bradford who is also with the CPS, he is a prosecutor, whom you also met today and

as you already are aware, I'm Chief Inspector Kelvin Armstrong, I will be leading this interview with you.''
Tom jerked his head fearfully to look at each one of the officers. He was surrounded. The door was shut. Two tape recorders sat side by side near the edge of the Inspectors desk.

''We'd like to ask you some questions, is that okay?''

''Yeah. I think so''
''You have nothing to worry about, you've been here a couple of time in the past, maybe not in this particular station but you've definitely gone through an arrest before, yes or no?''

''Yeah.'' replied Tom.

''Before I start the questioning, I want to be sure that you understand your rights. First of all, you have the right to remain silent. Understand?''

''Uh, huh.''

''You don't have to talk if you don't want to, but if you do, anything you say can and will be used against you in court. Understand?''

''Uh huh.''

''Are you literate, I mean can you read and write?''

''Yeah I can.''

''Very good, then read this and sign it. It says that you've been advised of your rights.''

Tom then signed along the dotted lines. Kelvin pushed the red button on one of the tape recorders.
''You understand this tape recorder is on?''

''Uh huh.''

''And the time is 17:50 hours on 13 February 2016.''

''Yeah.''

''What is your full name?''

''Tommy Blackstone.''

''Any nicknames that you are also known as?''

''Thomas or Tom.''

''Where do you live?''

''I live in a hostel accommodation in Croydon but sometimes go and visit my parents at the address where you came to see me in December 2015 and today.''

''Noted. So do you shuttle between two addresses?''

''Yeah.''

''Is that the hostel along Reeves corner?''

''Yeah.''

''What road is that?''

''Waterloo road.'' Tom paused, ''I live with other residents in the hostel.''

''How long have you lived in the hostel for?''

''Since I came out of prison.''
''Do you have any friends in this residential hostel?''
''Yeah.''

"What are their names?"
"Gary and I have always been together."
"What do you mean by being together? Are you partners?"
'No I'm not gay. We are just friends; we came back from prison at the same time."
"Oh I see. Do you know Mr Frederick, the hostel Manager?"
"Yeah, I know him, he is a nice man."
'Ok, do you go out drinking along with Gary and his friend Neil and with Neil's girl friend?"
"Yeah."
"What sort of drinks do you normally drink when you go out together?"
'Vodka and tonic, wine, champagne, lemonade…yeah."
'Have you ever requested for Clicquot, 1948 – a very good and expensive wine?"
"Yeah I like that drink."
"Was that the drink you asked for from the waitress on the evening you went out for drinks with Steve?"
"I can't remember the name of the drink." he breathed deeply looking at Kelvin.
"Do you know late Mr Steve Claxton?"
"Yes I do, he was my half-brother."
"Did you grow up together with him?"
"No."
"I met him for the first time in England, but he was born in America."
"Tell me what happened on the day you both went out together?"
"I took a train from Croydon to meet Steve in London."
"Where in London did you both go to?"
"I met Steve in West-End, one of the restaurants there, he was already waiting for me at the station before I arrived, it was his idea that we hang out."
"Are you saying that you really did not want to go out for a drink with Steve?"
"No that is not what I mean."
"Were you also keen to go out for a meal and a drink with Steve?"

''Yeah.''
''Who paid for the drinks and the food?''
''Steve paid; I only work in the factory as apprentice.''
''What does the factory manufacture?''
''Some chemicals and cleaning products.''
''Where is the factory located?''
''South Norwood'' he said with hesitation, he then studied his shoes, I don't like these your questions, what have I got to do with Steve's death?''
Kelvin pushed another button and the recorder stopped. He breathed deeply again at Tom before asking if he would like to go for a smoke. Tom is a drug addict and his hands have started to shake in discomfort. The interview was paused, Tom was escorted to have a smoke and he was followed back to the interview room.
Kelvin again punched the green button of the recorder for the recording to restart. Tom dropped his head, his face twisted – his expression sobered.
''What time did you get to London?''
''At about 5:30pm, I can't really remember exact time, but it was before 6pm.''
''What is the name of the restaurant you both visited?''
''I can't really remember the restaurant name, but I know it is close to the West End station.''
''What did you drink and eat?''
''Beef Lasagne and some chips, then Clicquot, 1948.''
''That is your favourite drink. Isn't it?. Steve really wanted to give you a treat.''
''Yeah we both enjoyed the evening.''
''Did Steve come to West End with any letters?'
''Letters?...hmm… yeah he did.''
''Can you remember what was inside the letters.''
''Something that grand-dad had written to Steve.''
''Did you travel with Steve to the US to meet your grand-dad and grand-mum?''
'Yes he did, he paid for our flight.''
''And how did that make you feel?''
''Good.''

"Could you tell us how you got to meet your half-brother Steve, since you did not know him before he came to England to study accountancy?'

"It was a miracle how I got to meet Steve here in London."

"Tell us about this miracle!"

"I was involved in a motor car accident when I went out with Neil, we were out in London when the accident occurred; the car rolled to its side when one of the tyres burst at full speed, the car somersaulted in the middle of the road rolling itself as the driver loses control. It was an extreme level of car damage and I was lucky to be alive. All I could remember was that I woke up in St Thomas Hospital in London with a man by my side. He introduced himself to me as Steve. He said his fiancée was admitted into the same hospital at the time. He saw the medical team discussing about the man on the stretcher (me) who had no family to sign documents on his behalf as it was an emergency. That was when he asked for my name and he was told my name was Tom Blackstone, and he stepped in as if he was the only family that I had. When my medical records was retrieved from the central National Health Service (NHS) system he discovered Blackstone was my adopted name and that Bradford was my biological parent's surname. He became curious because his grand mum had told him that he had a half-brother whose name was Tom. To cut a long story short fate brought us together to meet. We are brothers born by the same mother. He grew up in America but came to study in England. He is a qualified chartered accountant."

"That is a moving story of how two brothers came to meet one another for the first time without their parents being involved in the meeting. How did that make you feel to know that you have a brother who was trained to be a chartered accountant?'

"Well I never knew he existed, it was him who knew that he had a half-brother somewhere, because our grand-parents had told him that my mother had a child named Tom somewhere in England, so at least he had that information which I never had the privilege of knowing."

''Would you say that Steve was more excited to know that he had a half-brother and that he had met him?''
''Yeah he was thrilled that he found me.''
''And what about you, were you excited that he found you?''
''It was good to connect with him, but I am not sure he really would like to have anything to do with a low life like me.''
''Why do you say that?''
''Well when the Police were about to nick me after the London riots I called his number and he never picked it up.''
'At what point in time did you lose contact with Steve?'
'Before I went to prison after the London riots in 2011'
''Tell us what happened at that time?''
''When I was arrested I tried to call Steve so that he could help me out to maybe get a lawyer or something, but he did not pick up his phone.''
''Why did he not pick up the phone?''
'Initially, I thought he did not want to have anything to do with me, but I was wrong. I later found out when we went out that he had changed his phone number, so I was ringing a number that he was not using anymore.''
''How did that make you feel towards Steve before he explained to you that his number had changed to a new one?''
''No hard feelings.''
''So when did you re-connect with him?''
'When I got out of prison.''
''Was it Steve who called you on your number?''
''Yeah he was the one looking for me.''
''So you really did not feel that he had treated you rightly because initially, when you could not get Steve to pick up his phone, you felt that he probably did not want to have anything to do with you. Little did you know that his phone number was changed without you knowing about that. Is that correct?''
''Yeah that is correct''
''Steve did not and never treated you like a low life, did he?''
''No never, he was kind to me.''
''Was he sorry to hear that you were arrested and went to prison for the London riots?''
''Yeah he was sorry for me.''

'Ok. About your friend Gary, can you tell us more about him.''
''What? We keep each other company in the hostel.''
''Does he work?''
''No he is on income support.''
''Was he the one that taught you how to smoke weed and substance?''
''I don't know.''
''What don't you know?''
''Don't remember, I swear I don't remember.''
''Are you trying to cover up for your friend Gary?''
''No comment.''
''Is it true that you were not happy that your mother never mentioned your name in a letter Steve showed you on the evening you went out for drinks, that you got jealous and went ahead and carried out your violent attack of poisoning your half-brother?''
''No comment.''
Kelvin pushed another button to stop the recorder. ''We'll type this up and get you to sign it.''
Tom fidgeted and shivered as he replied ''Can I go home now?''
''No you are going to be taken into detention until your mum visits you with a lawyer and we will ask you some more questions maybe tomorrow.'' Kelvin revealed.
Sweat trickled down Tom's spine.

Chapter 16

Keith Bradford, 14 February 2016

When I set my eyes on Tom for the first time in his parent's home, my heart sank within me. I don't need a DNA result to tell me that Tom is the son that Teresa had with me. His body was a small version of mine, like a son version of a father. Shame spiralled through me as I stood there. I burned with humiliation. My heart crept into my cheeks and my expression sobered. I watched Kelvin do the talking as I studied Tom's physical appearance.
I felt sadness and joy together as my vein popped out of my neck. When I set my eyes on Tom yesterday, there was a striking resemblance that I could not deny. Everyone in that living room yesterday could see the genes from afar. His eyes were crystal blue like mine, his eyebrows was wide and dark like mine, his skin was florid and luminescent like mine.

The only difference on his skin that I have never had were tattoos. I could not stand tattoos. He had a broad forehead with prominent brow ridge, his Adam's apple was protruding and his nose long and pointed like mine. Standing there was a handsome young man with gleaming white teeth; he was rough and unkempt with few of days' growth of beard while I was clean-shaven.
He kept long hair while I was going bald without a choice. His hair colour was brown which was mine when I was his age. He was well over six feet tall, lean and long-legged just like me - that was exactly what I looked like when I was about his age.

When I abandoned Tom when he was eighteen months old, I did not know that he would grow up to look almost exactly like me. If I could turn back the hand of the clock, I would have done things differently from the choices I made in my past.

I started my career as a Law Attorney after I graduated from the university in Pennsylvania. I met Teresa and we got married. Her parents both lived in the States. Our wedding was well celebrated. We agreed that she would travel down with me to the United Kingdom where we lived and settled. We had a son, we named him Thomas Kennedy Bradford. Teresa suffered from depression after the birth of Thomas. I was so into my career, we lived in a terraced property in Kensington. Teresa was a practicing nurse.
When Tom turned 12 months old, she went back to work after a long maternity leave, but it only made her depression worse, she then began to take drugs at work and she soon got into trouble, and was caught injecting herself with heroine while at work when she was served with several warnings before she was taken to a disciplinary and eventually lost her license to practise as a nurse from there things got worse for her.
I did all that possibly could be done to save her job but Teresa had gone too far into drug abuse. By that time, she was reinstated to practice her profession as a nurse but she was not emotionally stable to return.

When Tom was eighteen months old, I moved out of the house that we bought together. I had a very busy career as a prosecutor and my marriage to Teresa had ended. I walked away leaving everything. I started well with Teresa. I loved her genuinely. I have not loved any other woman as I loved Teresa. My career was overwhelming, so overwhelming that it began to eat me up and it had its toll on me when I also had a young family. I could not cope handling the two. And so I left Teresa with our eighteen month old son known today as Tom.

I flourished in my career but I have never had any serious relationships after I abandoned Teresa. My investigation into what Tom had become brings me shame. It is often said that when a young child is caught in between a bitter divorce of his/her loving parents, the consequences could be grievous. That was the case with my Tom.

I wept and my heart bled when I found out that his name had changed from Bradford to Blackstone. Kelvin and I had checked the history of Tom's life in social care. Frederick managed the hostel where Tom had lived in the past and the residential hostel confirmed that he had been in and out of living with them in the past; he has been moved around several families picking up all sorts of habits as he grew up.

I cannot forgive myself for leaving Teresa, but the consequences of not looking back and going to search for Tom was my greatest failure. What happened was I heard that Teresa was taken into rehabilitation and that she had travelled back to America where her parents lived. I never knew that she had married Brian Caxton and given birth to Steven. There is a stack of difference between the upbringing Steve had and that of Tom. Steve was brought up by his grandparents and even though he was an orphan, he understood love and care. Sadly, Teresa died during the birth of Steve while she was in rehabilitation in Arizona. However, his half-brother Tom was the complete opposite. Tom was taken away from his vulnerable mother, and that was when all hell broke loose, as he was so unfortunate with the homes he was placed in while he was in social care, so many times, he ended up on the street where he made the wrong choices, he ended with the wrong families, with the wrong friends and role models on the street who were gang stars. Moreover, by the time James and Rebecca adopted him, there was not very much they could do to save him, his character was already negatively made, and it was hard to reform a teenager. The harm had been done, and as they tried to mould Tom, the couple became a victim themselves as their daughter became victim of rape. Need I say anymore? My heart cries out very loudly. I cannot stop sobbing. Do not weep for me, but rather let us join hands to prevent such incidents from re-occurring in our world.

Sometimes it is hard for some professionals to balance their work life and home simultaneously. You don't have to mix the two, at least I know if I had taken a career break to look

after my home, perhaps Tom would not have suffered this much neglect. Moreover, perhaps Teresa would still be alive today!
Most times, we try to eat our cake and still want to have it. We cannot have it all. We do not have to be super perfect. We can just be ourselves, live each day as it comes and go with the flow.

What is the point of bringing children into this world, if we cannot look after them or at least impart positivity in those children.

And as a prosecutor and successful attorney in the US and the UK, I have everything that you could say money could buy in and out of, but Tom is my son and I could not put a price on that. I now blame myself for not investing quality time with him when it really mattered.

I have pulled out of the prosecution team on the murder trial of Tom, I have to liaise with the defence team to negotiate a plea bargain if the allegations against Tom is true that he committed murder.

Like I always say 'an accused person is presumed innocent until he is proven guilty' and 'the burden of proof (the onus probandi) is on the prosecution to prove their case beyond all reasonable doubt'

I am going to use every strand of hair on my skin to save my son from life imprisonment if he actually did not do what he is accused of.

The defence counsel would mitigate going by all the circumstances surrounding the case and Tom's life…''The Defence Presumption of innocence.''

Chapter 17

The Trial, 2nd May 2016

On the day before the trial, Howard Sullivan who was the Defence Counsel woke up at 3:00a.m with a headache and knot in his stomach that he attributed to the trial. He got so nervous before a trial that he can neither eat nor sleep. His doctor gave him sedatives, but was still so jumpy no one spoke to him on the opening day. He still felt this way after hundreds of these trials. He had a couple of martinis with a Valium, after which he lied on his desk with the door locked and the lights off until it was time for court. His nerves were ragged which resulted in him being ill-tempered. Keith Bradford had stepped back from the trial, he could not be prosecuting his own son. Someone else would be doing that. Keith knew Howard Sullivan from their University days. Was the trial of Tom going to make Keith or mar him? This is the first time in his career that Keith was so keen on the outcome of the defence team. The accused person was his own son.

2nd May was the first day of the trial, Judge Archibald Magnusson rapped his gavel at three and the courtroom came to order.
''The State may examine the panel,'' he said. The prosecuting attorney stood up on his feet magnificently, he then walked honourably to the bar, and then stood and gazed pensively at the spectators and jurors. The three artists stood in a corner sketching him; and he was enjoying the euphoria of posing for just a moment for the artist to capture his posture. Smiling transparently at the jurors, Nigel Stanley introduced himself. He explained that he was representing the Crown prosecuting service, the State. He had served as their prosecutor for over a decade now, and it was an honour for which he would always be grateful for the opportunity. He then looked in the way of Steve Caxton's family, and pointed at them and told them that they were the ones who had elected him to represent them. He

thanked them, and hoped that he would not let them nor the Crown down. He admitted that he was nervous and frightened. He had prosecuted thousands of criminals, but no two cases or trials is exactly the same. He felt scared because of the awesome responsibility the people had bestowed upon him as the man responsible for sending criminals to jail and protecting the community and people. He was scared because he might also fail to adequately represent his client, and the people of London. Looking at the Juror he reminded them that the reason they were all there is to ensure that true justice is done. The right to a fair trial, a constitutional right exercised without intimidation. A life had been brutally cut short in this case and it was his role to get to the bottom of establishing the facts through evidence, to prove beyond all reasonable doubt that the accused person is liable for the murder of Steve Caxton. He was the state lawyer, and he was united with the people to seek justice, to save our society from brutal murders. He was not there to just make a smooth speech, neither was he there to deliver a sermon with eloquence, the stability of their society is crucial, even the future of human race, depended upon a guilty verdict.

Nigel Stanley spoke boldly without notes, and he held the courtroom captivated as he portrayed himself as the underdog, the prosecutor and friend to society, a partner of the jury, who, together with him, would find the truth, and punish the accused person for his monstrous act of brutal murder.

Howard Sullivan, the defence counsel barely waited for Nigel Stanley to finish his introduction before he jumped to his feet, with a frustrated look on his face, (…his body went stiff with anger and irritation by what the prosecuting attorney was saying about his client.) "Your honour, I object to this, the prosecutor is not standing here to select a jury for this case and in this trial. We are not in this court for rhetoric, which is what he is doing, it is not for him to interrogate the panel. My client is innocent, the onus of proving otherwise in this case is on the

prosecution (onus probandi), and the burden of proof is on the prosecution to prove its case beyond all reasonable doubt.
Judge Archibald Magnusson yelled ''Sustained!'' into the microphone in front of him. ''It is either you have questions for the panel or you don't, make up your mind on that before you take a seat.''
''I apologize, Milord,' Nigel said with a line etched between his brows as he pretended to be hurt. Awkwardly Howard Sullivan had drawn first blood to make him sit up.

Nigel looked in the direction of Steve Caxton's family, to his grand-mother Phoebe, Evelyn, and witnesses from the restaurant where he last ate and drank before he died in the train and a Chemical weapon professional expert and some of his colleagues from CPS was on this case. He then looked back at the juror - he was masterful, and he'd obviously done his preparation well. He was a skilful orator, and held the courtroom in the palm of his hand, he would say something funny so everyone could laugh to relieve the tension in the courtroom.

Judge Archibald Magnusson looked at Nigel and stopped him at 4:50pm, since he knew that if he did not put an end to Nigel's speech he would continue in full stride and he would finish off in the morning if he had his way.
The Judge adjourned until nine the next morning. The defence counsel spoke to his client Tom, before engaging in a long conversation with the Rebecca, James, the Psychotherapist, Neil, Gary and Frederick. Tom looked at them all sitting in the front- row, they gave him a positive look that they would see him tomorrow.

The court deputy was on standby with the handcuffs, which he put on Tom, then led him into the holding room and down the stairs, where he was taken to jail.

Chapter 18

Day 2 Trial, 3rd May 2016

At nine, in the morning, the sun rose quickly in the east and in seconds burned the dew off the thick green lawn surrounding the trial court. Judge Archibald Magnusson said good morning to the standing-room crowd. Nigel Stanley stood to his feet announcing to his honour that he had no further questions for the panel.
Defence attorney Howard Sullivan rose to his feet, gazing into the eyes of the jury. He was articulate, eloquent, young, and an orator with track record of making a success in capital cases. He had a loud voice that could wake up any sleepy head, and he was full of confidence but was not over-confident in his approach. He was warm, learned, educated and yet colloquial. As he rose to his feet, he introduced himself again, and his client, then he looked in the direction of the Psychiatrist Doctor, Tom's adoptive parents, and his friends, Gary and Neil. He then looked back at his client Tom and glanced at his notes where he had scribbled all over the pages.

The Jury did not know what he was about to say so his first question took them by surprise. ''Please take a look at this young man.'', he looked at the jury again before looking back at Tom. ''Can we prove that Tom Blackstone did what people said that he did, and if he did, could anyone in his right frame of mind do such a thing?'' he paused ''Why should the prosecution accuse an innocent young man of murder when there is a possibility that the deceased in question could have in actual fact taken his own life and (who would have been able to commit suicide.) That is the conundrum to unravel in this case'' They all were quiet, none of the jury answered, though a few of them wanted to respond, they were not certain of the appropriate response to give under the circumstances. Howard looked at each and every one straight into the eye, he knew some of them were confused, and he also knew that some of them had started to lean in the direction that he wanted them to think which was - the possibility that his client either did not at all do what he is being accused of doing, or that he was insane when he did it! How could the prosecution prove that his client poisoned the deceased when he was not actually caught in the act? It was at this point that he decided to leave the jury to ponder on those facts.

''I have nothing further to add at this point Your Honour, thank you.'' he said, with his awe transforming their faces, he gave them a half-smile. The prosecutor stared at him before starring at the Judge who was astonished and bewildered.
''Is that all?'' The Judge asked. ''Is that all, Mr Sullivan?''
''Yes, sir, that is all Your Honour.'' He had ended his introduction in less than twenty minutes, and the jury were still in shock at his organised tactics compared to the Prosecution's one and a half hour address the day before.
Judge Archibald Magnusson cleared his throat and looked down at the jury. ''Ladies and gentlemen, you have been carefully selected to serve as jurors in this case. You also have been sworn to fairly try all issues presented before you and to follow the law as I instruct. According to the laws of England, you will be sequestered until this trial is over, Some of you are on jury service and you have been given time off work for two weeks, though you may have to extend your jury service beyond the period stipulated for you and like I already said you will be sequestered until this trial is over. Do you understand what that means?''
''Yes.'' they chorused.
''This is a murder trial, which mean you will be housed in a guest house and will not be allowed to return home until it's over. This is a sacrifice that you have chosen to take in service for your country, it is what the law requires and you will feel some discomfort and hardship. I am going to end today's court session for recess, so that you all can go and rest until tomorrow morning. Each night you will stay at the guest house at an undisclosed location. Judge Archibald looked at each and every member of the jury; they appeared bewildered by

the thought of not going home for several days. The Judge then banged his gavel and the courtroom began to empty.
The jurors were made up of six men and six women; four were black, four were white, and four were Hispanic; there was a clergy, a midwife, a Professor, a bricklayer, a dentist, a pharmacist, an automobile trader, a contractor, a high school teacher, a bartender, a newsagent shop owner and a housewife.

Chapter 19

Day 3 Trial, Part 1, 4th May 2016

Twelve members of the jury were escorted by deputies, bailiffs and security men, They went up the back-stairs to the jury room, where tea, coffee, biscuits, and croissants were waiting. The bailiff announced it was now nine o'clock and that Judge Archibald was ready to start, who then led the jury into the crowded courtroom and into the jury box, where they sat in their designated seats.
"All rise…" Mr Reuben Gibbs commanded.
"Please be seated." Archibald said as he fell into his black leather chair behind the bench.
"Good morning ladies and gentlemen" he said looking in the direction of the jury. "I believe you all had a good rest last night and you are ready for the task of today?'
They all looked back at the Judge in affirmation.
"It is good practice for me to ask you some questions before we continue, "Did you discuss this case among yourselves?"
They all shook their heads in denial.
"Very well then. If anyone attempts to contact you and discuss this case or influence you in any way, I expect you to notify me as soon as possible. Do you understand?"
'Yes' they nodded.
"Now at this time we are ready to start the trial. The first order of business is to allow the attorneys to make opening statements. I should caution you that nothing the attorneys say is testimony and is not to be taken as evidence. Attorney Nigel Stanley do you wish to make an opening statement?"
Nigel Stanley rose to his feet "Yes Milord"
"Very well then, you may proceed" Nigel walked to the jury box and stood behind it, This was a move that he had done so many times in his career, he took a look at his legal note pad, (…at the moment all eyes in the court were on him, which was something he took advantage of and secretly loved.) He commenced his statement by thanking the twelve member of

the jury for taking up the challenge for being there, for their commitment, their sacrifices on jury service; and he thanked them for their citizenship. He went about how very proud of them he was and reminded the jury of the responsibility on their shoulders as well as his own shoulders, the expectation of the people from the Crown and the prosecution service on this case. He went on about himself and his thoughts on the trial, and his hopes and prayers that he would do a good job for the people of this country and for the crown and state. Nigel Stanley was used to the same rhetoric each time he made his statement before the court. The defence sat there listening to what Howard Sullivan thought to be unnecessary gushiness and extravagant pseudo sincerity being demonstrated by the prosecution.

Nigel Stanley was used to reiterating the role of the prosecution, how they are always after justice and after the interest of the state. How they are the good ones, who are always seeking to right the wrongs of injustice and punish a criminal for some heinous crime; to ensure that they were put behind bars so they wouldn't stand a chance of doing it again. He said it was up to himself and the twelve members of the jury to seek and establish the truth, the whole truth and nothing but the truth. The only reason why they were gathered here was to seek truth and justice, to search diligently for the truth. He said he was the people's lawyer and it was their job to ensure that justice was not only done, but that it is manifestly and undoubtedly seen to have been done in this case.

He then said the murder of late Steven Claxton was an evil deed. It was a calculated murder, a gruesome and senseless murder. Steven was a young man in his prime, he had worked very hard to come to England leaving his aged parents Phoebe and Matthew behind in Pennsylvania, he had studied at the London School of Economics to become an accountant and he was a happy man, in a happy relationship with his fiancée who is here today with them in this court as a witness, his surviving grand-mother was there as well also as a witness, he had everything going good for him, a good job in the city, he was well meaning to his only brother whom he took out for a drink on the night that he was rushed to the hospital after a meal with him. The accused person was the last person to wine and dine with the deceased, he was the last to have any meaningful conversation with Steven Claxton, and by the time the deceased got inside the train he began to convulse as he fell on his face and choked to his death as he was being rescued by fellow passengers. It was too late, there was nothing that anyone could have done. We are here to establish the onus probandi, the onus of proof beyond all reasonable doubt. The burden of proof in this case is 'The Onus probandi of invisible cyanide'. We have to prove how the use of a deadly invisible weapon of cyanide was used in this murder trial on the deceased. This case was a case of a very violent crime, it was death in a public place, it might have taken place out of hatred and jealousy. A motive that the prosecution has to prove in this case.

The only regret that the deceased could ever have is that he invited his long-lost half-brother out for a free meal and drink out in the west-end, what he did not know was that he was about to dine with the devil.

The family of Steve Claxton deserve justice, society is not a lawless one where vigilantes roamed the streets at free will - where there is no police, no jails, no courts, no trials, no juries nor the state to protect the people. Nigel paused to allow the jury and the courtroom to absorb and ponder on those last words. He drove home his message and point, The jury looked in the direction of Tom Blackstone, they looked at him with no compassion for what he was being accused of.

Nigel Stanley again starred at his legal note pad, he continued on how the crown was there to prove that Tom Blackstone had planned to kill his half-brother in cold blood, and he spoke about how Tom had knowledge of chemicals from the job that he had done in the past, how he had gotten so jealous of Steve and had resentment for him when he did not pick up his phone before Tom was arrested during the London riots, and how he wanted to inherit the house that Mathew had left behind, how he was greedy and selfish. He purposely used cyanide to dispatch his victim - Steven. Tom knew what he was doing while he committed the murder, he knew that even with some concentration of cyanide in the drink, his victim would pass out before he even entered the train, he measured the dose and calculated when he expected his victim to slump. This young man named Tom was the face of evil.

Nigel Stanley asked the jury to imagine that Steve Claxton was their son who was murdered in cold blood by poisoning. He gave the life history of Steve, how he became an orphan when his mother died during his birth and how his dad had died during the Twin tower incident on ground zero in September 2001. He praised Phoebe and late Mathew for being hero grand-parents who took up the challenge of bringing up their grand-son from birth after the death of their daughter up until the time he graduated as an accountant in London. Howard asked the jury to try and imagine if Steven was their son, their grand-son, their brother, their nephew whose life had been cut short in his prime out of jealousy, greed and a senseless act of violence through poison.
Objection! Shouted Howard Sullivan.
Sustained! Judge Archibald shouted back. Nigel pretended not to hear the judge shouting, but he continued with a gentle and soft voice in asking the jurors how they would feel if Steve had been a member of their family.
The murder of Steven was gruesome and senseless, Nigel continued his address. There was no excuse for the violent attack on the deceased, ladies and gentlemen of the jury, the verdict for this crime must be guilty. The man did not commit suicide. He was murdered in cold blood. Tom was not insane when he did what he did. The law must now take its course.
Judge Archibald, looking into the distance cleaned his glasses, rubbing them with a handkerchief, or he would usually clean them throughout the trial.

The prosecutor and defence attorney each had an hour for their openings, and the lure of that much time proved irresistible for the prosecuting attorney - Nigel kept on repeating himself, and finally, the artists quit sketching, the reporters quit writing, the judge repeatedly cleaned his glasses a couple of times . The juror began to look bored stiff as they searched for other points of interest around the courtroom. None of them slept, although they were sorely tempted at times.
Judge Archibald removed his glasses again, held them upward in the light, blew on them, rubbed them as though they were blurry or greasy. He remounted them on his face like he'd done so many times before. He repeated the episode of cleaning and mounting his glasses ten minutes later. The longer Stanley dragged his introduction, the more Archibald repeated the glasses cleaning exercise.
After about thirty more minutes, Nigel rounded up his statement and the courtroom sighed.
Archibald announced a fifteen minutes recess; he lunged off his bench, through the door, past chambers to the men's room. Inside the jury box, the jury resorted to sleeping, glaring, snoring, squirming, checking their watches for what the time was. The last thing they need is a long trial, what they require are the facts, so that they could give the verdict.
Unlike Nigel, Howard Sullivan presented a brief opening, he purposely made it even shorter after Nigel's lengthy introduction. He gave a brief history of the childhood of Tom and how vulnerable he was. How he could not have committed the crime he was alleged to have committed, he asked the jury to try and imagine the stages of growth and development that Tom had passed through in his childhood, how disturbed he had been mentally and circumstantially. The deceased was not there to share with them his own side of the story, and they cannot presume that he was innocent; my learned colleague Nigel had just said that he was an orphan who had been through trauma!

Objection! shouted Stanley.

Objection sustained Archibald, shouted out. Howard pretended not to have heard the judge shout but continued in a soft voice …'The deceased must not have been a happy man as we are being told and made to believe, there could have been underlying issues that we do not know about that must be established, but we have to go by the facts in front of us. My client Tom on the day he was invited out for drinks by his half-brother, and went out to have fun and not to take someone else's life. If the glove does not fit ladies and gentlemen then you must acquit my client and set him free to go back home and carry on with his life with continued rehabilitation for his drug addiction. Howard asked them not to convict Tom Blackstone but to send him home to his long lost biological dad who had just found him after decades of practise as a prosecutor for the state. His client was unfortunate young man if truth be told, but then let it be established here.
''Can anyone tell me why the deceased would not have committed suicide?''
Objection! Stanley shouted at Howard.
Objection sustained! Archibald shouted down.
Howard finished his address shortly after he started, and left the jury with a marked contrast in the two approaches and styles of address.
''Is that all?'' Archibald asked in amazement.
Howard nodded affirming that he had finished before sat down next to his client; Tom.
''Very well Mr Stanley, you may call your first witness.''
''The crown calls Miss Evelyn Blackstone.''
The bailiff went to the witness room and came back with Miss Evelyn Blackstone. He led her through the door next to the jury box, into the courtroom where she was sworn in by Mr Reuben Gibbs and then he seated her in the witness chair.
''Could you speak into the microphone.'' he instructed Evelyn.
''Yes sir.'' she replied, her eyes darting everywhere.
''Miss Blackstone, could you please tell this honourable court your full names and where you live?'' Nigel asked the corners of his eyes crinkling.

'My name is Evelyn Blackstone. I live at 406 Bevington street, Jamaica road, South East of London.''
''Could you tell the court who Steve Claxton is to you and, what do you know about him during the period that you met him and the time that his life was cut short under tragic circumstances.''
''I first met Steve Claxton in the University in our first year studying Accountancy and Finance, so basically we were class mates.''
''Could you tell this court about the kind of person that you know the deceased to be?''
'During our first year in the accountancy department, Steve and I began to see one another, we developed a healthy relationship throughout our campus life, and we continued our relationship after university and we were just starting to plan on getting engaged and get married in the near future'
''Did the deceased share any story about his parents and grand-parents with you?''
''Yes Steve lost his mum during his birth and his dad died during the twin towers incident.''
''Would you say that he was a person who was emotionally disturbed, or depressed in any form?''
''No not at all.''
''What makes you say that?''
'Steve is a happy, jolly good fellow who had everything going on for him. He always was very proud of his up-bringing by his grand-parents in Pennsylvania, he was an American born and bred, he only came to further his education in England. He was a happy man and we had a healthy relationship and was looking forward to getting married. He was very generous too. I understand that he bought the drink and food for his brother when he invited him out for drinks, it is sad that anyone would do what they did to Steve. Steve's death was really very tragic.''
''In your opinion do you think that Steve was the kind of person who could take his own life?''
'Never! not in a million years, there was no need for him to do such a thing. He had everything going for him, he was such a

lovely person, his grand-parents would testify to that, he was a good guy to everyone that came into contact with him and he treasures having a family. Steve was not the kind of person that would commit suicide.'' she became emotional and started to sob profusely.
''Thank you Evelyn for your answers.''
Evelyn continued to sob as the memory of Steve flooded her thoughts.

The court was silent for few minutes before Nigel Stanley continued with his questioning.
'Are you alright to carry on?'
''Yeah.'' she said as she pulled herself together to continue with answering the questions being put across to her.
''When were you planning on getting married to Steve?''
''We were thinking of tying the knot next year, he just proposed to me two months ago.''
''Steve's nan must have been very glad to hear that all that was happening in Steve's life.''
''Do you know the accused person Mr Tom Blackstone?''
''Yes I do.''
''How so?''
''Tom was adopted by my parents; his surname was changed to my parents name after his adoption.''
''How would you describe the accused's behaviour when he lived with you and your parents''
''The only regret I have is that I did not know that this Tom was the same man that Steve referred to as his half- brother that he connected with'
''What do you mean by that Evelyn?''
''Tom is the face of evil?''
''What do you mean by calling Tom evil Miss Evelyn Blackstone?''
''He was sent packing from my parent's home because he raped me.''
''Objection!'' roared Howard Sullivan as he sprang to his feet he shouted out ''The criminal record of the victim is inadmissible!''

''Objection overruled!'' shouted Judge Archibald affirmatively. 'Miss Blackstone you may continue with your answers to Mr Stanley's questions regarding the rape.''
'Milord this trial is not a rape trial, my learned colleague's question is not relevant to the allegation in this case, Milord - the criminal record of the victim is inadmissible!''
''Mr Stanley you may proceed with your questioning.''
''Mr Howard the questions are relevant to help the jury to make an informed decision about the character of the accused person.''
'Miss Blackstone, you said that your parents asked the accused person to leave their home, was that after the incident of the rape occurred?'
''Yes sir.''
''Right. Did you not know that the Tom that your boyfriend called his half-brother was the same man that raped you when he lived with your parents?'
''No, Steve had not yet introduced Tom to me in person, he just said he'd found his half-brother, born by same mother but not by the same dad.''
'Did you ever share your experience that you had with your adoptive 'brother' with Steve?''
''Yes I did.''
''How did he take it?''
''He was so sad and sorry that the incident ever happened to me.''
''Do you think that if Steve knew that his half-brother was capable of raping and committing such an offence that he would invite him out for a meal and a drink that he himself paid for?''
'No he would not. I regret that I did not know that Steve went out dining with evil'
''Objection, mind your use of words Miss Blackstone.''
''Objection overruled. Continue Mr Stanley.''
''Miss Blackstone what else can you tell this court about the person of Tom Blackstone?''
''Tom had a lot of mood swings and depression, he was on drugs and addicted to substance misuse.''

''Do you think that Tom is capable of killing anyone?''
''Objection! Objection Milord!'' yelled Howard, waving his arms and looking desperately at the Judge, my client is presumed innocent until he proven guilty. The only onus that the prosecution has is to prove their case beyond all reasonable doubt, therefore, by the prosecution asking Mrs Blackstone whether my client is capable of killing is unprofessional and out of order Milord.''
''Objection sustained! Sustained!''
''He should be admonished, your honour, Howard demanded, his face and eyes were full of anger, his voice had gone blue with rage.''
Pretending not to hear his Lordship's sustaining Howard's objection, Stanley continued with his questioning.
'Miss Blackstone, when you were in courtship with the late Steven Caxton, did he ever mention that he had a brother whose name is Tom Blackstone?'
'He did mention that he had miraculously met his half-brother and that he found out his name was Tom, but he never told me his brother's surname, I never knew it was the same Tom that I knew.''
''Assuming you knew that the Tom that you had previously known was the same man that Steven had found out to be his half-brother, what would you have done?''
''I would have unreservedly warned Steven to be careful of his half-brother because he is dangerous and notorious man.''
''Objection! Your honour.'' shouted Howard.
''Objection overruled, you may continue with your questioning.''
''Miss Blackstone you have referred to Tom as a dangerous and notorious man because of the experience that you have had living with him, when your parents adopted him.''
''Yes sir,'' she said as her eyes watered.
''That is all for this witness your honour, nothing further'', Nigel Stanley announced.
''Cross-examination, Mr Howard Sullivan?''
Howard saw this as an opportunity to wake up Archibald and Nigel. He could see why Evelyn had been brought by the

prosecution team to establish that the deceased was a happy man and could not have committed suicide. Howard saw an opportunity that he could not pass up in order to redress the issue. This was the chance to set the right tone for the defence in this trial. He was ready to reveal areas of vulnerability in the life of the deceased that he thinks the last witness – Evelyn was not letting on; he was going to drill her with some questioning. Maybe Nigel had coached her on what to say but things were about to change when he started his cross-examination.

''Yes your honour, I only have a few questions for Miss Evelyn Blackstone,'' Howard said as he made a move behind Nigel through the podium. The Jury looked at each other. The prosecuting team, and district attorney, all looked at one another, as if to say they knew Howard is not up for revenge.

''Miss Evelyn Blackstone, when you first met the late Steve Claxton in the University, did he ever mention to you that he was an orphan?''

''Yes we both shared our history and background with one another when we met. Steve's mum died during his birth and, his grand-parents looked after him from birth up until he came to England for his university education.''

''Did you know the circumstances that led to the demise of his parents?''

''He lost his dad under tragic circumstances in the twin tower disaster at ground zero.''

''So he was not a 100% happy person like you portrayed him to be earlier?''

''Of course Steve was a happy man, he had everything going for him, - a good job, and we were engaged to be married.''

''Did Steve tell you the circumstances that led to the demise of his mother?''

''She died at child birth.''

''And was that all he said to you about his mother?''

''What else would he have said about his mother that would have made him very sad apart from her death?''

''Well that is the question that I am asking you Miss Evelyn Blackstone, you were his girl-friend, you were close to him,

he told you a lot about himself and his family. Could you tell this court what you know about Steve's late mother?''
''I have already told you what I know about late Steve's mother, unless there is something that you know that I do not know.''
''Did the deceased ever mention to you that his mother was a drug addict, and was in rehabilitation at Arizona where she was receiving treatment when she was pregnant with the deceased and lost her own life giving birth to him...''
''Yes I knew that his mum was poorly but Steve was not affected by it because she was not alive when Steve was growing up, he grew up to be told the story, his grand-parents nurtured him to be a happy child in the United States.'
''I put it to you Miss Evelyn Blackstone, that you knew that Steve was battling with issues that constantly made him sad, he was a lonely child, that was why he came to England to look for his half-brother. He was an orphan, his grand-parents were aged and he was scared of not having any family left on the face of this earth.''
''Objection, Objection your honour, the emotional state of the deceased's mother is irrelevant and inadmissible in this trial!''
''Objection sustained!''
''Thank you, your honour,'' Stanley exclaimed, with gratitude that Archibald had indeed done him a great favour by sustaining the objection.
''Miss Evelyn Blackstone, you told this honourable court that you and the late Steve were engaged to be married.''
''Yes we were.''
''You certainly at this point knew everyone in Steve's family, except his half-brother Tom.''
''He was about to arrange for me to meet his half-brother after his taking him out for a drink to tell him that he was going to get married and that he would like him to be his best man.''
''You expect this court to believe that you did not meet Tom at all before Steve died.''
''Yes I did not meet Tom through Steve, if I did; I would have told Steve that his half-brother was not worth the trouble.''

''Steve only had Tom as his sibling, they got on and there was no misunderstanding between them. Tom was not a danger to Steve, he was company to Steve who was lonely and deeply sad, he was going through loneliness.''
'No. Steve was not lonely; he did not need Tom to be happy. Tom is not capable of making anyone happy, I can testify to that.''
''Evelyn, I put it to you that you are misleading this court. You knew that Steve was depressed, he was an orphan who had lost his mother under tragic circumstances. His father too died during the twin towers tragedy, he was dealing with a lot of emotional trauma. It was when his grand-parents decided to go and look for his father when he was at the age of eleven years that they found out for the first time that his father had died. Steve was suffering silently. He was a sad man. His emotional trauma was what pushed him to look for his half-brother. He took his own life at that meeting with his half-brother. He put poison in his own drink and he drank it.''
''Why would Steve do such a thing, he is not even capable of hurting a fly much less of killing himself. He was an angel, I believe that someone maliciously took Steve's life.'' she began to cry again, then wiped her eyes and cried harder, she repeatedly burst into tears and bawled uncontrollably as the shouting erupted.
''Steve was at his lowest moment when he invited Tom out for drinks. He took his own life.''
''No, no stop all these lies, you did not know Steve, and he did not take his own life, he could not have, she managed to keep the microphone by her face, she wept, her wailing continued echoing through the entirely astonished and stunned courtroom.''
''Objection Milord, Objection your honour, my learned colleague should be admonished, your honour, he should be admonished.'' Stanley repeated himself with anger, in his voice.
'I'll withdraw the question.'' Howard replied loudly as he returned to his seat.

Stanley again asked the jury and the judge to admonish Howard and he urged the jury to disregard the last question.
Judge Archibald asked Stanley if he had any redirect. Stanley answered ''No,'' he then dashed to the witness stand with a handkerchief to give to Miss Evelyn Blackstone, who had buried her head in her hands who was sobbing and shaking uncontrollably.
''You are excused, Miss Blackstone,'' Archibald said. ''Bailiff, please assist the witness.'' The bailiffs carried out the Judge's instructions. Evelyn was led down from the witness stand. Archibald looked in Howard's direction until Evelyn was gone and everyone went very quiet. The jury was told by the Judge to please disregard the last question put to Evelyn regarding suicide.
The judge excused the witness from further questions and he recessed until 2:45pm.

Chapter 20

Day 3 Trial, Part 2, 4th May 2016

The court resumed at 3pm.
''All rise...'' Mr Reuben Gibbs yelled.

''Please be seated. Any other witness Mr Stanley?'' asked Archibald.
''The State calls Mrs Phoebe Brynhild,'' Nigel announced.
Mrs Phoebe Brynhild was brought from the witness room above the courtroom. She was sworn in by Mr Reuben Gibbs, and was seated. Phoebe was late Steve Caxton's grandmother; she was his late mother Teresa's mother. Phoebe and Matthew had looked after the deceased ever since he was born after the tragic incident of his mother dying at child birth. Phoebe was now 85 and frail. She was flown to England from Pennsylvania by the prosecution team to testify and witness the trial. She knew a lot about her grandson who had been murdered. Though she's frail but she knows that she has to be at the trial for the sake of her late daughter, late husband Mathew and her late grandson Steve.
''You are Mrs Phoebe Brynhild?'' Stanley asked.
''Yes I am.'' she replied with a fragile voice.
''Mrs Phoebe Brynhild, you will remain seated throughout the questioning. If you require to use the rest room or to have a break, please do not hesitate to ask for a break. If for any reason you would like me to repeat any part of my question or the whole question, please do not hesitate to ask for a repeat.''
''Thank you.'' Phoebe replied.
''Can you please tell this honourable court your name, where you live and what you know about the deceased.''
''My name is Phoebe Brynhild. I have lived in Pennsylvania ever since I was born, and I am an American.''
The Jury looked at each other, some with a smile as they looked at Phoebe graciously.
''How would you say the deceased person related is to you?''

''Steve is my grand-son. Matthew and I lost our daughter in 1990 when she was giving birth to Steven; we both were in our sixties. We started looking after Steven as he had lost his mother tragically. We nurtured him from cradle till he left US to study accountancy in England.''
''Would you say that Steve suffered from any form of depression or emotional trauma due to the loss of his mother as he grew up…''
''No. not at all. Steve was emotionally balanced.''
''What about his dad?''
''Yes his dad's name was Brian Caxton; he was also an accountant, practising before his life was cut short by the twin tower incident on 9/11. Steve was only eleven years old at the time.''
''That must have been another tragic incident for you and Mathew to deal with.''
''Did your daughter Teresa own any property apart from the one that you and Mathew would have made her a beneficiary of?''
''Yes Teresa owns a house in England.''
''Can you please tell this court how Teresa came about this property?''
''She bought it with her first husband Keith Bradford.''
''How did she manage this property when she was unwell?''
''She asked the estate agent to manage it for years because the only son of her marriage to Keith had been taken into care while she was unwell with addiction.''
''And who has been in charge of the property since the death of Teresa?''
''Our family lawyer.''
''Have you ever met Tom Blackstone?''
''Yes I first met him when Steve brought him to the US during Mathew's funeral.''
''While Tom and Steve were in the US, was there any information that you revealed to them, that you thought they both should know because they were half-brothers?''
''Yes I was pleased when Steve told me the circumstances in which he met Tom after a motor accident which Tom survived

by some miracle. I told both young men that Matthew would be pleased in his grave that fate had brought them to meet after the death of their mother.''
''Did you mention the property that Teresa had left behind and how she came about it?''
''Yes, I explained to Tom and Steve that they both owned the property and that the lawyer was looking after it and that it was my joy for it to pass to them both.''
''And what was the response of Tom and Steve?''
''Tom said he would never have thought in million years that his parents whom he never knew would ever have anything for him. Steve did not say anything because he was never in need, Mathew had made him aware that he was the sole beneficiary of what we owned and that we hope that he would one day find his half-brother, if he did then they could share our real estate.''
''What else did Steve say to you while he visited you in Pennsylvania?''
''He was very happy to tell me that he was engaged and planning to get married.''
''Did he appear as a man who was depressed or sad in any way?''
''No. He was very happy, in-fact it was one of the times that I've seen him at his happiest.''
''Did Tom make any comment that would make you suspicious that he could be a danger to Steve or to the family?''
''At the time I laughed because I did not perceive it to mean anything, but right now…my perception of what Tom said has changed.''
''How do you mean and what did Tom say?''
''Tom said does it mean that the house in England would be owned by Steve and his spouse when they got married?' she paused, ''I then explained that should not be the case because the lawyer will ensure that both young men get their share of their mother's property.''
''What was Tom's response to your answer?''
'He again said he would never have thought that his parents left anything for him, he said how he hardly even knew them,

he also lamented that he was taken into social services care instead of being looked after by his parents.''
''What then did you say Mrs Brynhild?''
''I comforted him asking him not to think of the past, but to look to the future.''
''And what did he say?''
''He thanked me.''
''Would you say that there was a big difference in the personality between these two young men?''
''I think the biggest difference between them is that one was lucky to be brought up in a happy home, while the other young man had gone through social care and various families. It is very sad.''
''If you were asked to be the judge or a jury member for a second, would you ever think that Tom could plan Steve's murder?''
''Yes I think Tom is responsible for Steve's death. Like the story of Cain and Abel in the bible, nothing is impossible between people if there is jealousy instead of love. Steve's life was cut short by a violent crime committed by someone. It is a senseless act and whoever has taken my grand-son's life will never know peace, if it is Tom then he too will die by the sword.''
Howard Sullivan stood to his feet as he shouted ''Objection! your honour, Objection! Admonish him your honour, my learned colleague is out of order!, He must be admonished.''
Howard said shaking, ''I ask that the question Stanley just asked Phoebe on her being a jury or judge in this matter should be stricken from the record and the jury be instructed to disregard it your honour!'
''Objection sustained!'' The Judge pronounced.
Looking at Howard with a smile and then turning to the Judge, Nigel said 'I'll withdraw the question your honour.''
''I ask the Jury to disregard the last question from Mr Nigel Stanley.'' Archibald instructed the jury.
''No further questions for Mrs Phoebe Brynhild Milord.''
''Mr Howard do you have any redirect examination for the prosecution witness?''

''Yes sir.''
''Very well, you may proceed.''
''Mrs Phoebe Bryhild, could you tell this honourable court at what age you told your grand-son that his mother had died during his birth?.''
'Mathew and I told him when he was 11 years of age, he understood the fact that we were his grand-parents, and he also understood that we were left with no choice but to bring him up after the loss of our own daughter who happened to be his mother.''
''And did you and your late husband not think that this news was too much for an 11 year old to take all inside his fragile mind.''
''At that age he was getting ready to go to high school, and we thought it was the right time to make him aware about his parents.''
''Why was his father, who was alive at the time his mother died not take up the responsibility of bringing Steve up?''
''Brian was an accountant who was practising in New York at the time Teresa died, and he worked round the clock and could not shoulder the responsibility of looking after a new-born baby, that is something that a woman would do a better job of.''
''And how many times did Brian travel down to Pennsylvania to visit his son?''
''Initially he visited his son when he was a baby, but later we lost contact with him when he moved house and changed his job.'
''So basically you and the late Mathew lost contact with Steve's father?''
''Yes we did.''
''And do you know the effect of not having his father would have on him psychologically as he was growing up?''
''How do you mean?''
''Many children of Steven's age would have grown up with their mother and father and not with their grand-parents alone, is that not the conventional way?''

‘‘Are you telling me that we did the wrong thing by taking Steven on to look after him after the death of my daughter? I don’t get your point sir.’’
‘‘What I am saying is that you deprived Steven of the bonding that he would have had with his biological father, Brian.’’
‘Of course we did not do anything like that. After we told Steve that his mother died during his birth, we then went on a journey to look for his father Brian. Steve was only 11 years of age when we discovered that his dad had died in the twin towers disaster on 9/11. And what do you expect us to have done? Of course we continued to look after him.’’
‘‘My point exactly, you continued to look after Steve and to bring him up, but this young man had an underlying traumatic disorder which was caused by the news of the death of his parents, he was an orphan.’’
‘‘My grandson did not suffer from any emotional or psychological trauma, he grew up emotionally sound like any other child and he proceeded to study Accountancy at University. I don’t know what you are talking about.’’
‘Did you take Steven for any bereavement counselling after telling him about the loss of his parents?’’
‘‘Steve was only 11 years old when we told him about his parents; Matthew and I were the only family that he had.’’
‘‘Did you know whether your late daughter suffered from suicidal tendencies when she battled with drug addiction?’’
‘‘No, Teresa was not suicidal.’’
‘‘How did you know that when you did not live with her in England before she moved to the US for rehabilitation?’’
‘‘My daughter had never been suicidal you can take it or leave it, that is the fact.’’
Looking at the jury, Howard smirked then said, ‘‘The late Steven had an underlying emotional sadness within him. He could not wait to meet and bond with his half-brother Tom. He needed family. He longed to feel the gap of having been alone without his parent or sibling all his life. This man lost both of his parents under tragic circumstances, and he only lived to hear the sad stories which had left him with depression in a dark and lonely place in his life, he had a subtle mental

health disorder as the lone child that he thought he was, and he was left with no other choice but to contemplate and execute the taking of his own life through poisoning. We cannot rule out the fact that he did not inherit suicidal traits or tendencies from his late mother. Is that not the case with your grandson Mrs Bryhild?''
Phoebe did not answer the question, she sobbed bitterly, and she dried her tears with handkerchief which she took out of her handbag. Anyone would be sorry for her except for Mr Sullivan. The memory of the loss of her daughter and grandson flooded her thoughts.
''Objection your honour! Your honour Objection! These facts are not substantiated with any evidence, it is inadmissible and Mr Sullivan knows It!'' shouted the Prosecutor.
''Sustained.'' replied the Judge.
The defence has no further questions for the witness your honour.'' Howard said with a frosty look and at 4:55pm Judge Archibald said goodbye to the jurors with strict instructions: ''If anyone attempts to contact you and discuss this case or influence you in any way, I expect you to notify me as soon as possible. Do you understand?' '
They all nodded affirmatively and politely as they filed from the courtroom. Judge Archibald Magnusson banged his gavel and adjourned until nine in the morning.
''Court!'' Reuben Gibbs yelled, and everyone stood up. The Judge stepped off the bench, went through the door, past chambers to the men's room and then into his Chambers afterwards. He did not leave his chambers until 8pm before calling it a day.
Phoebe was taken into a quiet room where she was given a glass of water to drink and to take her medication. She needed to recover from the questioning. The prosecution team made sure she was looked after as the court trial was all getting too much for her to cope with considering her old age. Phoebe was a crucial witness for the prosecution.
''I hope you'll be able to get some sleep tonight when you get back to the guest house.'' Stanley said with empathy.

''How can I close my eyes to sleep tonight after all these questions, how can someone assume that Steve took his own life?, it makes me feel sick…'' she said as she broke down in tears again.

''Let's go and get you a nice meal in town, I'm afraid you have to take your mind off today's trial, your well-being is more important than anything else. We cannot bring back either Teresa or Steve, they are now at peace somewhere above in heaven and you should be at peace too here on earth. You will soon be back in Pennsylvania where you can put all of these behind you. '' Stanley said and Phoebe's eyes lit up but her pupils were dilated, her lips parted releasing a smile on her face.

Stanley held Phoebe's hands as he escorted her to the car waiting outside the court building and she was driven back to the guest house where she stayed before she travelled back to the United States.

Chapter 21

Day 4 Trial, Part 1, 5th May 2016

On the 4th straight day since the trial began, the court room was packed by 8:45am. All the seats available in the court were taken by spectators. As the court room door was opened, the crowd filed inside slowly through the metal detector, past the careful eyes of the security and finally into the courtroom. The front row was reserved for Gary, Neil, Fredrick, the mental health experts and the psychotherapist, Tom's biological father, Keith Bradford. Prosecution witnesses were all seated: the pathologist - Dr Jeremy McWhinney, the chemical poison expert, the Late Steven's family and his girlfriend sat down together; Phoebe, Evelyn, James and Rebecca.
Cameras and reporters were sitting on the front lawn in abundance, the trial was the only topic of conversation and reporting. At about 8:50am Tom Blackstone was escorted from the small holding room. There were half a dozen officers surrounding him, his hand-cuffs were removed by one of the many officers and was led to his chair. The prosecutor and defence attorney took their places in the court room. The bailiff was stationed near the jury box, and, thereafter, opened the door and released the jurors to their assigned seats. Mr Reuben Gibbs was watching all this from the door leading to Judge Archibald's chambers, and when everyone was seated and it all looked perfect as the court room grew quiet at 9:00am on the dot, he stepped forward and then yelled 'All rise for the Court!' The Judge walked inside in his black robe, he loped to the bench and then instructed everyone to take a seat. Archibald greeted the jury and questioned them about what happened or didn't happen since yesterday's adjournment.
''We are ready to proceed Milord.'' Nigel Stanley announced.
''Call your next witness,'' Archibald ordered Nigel. The Chemical poison expert and pathologist were brought in by the District Attorney. The pathologist ended up being very thorough and the doctor took the stand that morning fully

laden with photos of the autopsies and several anatomy charts to support the prosecuting team's evidence. Nigel wanted the jury to hear and know the circumstances under which and how he had died. He had a right to prove it. The prosecution would prove that it was cyanide poison that actually killed Steven and how his post-mortem results confirmed the fact before the court. And so, with his prosecutorial overkill, Nigel was determined prove that the invisible cyanide was the weapon used for the murder of Steve in this case. The anatomy charts were placed on easels before the jury, he had a plastic version of the human physiology and intestine to demonstrate the effect of changes in the internal organs of the victim after the poison entered his body. So many times Nigel would ask a question, and then elicit a response, he would ask a question to drive home the point that he had already made.
"You may proceed with your witness Mr Stanley or we will never leave here today."
"Yes Milord, the state calls Dr Jeremy McWhinney."
"Can you please tell this court your name, which hospital you work at, and where you live?"
"My name is Dr Jeremy McWhinney, I am a Consultant Pathologist, I work at Merseyside Hospital in London and I live in London."
"How long have you worked as a Consultant Pathologist?"
"I have practised for thirty-five years as a Doctor, twenty years of which I have practiced as a Consultant Pathologist."
"How would you describe what you do to a layman?"
Howard stood to his feet, "Your Honour, we would be glad to stipulate as to the causes of death." Howard announced with great frustration.
"No we won't." Nigel replied as he proceeded to repeat the same question that he had just asked the pathologist. Howard fell back into his chair, shaking his head as he looked at the jurors.
"Yes Dr McWhinney, before I was interrupted; how would you describe what you do to a layman?"
"Pathology is the study of the causes and effects of disease or an injury, incorporating a wide range of bioscience research

fields and medical practices such as diagnoses of diseases through analysis of tissue, cell, and body fluid samples. A physician practicing pathology is called a pathologist.''

''Thank you Doctor. Can you explain to the court the results of the post-mortem carried on the deceased in this case?''

''The late Steve Claxton died within between thirty minutes to an hour after exposure; he had respiratory failure compounded by lactic acidosis and rhabdomyolysis. After post-mortem examination we found out that the deceased had drank cyanide.''

''Doctor, can you please explain to the court what this substance called Cyanide is?''

''Cyanide is derived from the seeds of Prunus family, (which includes cherries, apricots and almonds) and it is rapidly lethal. It works as a mitochondrial toxin, inhibiting cytochrome c oxidase in the electron transport chain, thus preventing cells from aerobically using adenosine triphosphate for energy. High concentrations leads to death in minutes; the cyanide-haemoglobin complex can cause the skin to remain pink (in contrast to the cherry-red of carbon-monoxide poisoning), despite cellular hypoxia.''

''From the post-mortem examination, could you explain to this court the cause of death of the deceased?''

'The deceased died from cyanide which prevented the cells of his body from being able to use oxygen, the chemical inhibits an enzyme in the mitochondria of cells from doing it's vital job of capturing oxygen and transporting it into cells. Symptoms that victims of cyanide poisoning exhibit before their death include general weakness, shortness of breath, confusion, headache, dizziness, excessive sleepiness and bizarre behaviour. The symptoms usually progress to seizure, coma and eventual death. Cyanide exists as a gas, a liquid or in solid form.''

Nigel Stanley looked at the jurors one after the other, then he looked at his legal notepad before asking Dr McWhinney the next question.

'The late Steve died inside the train and that was about half an hour after he had his last drink in the restaurant. Doctor, how

long does it take before the victim slumps after exposure to the poison?''
''High concentration in the body leads to death in minutes.''
''Do you consider the dose of cyanide found in the deceased's body during post-mortem examination to be of high concentration?''
''Yes there was high concentration of cyanide according to laboratory tests carried out.''
''Which means the deceased would have convulsed and died almost instantly of respiratory failure on the day in question?''
''Yes.'' replied the doctor.
''Can you explain the photos of the autopsies and several anatomy charts to the court?''
''Pointing at the charts with his pen he showed the jurors the pink skin of the deceased caused by the cyanide-haemoglobin in contrast to the cherry-red of carbon-monoxide poisoning, despite cellular hypoxia.''
''What other symptoms does the anatomy charts suggests?''
''The deceased before his death must have had chronic ingestion causing a variety of symptoms ranging from generalised weakness in the victim's body, confusion and bizarre behaviour, through to paralysis and liver failure before the victim slumped to the floor to meet his death.''
''What other symptoms did the deceased's body suggest on your anatomy charts?''
''The deceased suffered excessive salivation, lacrimation, instant and involuntary urination, involuntary diarrhoea, gastrointestinal distress and Ernesis.''
''How was this cyanide consumed by the deceased, was it put inside his food or inside his drink?''
''The post-mortem suggests that he drank cyanide in his sparkling wine.''
''As a Consultant Pathologist you testify and are a witness in this case to the fact that the victim of this murder died of cyanide poison that was put in his sparkling drink on the day that he died?''
'Yes I do so testify and witness.''

''That is all for the witness your honour.'' Nigel said as he suppressed a shudder.
Through the examination of Dr McWhinney by Mr Nigel Stanley, it was determined that the deceased had been poisoned while he was in the restaurant, and collapsed when he climbed into the train. The symptoms and evidence of his cause of death was cyanide which was meant to kill him instantly, the restaurant where he met Tom was a few seconds to the train that he boarded and as soon as he got onto the train he slumped instantly. The passenger pressed the emergency button to call the attention of the train driver. After which the train could not proceed until the ambulance arrived. The late Steve was then rushed to the hospital but he died while on the train. The doctor at the accident and emergency room recorded that he was brought in dead' on his file.

The doctor finished at 11:45am and Judge Archibald, looking tired and numb with boredom, awarded a one-hour and thirty minutes lunch break. The bailiff led the jurors to the jury room located upstairs on the second floor where their lunch was already waiting for them. Their assorted sandwiches were lined with cheese, ham, bacon, lettuce, avocado, chicken, bacon and tomato nicely laid on polystyrene plates. There was a chess game on the table for anyone interested in playing chess. The bailiff reiterated that they were forbidden from to leaving the courthouse.

Chapter 22

Day 4 Trial, Part 2, 5th May 2016

The court resumed at 2pm.
"All rise..." Mr Reuben Gibbs commanded.

"Please be seated." Archibald said, removing his glasses. "Howard, any cross-examination?" he asked.
"Yes just a few."
"Very well then, go ahead."
"Dr Jeremy McWhinney, you have medically established that the deceased died of cyanide poison which was put inside his sparkling drink on the day that he died. Is that right?"
"Correct."
"Doctor, can you confirm what you said earlier that a high concentration of cyanide in the body leads to death in minutes."
"Yes I did."
"Can you also confirm that you said that you consider the dose of cyanide found in the deceased's body during post-mortem examination to be of a high concentration?"
"Yes there was a high concentration of cyanide according to laboratory tests carried out."
"Which means that going by these facts, the deceased after drinking the poison ought to have convulsed and died inside the restaurant and not an hour later considering the dose of cyanide you found in his post-mortem?"
"I suppose so."
"Do you agree with me that the cyanide that violently killed the late Steve was consumed orally within minutes of entering the train or just before boarding the train, and that it was that dose that caused Steve to slump, convulse, collapse and go into coma."
"It is possible."
"Do you also agree with me that the cyanide that violently killed the late Steve may not have been from the drink that he

drank, but may have been in another form as you described earlier that Cyanide exists as a gas, a liquid or in solid form.''
'Do you agree with me that there is a balance of probabilities here and that the cause of death could have been suicide and not murder as your report presupposes?'
''Suicide?'' replied the doctor.
''Yes, suicide, I mean the deceased put something in his own mouth to take his own life and that it is this substance he took that actually caused him to slump.''
Nigel jumped and roared, ''Objection! Objection! Improper question!''
''You don't have to answer.'' Archibald said loudly.
''Objection! Objection your honour!'' Nigel continued, standing on his toes.
''Order! Order!' Archibald banged his gavel.
The doctor kept quiet - not answering whether his pathology report on the death of Steve was murder, or whether suicide was a possibility as presumption of innocence of the accused person that was raised by defence counsel. Nigel was silent. Howard knew what he had done, who walked to his chair and said looking directly at the Judge, ''I'll withdraw the question.''
''Please disregard,'' Archibald instructed the jury.
The court was quiet for about four seconds as the jurors looked at each other. For the first time since the beginning of the trial, the defence counsel had pointed out a very important point based on the facts on the report of the consultant pathologist. The look on some of their faces confirmed the prosecutions worst fear. The defence had raised an important point that cannot be overlooked by the jurors.
''Can you call your next witness.'' Archibald said looking at Nigel, ''Where is Inspector Jasper Willard?'' asked Archibald.
''He is here Milord. The State calls Inspector Jasper Willard, ''Nigel announced. The Inspector swore to 'tell the truth, the whole truth, and nothing but the truth, so help me God.' He then sat in the witness stand. Jasper Willard was in his early thirties, of mixed race, a matured cop, who with his hard work had rose to Inspector rank and he was eager to ensure justice

was done, and was ready to please and to make an impression in making the London streets a crime free zone. He stood out as a prosecution witness. Nigel Stanley addressed him from the podium.
''Go ahead with your examination Mr Stanley.'' The Judge said.
''Yes your honour.'' he paused ''Inspector Jasper Willard, what is your position with the London Metropolitan police?''
''Police Inspector sir.''
''Inspector, could you tell the court whether you were able to check the body of the deceased for any vital signs of the cause of death?''
''No sir.''
''Why not?''
''From the appearance of the body, there was no reason to doubt that the deceased was dead and, by the time we got to the scene, the deceased had been dead for some time. We try to avoid contaminating the evidence.''
''Would you consider that as your usual practice and training?''
''No, not really sir, it has been the practice for some time and it is just by analogy from past cases where some police cops were accused of contaminating the evidence.''
''What did you do when you saw the late corpse of the victim?''
''I called the station and spoke to the Chief inspector at the headquarters.''
''And what happened after you spoke to him?''
''He directed the criminal investigation department to come down to the scene of crime.''
''Can you brief this court on the coroner's report on this case?''
''The death of the late Steve was reported to the coroner after a post-mortem had been carried out on his corpse by the consultant pathologist.''
''What was the nature of death that was reported to the coroner in this case?''

''According to the report to the coroner, the cause of death was murder. The coroner investigated the death as it was reported to him. The coroner made necessary inquiries to find out the cause of death of the deceased. He ordered a post-mortem examination and he obtained witness statements and medical records. He held an inquest.''
''Who made witness statements for this case.''
''The train passengers and train driver present when the victim slumped inside the train.''
''Do you have the statement with you?''
''Yes there are 4 statements from witnesses: one from the restaurant staff and three from train passengers.''
''Can you give the statements to the jurors to read.''
The court bailiff took the statements to the jurors, waited for them to pass the exhibits round to one another as they read the content, he then collected it when they had finished reading all four statements and took them back to Inspector Jasper Willard. Basically, the four statements confirmed what the witnesses saw before the late Steve slumped while on the train. Evidence of symptoms that the deceased exhibited after his exposure to cyanide which led to his death, these symptoms included general weakness, shortness of breath, confusion, headache, dizziness, excessive sleepiness and bizarre behaviour. The eye-witnesses confirmed from their statement that the deceased slumped on the train and he progressed to a seizure after which becoming coma like and eventual death.
Looking directly at Inspector Jasper Willard, and then back to his legal notepad where he had lots of scribbles, Nigel looked back at Inspector Jasper Willard before asking him more questions.
''In this case could you tell the court who reported the death of Steve to the Coroner?''
''The Police did because the death occurred in suspicious circumstances and the death was unexpected and sudden in a public place on the day in question. The victim died before the ambulance reached the hospital emergency room.''

"Can you tell this honourable court whether the coroner was satisfied that Steve's death was from natural causes or suicide?"
"No the coroner did not report that the death of Steve was due to suicide."
"To the best of your knowledge, did the coroner first gather information to investigate whether the cause of Steve's death was due to natural causes and if a doctor can certify the medical cause of death."
"Yes the coroner made sure that the protocol and procedure was observed. From the police report, the police were asked by the coroner to gather information about the death of the deceased. The police then spoke to the family of the deceased and from witnesses who were present when the death happened."
"And who was there when the death of Steve happened from your report?"
"The ambulance staff, the train driver and passengers."
"Inspector Jasper Willard, can you tell this court who was the last person to have a meal and have a drink with the deceased before he boarded his train?"
"Mr Tom Blackstone was the last person that saw the deceased alive before he boarded his train at the station."
"Do you have on CCTV camera activities on the train platform where both men stood before they parted their ways, I mean before the deceased boarded the train?"
"Yes we do, we could ask for footage from the National rail service."
"What about the restaurant where Tom and the deceased had their drinks, do we have any footage to show us the activities that transpired inside the restaurant?"
"We will find out with further investigation sir."
"Thank you Inspector Jasper Willard. No further questions."
Judge Archibald turned to Nigel.
"That is all for the State witness Milord." Nigel Stanley said as he again flipped through his legal pad and glanced at the jurors. They all stared back at Nigel Stanley as he looked into the eyes of the gentlemen and women in the jury – professor,

the midwife, the house-wife, the mechanic, the high school teacher and the others...he wondered if they would be fair in the case of Tom Blackstone. Looking into their eyes a second time he said, ''Ladies and Gentlemen of the jury you hold the defendant's future in your hands. Listen carefully. Please think for yourself. Be fair in this case. Let justice not only be done in this case, let it be seen to have been done even twenty years down the line, the world is watching us, people are waiting to see justice dispensed in this case.''

Howard slumped into his chair as he looked sadly at the pathologist first, and then disdainfully stared at Inspector Jasper Willard.

''Howard any cross-examination for Inspector Jasper Willard?'' he said as he was removing his glasses from his face.

''No your honour.'' He rose to his feet with so much effort as if he had been thrown out of the boxing ring by an opponent, wondering whether he would soon bounce back to good form to climb back into the boxing ring.

''Mr Nigel Stanley, do you want to call your next witness?''

''Milord the State rests.''

''Very well then, good.'' Archibald replied. He excused the jury with strict instructions against discussing the case. They nodded politely as they filed from the court room. He banged his gavel and he adjourned the case until 9.00am the next morning.

Chapter 23

Day 5 Trial, 6th May 2016

Archibald Magnusson arrived early to his chambers at 8:15am. He called Reuben Gibbs into his chambers to ask if all papers were up to date. ''Is the court room ready, Mr Gibbs?''
''Yes, sir.'' ''Very well then. Let us proceed.'' At exactly 9:00am Archibald seated the courtroom. All the jurors were fully seated.
Looking in the direction of Howard Sullivan and the defence team, the judge instructed, ''You may call your first witness.''
''Dr Bartholomew De La Pole,'' Howard announced as he moved to the podium. Nigel wore an unimpressed look. Dr De La Pole was sitting on the same row as the family of the accused next to Tom and his father Keith Bradford. Reuben Gibbs conducted the swearing in. The doctor was then led to the witness stand and delivered the standard orders to speak up and use the microphone so that the jurors and the judge and indeed everyone present in the courtroom could hear what he said.
Howard looking in the direction of Dr La De Pole.
''State your name please.''
''Dr Bartholomew De La Pole.'' He looked at Howard as if to say ''why do you ask a question that you already know!''
''What is your address?''
''24 Bevington Street, Jamaica road, London.''
''What is your profession?''
''I was primarily a physician before joining the Police Force. I am a trained Forensic Medicine Expert. I am a Death Scene Investigator for the Force.''
''How long have you practised as a forensic medicine expert?''
''Thirty odd years.''
''How would you describe your role as a forensic medicine expert?''

''Medical expertise is crucial in death investigations. It begins with a body examination and evidence collection at the scene and proceeds through history, physical examination, laboratory tests, and diagnosis – in short, the broad ingredients of a doctor's treatment of a living patient. The key goal is to provide objective evidence of course, timing, and manner of death for adjudication by the criminal justice system. Death investigation is an integral part of my day-to-day job, although not always by medical professionals.''
''When you say that death investigation is an integral part of your job but not always by medical professionals, do you mean that a Consultant pathologist does not always have to visit the death scene as often as you do on a day-to-day basis.''
''That is correct. We all work as a team in crime investigations but a Consultant pathologist more often is hospital based to carry out inquest and post-mortem investigation on the dead body to ascertain the cause of death.''
''Dr De La Pole when you were called to the death scene to investigate the sudden death of the deceased from the viewpoint of a Forensic Medicine Expert what did you observe and what were your findings?''
''My findings are that the deceased had collapsed of chronic ingestion which had a variety of symptoms ranging from generalised weakness, confusion and bizarre behaviour through his paralysis and possible liver failure. There was severe salivation, lacrimation, urination on his trousers, gastrointestinal distress, diarrhoea and ernesis. The deceased started to convulse inside the train and that was after almost an hour after his drinking a poisonous substance.''
''Dr De La Pole in your findings what chemical poison did you report killed the deceased?''
''Strychnine''
''Could you explain to this honourable court the symptoms of poisonous death by cyanide and that of strychnine?''
''In a lay man's terms cyanide poison would have caused the victim to convulse with a blue face almost immediately after drinking. Ordinarily a cachet would take only a few minutes to dissolve, unless it might have had a lining of gelatine or

some other substance. It might well be that the deceased might possibly not have swallowed it there in the restaurant while he was having his drink, he might have swallowed it later. On the other hand if he was poisoned with strychnine death occurs some few hours after exposure most commonly from respiratory failure compounded by lactic acidosis and rhabdomyolysis, in this case the deceased was poisoned in the restaurant while having drinks but the effect of the substance commenced when he boarded his train.''

''In essence, what you are saying to his honourable court is that if the effect of the poisoned drink took place in the train then the late Steven is more likely than not to have been poisoned of strychnine which he must have drank thirty minutes or more before boarding the train, on the other hand, he could have swallowed cyanide by himself as he boarded the train causing him to slump to the floor inside the train with some concentration leading to his death in minutes.''

''That is correct.''

''Do you agree in your findings alongside the coroner's inquest report that it was the effect potassium cyanide poison that caused the violent death of the deceased in the public place?.''

''Yes sir.''

''Therefore, if cyanide was the cause of death of the deceased, then, it must have been swallowed by the deceased by himself nearer his boarding the train or inside the train. This suggests that Steve more likely than not might have committed suicide or did in fact committed suicide. Is that right?''

''Yes sir.''

''Are you saying that when you investigated the death scene from your viewpoint of a professional Forensic Medicine Expert, you know that the poison of cyanide would have caused the deceased to convulse with a blue face within minutes and since he did not start to convulse within minutes after drinking the poison, your findings reported that another form of poison must have been used to kill him. However, you cannot rule out the fact that cyanide could have been

swallowed by the deceased himself before or just after boarding the train causing him to have taken his own life.''
''Yes sir, we cannot rule out suicide in this case if the pathologist result from the laboratory and post-mortem result finds cyanide in the deceased's corpse.''
''Thank you Dr La De Pole. Could you refresh the memory of the court on what sort of drink the deceased drank on the day?''
''Coroner's inquest report has it on record that he had an expensive wine Clicquot. He also ate a good meal lasagne and drank the best champagne.''
''Is it correct to say that your report emphasised that strychnine is a more likely cause of death in this case because a low dose was taken by the deceased and the effect of the poison started half an hour later after consumption?''
''Yes sir.''
''That is all for the Defence witness your honour.''
''Nigel Stanley do you want to cross-examine Dr La De Pole.''
''Yes your honour.''
''Dr La De Pole, when you visited the death scene investigating from the viewpoint of a Forensic Medicine Expert, did you see on the body or in the pocket of late Steve any traces of cyanide crystals on his body, in his pocket, in his hands or on his face?''
''No I did not?''
''But did you record in your findings that an intriguing story of violent death in public place had occurred, in this case a restaurant where two half-brothers had just met for drinks.''
''We recorded that a violent death in public place had occurred on the train, that was where the deceased slumped.''
''Did your report mention anywhere that the deceased swallowed a high dose of cyanide or strychnine?''
''The deceased died of strychnine but not a high dose of it''
''Are you then saying that a low dose of strychnine was taken by the deceased?''
''Well after taking the poison at the restaurant it took more than thirty minutes before the deceased slumped, so he must not have taken a high dose. With both cyanide and strychnine

victims of crime can convulse and slump instantly if a high dose of the poison is taken. From the facts of this case, the deceased did not react immediately to the exposure to the poison, if he consumed a high dose, he ought to have slumped right there inside the restaurant.''

''Dr La De Pole how do you expect this honourable court to see you as a credible witness? You just admitted that you did not find any cyanide crystals on any part of the deceased outer body, which means that he must have drank it in the restaurant. He did not swallow cyanide and that is why you could not find any trace of cyanide either in his pocket or in his hands.''

''I said the fact that he swallowed cyanide could not be ruled out in my viewpoint of the death scene.''

''So why was trace of cyanide crystals not found in the deceased pocket or hands?''

''How am I expected to know why traces of cyanide was not found on the deceased pocket or hands. I have just told you that in my opinion and in my report strychnine is the most likely cause of his death and that he did not have a high dose of it!''

''Dr Bartholomew La De Pole, you are a forensic medical expert and there are some discrepancies in your report and that of the consultant pathologist on the cause of death of the deceased.''

''How do you mean?''

''Well, the pathologist confirmed that the cause of death is cyanide and you said the cause of death is strychnine?''

''What I am saying to you is that both cyanide and strychnine could cause violent death, it depends on the dose that is taken by the victim, in my opinion I think strychnine is a more likely cause of death of the deceased in this case because of the time lapse between consumption and the time that he convulsed and slumped.''

''Is it possible for a high dose of strychnine to cause instant death of the deceased.''

''My report already tells you that the deceased did not die from a high dose of either strychnine or cyanide.''

''I put it to you Dr La De Pole that you are not true to this honourable court and that your account and viewpoint as a forensic medicine expert cannot be relied upon and therefore inadmissible in evidence. Your report is in conflict with the report of the Consultant pathologist and therefore not admissible.''
''Objection! Objection your honour! It is not for my learned colleague to decide the admissibility of evidence in this honourable court, which is for the Judge to adjudicate in law. Where there is conflicting evidence, the court decides on it, not my learned colleague.''
''Objection sustained, leave that to me Mr Howard Sullivan.''
'Yes your honour.'
'Any further questions Nigel Stanley?'
''The State rests your honour.''
His honour adjourned until nine the next morning. Nigel talked to his client Tom for a few moments while the crowd moved toward the rear. The court bailiff stood nearby with the handcuffs. Tom looked at his biological father Keith Bradford. Keith's eyes watered uncontrollably, they both had sat on the front row. They hugged each other. Tom would see his lawyer again tomorrow. The court security led him into the holding room and down the stairs, where the court security waited to lead him into jail once again.

Chapter 24

Day 6 Trial, 7th May 2016

It was now day six into the trial.
The nature of this case attracted the press. Hundreds of people were gathered at the front entrance of the court house: the local press, networks, the cable TV vans were lined on the street, their satellite dishes and camera crews ready to capture and transmit breaking news; several dozen police were keeping the peace.
Howard Sullivan was asked by one of his key witnesses (the psychologist) as they approached the court room: ''Who are all those people waiting for?''
''They are waiting for me.''
''Why?''
''Your guess is as good as mine.''
''This is a very good story line for their news, I suppose.''
''As the defence attorney Howard Sullivan approached the courthouse building, he pulled his clerk close to him and forged ahead. It was not long before they were spotted by the media, the cameras and reporters came rushing forward like the kicking team rushing downfield, with reporters aiming to sound bite for the evening news. They struck the microphones in Howard Sullivan's face and shouted from a foot away:
''Is your client Tom claiming plea of insanity?''
''Is this why you have a psychotherapist here today?''
''Are you going to use mental health to claim self-defence?''
To all the questions Howard answered, ''No comment,'', he just pushed ahead. They then went after prosecuting attorney Nigel Stanley, sticking microphones in his face and shouting at him:
''Do you think you have enough evidence to convict Tom in this trial?''
Stanley was irritated instantly. He then shoved the microphones and cameras away. With a disdainful look on his face he said: ''We have to wait for the court to determine on

whether there is enough evidence to convict the accused person, which is not the job of the media, or is it?''
''No.'' replied the newsman. Stanley's words had struck the reporters silent, the media circus felt embarrassed. The large crowd at the court entrance parted and allowed Nigel Stanley, Howard Sullivan and their clerks free passage into the courthouse.
They got off the elevator on the third floor and walked down the hall before turning into the corner leading to court room 307 which was Judge Archibald's courtroom.
Howard escorted his expert witnesses into the courtroom, up the centre aisle to the front row, as he was pointing out where they should sit, his eyes met with the prosecuting attorney who had his eyes fixed on Tom who was already seated. Stanley stared back at Howard.

The court convened at 9.00am. Archibald rapped his gavel and the courtroom came to order. Everyone looked in his direction. The Judge glanced at the spectator section, it was packed and crowded with gawkers gathered to witness the trial, outside the court building was also packed with reporters and the media like the Old bailey had never seen. Sitting at the back of the courtroom were the various groups of old men and some women who came to the courthouse randomly on a daily basis just like their age groups went to the golf course periodically or visiting Andy Murray or Serena Williams at the yearly Wimbledon tournament. On the top row seats were the general public who had lined up outside before daybreak to get a seat. The Judge could see the three rows of reporters taking notes and journalists engaging in discussions with some courtroom artists who were sketching portraits. Needless to mention there were several groups of lawyers, assistant prosecuting attorneys, and state court judges who viewed the trial as a continuing legal education. Judge Archibald was familiar with some of the faces he saw this morning.

Nigel Stanley rose to his feet, and with his eyes directly fixed on the jurors he said, ''Ladies and gentlemen, let us try to

imagine what the victim Steve Claxton went through, the victim was found lying on the floor as he boarded his train at the station. The evidence before the court is showing the report of the cause of the death of the deceased. And that is why I will ask you to return a verdict of guilty and life imprisonment. The poison used in murdering the deceased is cyanide, we have proven that this deadly poison prevented the cells of the body of the victim from being able to use oxygen. It inhibits an enzyme in the mitochondria of cells from doing its vital job of capturing oxygen and transporting it into the cells in the body. The victim in this case writhed in pain, he convulsed, had shortness of breath, became weak, was confused with dizziness had excessive bizarre behaviour which progressed to seizure, and then into a coma which led his eventual death.
Nigel Stanley then turned away from the jury, walked from the podium back to the prosecution table, knowing that he had just made a very effective opening statement, telling the jury exactly what he would prove and knowing that he could back up his words.

''Howard Sullivan are you ready to proceed with examining your expert witness?'' the Judges asked.
''Yes your honour.''
''Very well you may proceed.''
Howard looked from his notes to the podium.
''State your name, please.''
''Dr Cassandra Guideville.'' She answered, looking soberly at Howard.
''What is your address?''
''Two fourty-seven Glastonbury avenue, Middlesex.''
''What is your profession?''
''I am a practising medical doctor.''
''When did you qualify as a Doctor?''
''June 6, 1990.''
''Which University did you attend?''
''University of Bristol.''
''Is that an accredited medical school?''
''Yes.''

''By whom?''
''By the Royal College of Medicine and Council of Medical Education.''
''Which hospital did you do your houseman-ship and for how long did it take you to complete it?''
''I did my houseman-ship after graduation at The Guys and St Thomas's Hospital in London. I spent one calendar year doing it.''
''What would you say your specialisation is?''
''I specialise in Neuro-Psychiatry.''
''Can you explain to us what you mean by Neuro Psychiatry.''
''As a neuro-psychiatrist I work with patients with mental disorders which in most cases originate from a brain malfunction. Neuro-psychiatry is a growing specialty that involves combining organic (neurological) and psychological aspects of illness. Psychiatry is that branch of medicine concerned with the treatment of disorders of the mind. It usually, but not always, deals with mental malfunction, the organic basis of which is unknown.''
Howard gave Dr Cassandra Guideville a resounding look of affirmation, as if to say thumbs up for a job well done. His words were those of an expert.
''Could you describe to the jury what your professional training as a neuro-psychiatrist entailed?''
''The training we receive as members of the Royal College of Psychiatrist is very versatile and robust indeed. I spent two years at the North Wales Hospital in Denbigh Clwyd in Wales as a resident doctor in an approved training centre. During my residential training I engaged in clinical work with psychoneurotic and psychotic patients. I studied psychology, psychopathology, psychotherapy, and the physiological therapies. We experienced consultant psychiatric teachers and doctors who trained us and supervised us giving us instructions in the psychiatric aspects of general medicine, the behaviour aspects of children, adolescents, and adults.''
The jurors looked at each other giving Dr Guideville an affirmative look one after the other. Her words were coming from an expert who knew what she was saying. She appeared

to be a genius with a clever and intelligent outlook. She was articulate in the way she pronounced those words. Her vocabulary was rich. The jurors gave her a credible look.
''How long have you been qualified as a Doctor?''
''Twenty-nine years.''
''And how long have you practiced as a Neuro-psychiatrist?''
''Twenty-three years.''
''Can you tell the jury what it took you to become a member of the Royal College of Psychiatrists?'
'To be admitted as a member of the Royal College of Psychiatrists in the United Kingdom, a candidate must pass both oral and practical examinations as well as a written examination at the direction of the Board of Psychiatry examination Board.''
Howard walked two steps towards the Judge as he eyed Archibald who was watching Dr Cassandra Guideville intently.
''Milord, the defence presents Dr Mrs Cassandra Guideville as an expert in the field of psychiatry.''
''Very well so.'' Archibald replied. 'Do you wish to examine this witness Nigel Stanley?''
Stanley stood to his feet, glaring at his legal note pad. ''Yes, Your Honour, I have just few questions.''
''Dr Mrs Cassandra Guideville do you work as a full-time neuro-psychiatrist or a part-time neuro-psychiatrist?''
''I work part-time.''
''How many patients have you seen and how regularly in the last two years?' Stanley asked with a lot of confidence radiating from his voice.
''I see between two to three patients in a week.''
''You see only two to three patients in a whole week?''
''Yes.''
''Do you consider the job you do sufficient to give you the so called desired experience that you claim to have.''
''I am an expert you don't have to work sixty hours in a week to prove your professional competence, what you require is successful outcome of the effect of your medical advice on your patients.''

''How many times have you gone for a one year sabbatical leave in the last four years?''
''I was not on sabbatical leave, I was on study leave.''
''Well you were not working for two years. I put it to you that you are out of touch with your practice and you are not in the best position to testify in this case as an expert witness.''
Stanley stared at Dr Cassandra Guideville, gazed at his legal notepad, looked directly at Archibald, then he said ''Milord the Crown objects to this woman testifying as an expert in the field of psychiatry. She may be qualified but she obviously has not practiced full-time for a long time. She is out of touch and her witness expert evidence in this case cannot be admissible. This woman has spent about ten years out of the twenty-three years she said she has practiced for on maternity leave. She is always on study leave. She has not got enough experience to testify in this case.''
Howard tiptoed on his feet with his mouth ajar… ''Objection Milord! Objection! my learned colleague is discriminating against my witness on grounds of her sex as a neuro-psychiatrist. There is nothing wrong with a female practitioner going on study leave for as long as she wishes, that does not in any way diminish her expertise in her learned field as a professional. It is not the number of hours that you work that makes you a good doctor, it is the quality of your expert advice for which Dr Cassandra Guideville is certified to deliver and she has so delivered for the last twenty-three years. My learned colleague is making unwarranted excuses to discredit the prosecution expert witness. Milord this is sex discrimination and I raise an objection to the unprofessionalism being exhibited by my learned colleague. This level of discrimination is unacceptable your honour.''
''Objection sustained.'' The Judge ruled. ''Stanley, Dr Cassandra Guideville is a professional psychiatrist in her own right. Her professional body has not found her unfit to practice her profession, therefore she is a credible expert witness in this case unless her expertise is proven otherwise.'' Archibald explained to the defence and prosecution.
''May it please Milord.'' Stanley replied Archibald.

''Any further questions?''
''The State rests your honour.''
''You may proceed Mr Sullivan.''
Howard gathered his legal notepads, and walked to the podium, knowing the suspicion that the prosecution had just spitted over his star witness. ''Dr Cassandra Guideville have you recently or in the past examined the defendant, Mr Tom Blackstone?''
''Yes I have examined the defendant recently and also in the past regarding his mental health condition.''
''How many time have you examined him recently?''
''At least five times.''
''When did you conduct your last examination on him?''
''September 15 2015 and March 17 2016.''
''Could you tell the jury what was the purpose of this examination?''
''I examined the young man to determine and ascertain his current mental condition as well as his condition on the night when he had a meal and drink in a restaurant with his half-brother who is the deceased?''
'From your examination report on what date did Mr Tom Blackstone have a meal with the deceased?'
''I have it on record as the March 30 2015.''
''Why was it important for you to keep a note and record of that date and what happened on the day?''
''Well I need to study the behavioural pattern of Mr Tom Blackstone in order to medically determine his mental health on the day in question.''
''And where did this examination take place?''
''The examination took place at Roehampton Hospital in Putney, London in September 2015 and in the London Metropolitan Police station cell.''
''Was anyone else there when you conducted the examination, or was it just you and Mr Tom Blackstone?''
''Just Mr Tom Blackstone and I were present at the examination.''
''For how long did the examination last for?''
''Five hours.''

''How would you describe his mental health medical history?''
''It's a lengthy review, we tried to discuss the key issues like his childhood and so on.''
''What did you gather from his mental health medical history and his childhood?''
''Mr Tom Blackstone had an unstable childhood having lived with so many different families when he was in social care.''
''What effect or consequences would you say that had on his mental health?''
'A big effect.'
''How do you mean?''
'He was a drug addict who had battled with the abuse of substances for such a long time. This is evident in his suffering withdrawal most times. He is dependent on drugs, without which he cannot function.''
''How long has the drug addiction or substance abuse been going on in the life of Mr Tom Blackstone?''
''It's been going on for such a long time. Like he's been on drugs since the age of ten and by the age of fifteen he was very dependent on drugs that he injects himself to be able to cope with day to day life.''
''Dr Mrs Cassandra Guideville, I hope you don't mind me asking: are you a mother?''
''Yes I am a mother of three children.''
''How does it make you feel seeing the background medical state of this poor kid and how he has ended up?''
''It is very sad and would break any mother's heart.''
''So this young man was vulnerable to street crime because of his background, no role models to speak of, hopping from family to family, constantly running away from rehabilitation, living in several hostels in London, picking up the wrong friends, in and out of jail and so on. Are these some of the issues recorded in his medical records or if you wish to call it mental health records?''
Archibald's eye went to Tom and his dad Keith where they both sat next to each other. Keith wiped his eyes that were full

of tears with a white handkerchief before the State prosecutor burst into tears breaking down inside the court.
The court session had run throughout the day from 9am to 5:05pm. Archibald felt they had reached a point where they ought to call it a day, they have only had an hour recess the entire day. Howard still had a lot of questions to ask his star expert witness but at 5:10pm Archibald said goodbye to the jurors giving them strict instructions against discussing the case. They nodded as they looked at each other with their tired faces. Some of them were already nodding off, while others were yawning past the hour. They then filed from the courtroom. The Judge banged his gavel and adjourned until nine the next morning.

Chapter 25

The Kidnapping, Day 7 Trial, 8th May 2016

''Dr Mrs Cassandra Guideville,'' Howard said, with his eyes stuck on his legal notepad. ''Other than his childhood history and drug addiction, what other significant events did you note regarding Tom's mental history?''
''We discussed the return of his half-brother Steve and how they arranged to meet up for a meal and drink.''
''What effect did the sudden emergence of a half-brother turning up that he never knew have? and How was his mental health during this stage?''
''It was a mixed feeling effect on Tom.''
''How do you mean?''
''Tom did not know all his life that he had any half-brother from the same mother.''
''Did he mention that he resented his half-brother?''
''No, he did not…although he did once say that...''
''What did he once say to you Dr Cassandra Guideville?''
''He said that when he was arrested after the London riots, he tried to contact Steve but that he did not answer his call and that he ignored him, but he later found out when he was out of prison that the reason why he could not get hold of Steve on the phone was because Steve said he had changed his phone and he had a new number. Steve was not in the UK during the time that Tom was in jail.''
''Dr Guideville could you explain to this honourable court where Tom told you that Steve was when he tried to get him on the phone and couldn't.''
''Steve was on a world tour for three months.''
''Which part of the world was he at the time of the phone call?''
''He had finished touring Europe and Asia, he then travelled to West African countries when he was kidnapped by gun-men, his phone was confiscated and a ransom was demanded before he could be released by the kidnappers.''

''Oh dear, which country was Steve when this incident happened?''

''Tom said Steve was in Nigeria when the kidnapping occurred.''

''I really don't want to digress from the essential point, but it is clear from the facts here that Steve was in a helpless situation at the time and could not have answered Tom's phone call under the circumstances he was at the time. He did not mean any harm, when he eventually was released from captivity by his abductors, he returned safely to UK and on his return having escaped death from kidnappers in Nigeria, Steve went out looking for Tom, who was at the time living in a hostel in Croydon when he was released from jail.''

''Are you saying that they made up with each other and that there was no resentment of any sort?''

''Yes everything was normal. Steve never intended leaving or snubbing Tom at the time of his trouble, he was lucky to escape death in the hands of the gun-men in Nigeria while he was on holiday, his life was in danger and there was no way that he could help anyone under the circumstance he suddenly found himself.''

''Would you in your expert opinion think that Tom could murder Steve by poisoning him on the day that Steve died?''

''I don't think he is mentally able to be responsible for such an act.''

''Why do you say that?''

''Because a person is not criminally liable for an act or omission that occurs independent of the exercise of his will.''

''Are you saying that there is a presumption of innocence in his defence?''

''Yes.''

''Can you tell the jurors a brief account of Tom's childhood and the circumstances that led to him being taken into the state social care system?''

''His father and his mother separated and later on divorced when he was only eighteen months old.''

''Are you saying that he never grew up to know his father and that he never contacted him while he was growing up in the social care system?''
''Yes his father walked away from his wife and his son.''
''Do you know the reason why this happened?''
''From Tom's history record, his mother also battled with drug addiction and that was one of the reason's that led to her divorce. She also lost her license to practice as a nurse because she had serious substance abuse problems which caused her to lose her license and her job, consequently making her life miserable where she could not look after Tom while he was just eighteen month's old. That was when the state social security decided to take Tom away from his mother. He was taken into foster care.''
''How fortunate was Tom with the families that he was placed in while in the social care system?''
''He was a very unfortunate child according to the records.''
''Would you say that he picked up bad habits including drug use from the families he was placed?''
''I should think so.''
''It is either that is the case or not doctor?''
''Yes he picked up bad habits obviously from the families and fosters that he lived with as he was growing up.''
''Do you think that these issues were the main reason for his mental health deteriorating as he grew up into a young adult?''
''Yes, coupled with the bad friends that he picked up on London streets before he was arrested after the London riots in August 2011.''
''During your examination of Tom Blackstone could you explain to the jury the extent of the impact of his childhood on his behavioural pattern and on his personality.''
Dr Cassandra Guideville looked through glazed eyes at the jurors, She was well composed, she knew her facts and she was ready to deliver her expert witness role in this case.
Howard was determined to prove to the prosecution that his expert witness knew her stuff, she was a psychiatrist with years of experience, it did not matter whether she was a woman or not. She knew her stuff, she is an expert.

''Dr Guideville, in your twenty-three years of mental health practice have you ever come across the criminal responsibility test relative to the M'Naghten Rule?'' Howard asked.
''Yes I have, we refer to the M'Naghten Rule from time to time.'' She replied with a breath of confidence.
''Could you explain the meaning of this rule to the jury.''
''The M'Naghten rule is the standard for criminal responsibility in criminal law. The rule is any variant of the 1840s jury instruction in a criminal case when there is a defence of insanity: that every man is to presumed to be sane, and … that to establish a defence on the ground of insanity, it must be clearly proved that, at the time of the committing of the act, the party accused was labouring under such a defect of reason, from disease of the mind, as not to know the nature and quality of the act he was doing; or if he did know it, that he did not know what he was doing was wrong.''
''Can you break it down with simplicity and explain a little about the history behind the rule of M'Naghten.''
''Ok. Over a century ago in England, in the year 1843, when a man by the name of Daniel M'Naghten attempted to assassinate the prime minister, Sir Robert Peel, he mistakenly shot and killed the prime minister's secretary, Edward Drummond. M'Naghten fired a pistol at the back of Peel's secretary, Edward Drummond, who died five days later. The House of Lords asked a panel of judges, presided over by Sir Nicolas Conyngham Tindal, Chief Justice of the Common Please, and a series of hypothetical questions about the defence of insanity. The principles expounded by this panel have come to be known as the *M'Naghten Rules*, though they have gained any status only by usage in the common law and M'Naghten himself would have been found guilty if they had been applied at his trial…'' She paused and looked at Howard and the jury to see if she was making any sense to them from what she was saying.
''You may continue... we are all ears.'' Howard said.
''During his trial the evidence plainly showed M'Naghten was suffering from what we would call paranoid schizophrenia in neuro-psychiatry. The jury in that case returned a verdict of

not guilty, by reason of insanity. From this the M'Naghten Rule was established. It is still followed in England and enshrined in our criminal law.''
''In essence what does the M'Naghten rule mean?''
It was now 10:15am, Archibald had cleaned his glasses more than seventy-times-seven times and was not even midday or time for recess. The judge had drank more than half a dozen cups of tea. His bladder pressed forward the spillway. ''Time for the morning recess. We'll adjourn until 11:15am.'' He rapped the gavel and disappeared.

At 11:15am the court reconvened. ''Mr Sullivan you may proceed with your questions on the M'Naghten rule.''
''Yes Mrs Guideville you may continue with your definition of the M'Naghten rule.''
''The M'Naghten Rule is a simple principle which means that every man is presumed to be sane, and to establish a defence on the ground of insanity, it must be clearly proven that when the defendant did what he did he was labouring under such a defect of reason, from a mental disease, that he did not know the nature and quality of the act he was doing, or if he did know what he was doing, he did not know it was wrong.''
''How can you break that down in relation to Tom Blackstone?''
''Tom is a child who has made some wrong choices due to his mental health and state of mind. What I mean is that if the defendant cannot distinguish right from wrong, he is legally insane. Insanity is the expression we use as legal standard for a person's mental state or condition.''

''Mrs Guideville, based on your examination of Tom Blackstone in September 2015 do you have an opinion as to his mental condition if he was to be involved in snapping into any aggravated violent crime?''
''I do have an opinion after my medical examination sir.''
''What is your opinion?''
''Tom Blackstone needs rehabilitation for his illness and repeated suffering from withdrawal symptoms. How could the

same person go out for a meal with his brother, be a loving brother to him and yet suddenly become a cold-blooded murderer? This man often has a total break with reality which makes him snap in and out of who he is. This is my opinion of his behavioural pattern.''
Howard allowed those words from Cassandra to sink into the minds of the jury and the judge.
Dr Cassandra Guideville, based upon your observations of Tom and your diagnosis of his mental condition at the time he met up with late Steve in the restaurant on that evening, do you have an opinion, to a reasonable degree of medical certainty, as to whether Tom was capable of taking someone's life by using a chemical weapon in the form of cyanide or strychnine?''
''Yes I have.''
''What is your opinion?''
''Due to Tom's mental condition, there is a high probability that he was totally incapable of distinguishing right from wrong.''
''And as a psychiatrist, would you say that Tom was able to understand and appreciate the nature and quality of his actions?''
''Yes I do.''
''What is that expert opinion?''
''Tom was not capable of understanding and appreciating the nature and quality of what he was doing.''
''Thank you Dr Cassandra Guideville. No more questions for the defence witness Milord. I tender the witness to your honourable court.'' Howard looking fulfilled gathering his legal writing pad and walked with his head high and confidently back to his seat. He smiled at Dr Guideville as if to say 'Well-done you nailed it.''
''Nigel Stanley any cross-examination?'' Archibald asked.
''Yes your honour, but not many questions.'' Stanley said as he approached the podium.
''Dr Mrs Cassandra Guideville. I am not going to stand here to question your competence. What I would like you to tell this honourable court is why the accused person was previously

convicted and sentenced in the past for allegations of rape and theft. Why was the plea of insanity or his mental health not convincing to the juror to prevent him from being sentenced and going to jail?''
''Objection!'' Howard jumped out of his seat and sprung to his feet roaring almost like a lion ''The criminal record of the victim is inadmissible!''
''Sustained!'' the Judge said.
''Very well your honour,'' Howard said with a voice of relief. Stanley continued...''Are you at all aware of Tom's crime history before you conducted your mental health scrutiny and examinations?'
''Objection! Objection Milord!'' Howard cried out loud again looking at Archibald for mercy, ''Sustained! Sustained! You do that again and I will ask you both to see me in chambers. Did I make myself clear enough?''
''Milord Admonish him! He must be admonished your honour!'' Howard was irritated at Stanley's gushiness.
''I'll withdraw the question,'' Stanley said as he walked back to his seat.
''Milord that is not good enough, my learned colleague should be admonished!'' Howard reiterated.
''Are you giving me orders in my court Mr Sullivan?''
''I'll withdraw the statement Milord.''
''Very well then.'' Archibald then glared at Nigel Stanley before turning to the jurors and he said: ''Please disregard the last question by Mr Stanley.''
The jurors looked at one another in affirmation.
''Any more questions Mr Stanley?''
''Yes your honour.''
''Very well then, you may proceed.''
''Dr Guideville, you are a psychiatrist and you practice in a hospital where mental health patient are hospitalised so that they can receive treatment, is that correct?''
''Yes we call it Psychiatric hospital.''
''Right that is correct. Do you have a patient who has testified in court that they are mentally unfit to carry out their crimes of rape, theft, murder and yet when such a patient has been

acquitted and discharged by the jury and the judge, you and your colleagues admit such people into your hospital as patients?''
''How do you mean?''
''Exactly what I have said. It is clear enough for you to understand. I am not here for rhetoric. Is it right for this court to see you as a credible expert witness?''
''I don't see any reason why not sir.''
''Have you in the past stood as expert witness for the prosecution team?''
''Yes I have.''
''And when you stood as an expert witness for the prosecution, have you testified and said that it is possible for the accused persons to commit the allegations that have been made against them and you have said that they were not insane at all following on your medical examination?''
''Yes I have.''
''Have there been instances when your hospital then turned round after the trial to admit such criminals into your hospital to acknowledge and admit in your medical examinations that they are truly insane?''
''It is not my hospital that re-admits such patient after a trial, it is the publicly funded hospitals, not my own private hospital.''
''But you work there Dr Guideville.''
''Yes I do.''
''And that means you are part of the team of experts working in the hospital. Is that correct?''
''Yes.''
''If you were here today as a witness for the prosecution and not the defence you would be telling this court that Tom is capable of committing those crimes wouldn't you?''
''But that is not the case in this case is it?''
''What if it were the case and you were standing as witness for the prosecution, would you not be supporting your side and testify that Tom was not insane and that he is capable of committing the offence, that he knows the difference between the right and the wrong.''

''That is not the case in this matter is it?''
''The only reason why your mental health examination result and report today is saying that Tom is not capable of committing the crime put to him in this allegation of murder is because you are testifying for the defence team representing the accused person.''
''That is not true.''
''Dr Guideville, six years ago, to be precise in the year 2010, you testified that Mr Erik Randwer was legally sane and understood exactly what he was doing when he committed his crime, and the jury disagreed with you and found him not guilty, and since that time he has been a patient in your hospital, under your supervision, and treated by you as a paranoid schizophrenic. Is that correct?''
The look on Cassandra's face informed the jury that it was indeed correct.
''You have not answered my question Dr Cassandra Guideville.''
''Yes that is correct.''
Stanley looked directly at his legal pad to be sure of the next point he was about to make, he reviewed it then he looked up straight into Cassandra's eyes: ''Can you remember testifying in the trial of a woman by the name of Miss Edda Valka in September of 2013?''
''Yes I do remember the case.''
''Can you remember what that case was about?''
''It was a murder trial. Is that correct?''
''Yes.'' He paused ''And you testified and told the court that the 1st defendant in that trial was not legally insane. Is that correct?''
''Yes that was my testimony.''
''Ok. Can you remember that three other mental health practitioners and consultant psychiatrist testified on her behalf and told the jury that she was a very sick woman and that she was legally insane. These doctors were psychiatrists: Dr Agata Ellwood, Dr Davina Gregorio and Dr Elisha Seabrook. Is that correct?''
''Yes I remember.''

''Can you remember that you were the only doctor in the trial that testified that she was not legally insane?''
''Yes that is correct.''
''Can you remember the verdict of the jury in that case?''
''He was found not guilty.''
''By reason of insanity.''
''Yes.''
''Erik Randwer was admitted in the hospital where you practised as a neuro psychiatrist. Am I correct?''
''Yes.''
''How long has he been admitted in your hospital?''
''He has been admitted since the trial.''
''Can you tell the jury whether you normally admit patients and keep them for years and years if they are of perfectly sound mind without any mental health condition?''
Cassandra kept quiet… she then looked at Howard Sullivan who had no objection for the moment.
Nigel glared again at his legal notepad and said: ''I put it to you Dr Guideville that this court should have no basis admitting your expert witness as credible evidence. You and your team have appeared for the defence in the past testifying that the accused is not legally insane and yet your hospital has admitted the same accused person as a legally insane therefore capable of carrying out the allegation they have been charged to court for by the prosecution team just because you are on the side of the prosecution team and not because your medical report is honest and true.''
''That is not correct and why would I do such a thing? It is unprofessional thing to do.''
''That is what I would like you to explain to this honourable court. I put it to you that your witness report and psychiatric report compiled after your examination of Tom is not admissible by this court and in this case.''
''Objection your honour! Objection! It is not for Mr Stanley to say what the bench or jury determines to be admissible evidence. It is not for him to decide in this court. What he is required to do is to prove his case and he has not done so. My client is presumed innocent until he is proven guilty Milord.''

''Objection Sustained Mr Howard.''

''That is all for this witness your honour.'' Nigel stared at Cassandra with a wicked smile, and walked to his seat leaving her reeling in anger and frustration standing in the witness stand.

''Any redirect?''

''No your honour.''

The defence had no further questions for the expert witness and at five twenty Judge Archibald bid farewell to the jurors with instructions against discussing the case with anyone. The twelve men and women affirmed the instructions by nodding politely after which they filed from the court room. Archibald banged his gavel and adjourned until nine the following morning.

Chapter 26

Keith Bradford, Reflection

It is now the eighth day of trial, 9 May 2016. I was approached by the defence counsel to stand in the trial of my own son as a witness for the defence. For over 30 years I have represented the state as the Prosecutor. I have never appeared as a witness for the defence in any trial. All I have ever done is to be the prosecutor in all my law career. Today is an emotional day for me. Tom is a son I was never there to watch grow up. I was separated from Teresa and Tom when Tom was only eighteen month's old. It saddens my heart that I will be standing here today to attend the trial of my son for a capital offence of murder. It feels very awkward not to be the prosecutor. Nigel Stanley who will be questioning me is my colleague. We both have practiced as prosecuting attorneys. To face him in court today as a defence witness in the case of my son is something that I find humiliating to say the least. I do not wish the feeling I am having right now on my worst enemy. If you are not going to be there for your kids as they are growing up, please try not to have them yet. Wait until you are ready. If you have a busy career like mine, then think carefully before combining having a family with your career.

There is no point telling you that I woke up nice and early to go to court on the morning of 9 May 2016. I did not sleep throughout the night. I thought about my son, the kind of questions that I would be made to answer and why. I was wide awake reading other criminal law cases. It was pointless studying for a trial that you are not needed as a prosecutor. For the first time I felt the pain that parents of youth victims feel when their children are prosecuted for one offence or another. It is not a good feeling at all.
I dressed casually for court. I parked my car in my allocated bay as a prosecutor, it will be awkward for me not to park my car where I usually would. The rotunda was crowded by nine

o'clock. The spectators had learned that all seats were taken by eight-fourty-five. The moment the door was opened the crowd filed slowly through the metal detector, past the vigilant eyes of the court bailiffs and security and then finally into the courtroom.
Just before 9am, Tom was escorted from the small holding room. The handcuffs were removed by one of the many officers surrounding him. He smiled at me before going to sit down in his chair. The prosecuting attorney and the defence counsel took their places and the court room grew quiet. The court bailiff poked his head through the door beside the jury box, and, satisfied with whatever he saw, opened the door and released the jurors to their assigned and delegated seats. Earlier on Archibald had summoned the attorneys to chambers. He just wanted to make sure that they were all alive, well and ready for the day.

Mr Reuben Gibbs was watching everyone convening and well seated all from the door leading from the chambers, as when all was perfect, he stepped forward and yelled: ''All rise for the court!...''
Judge Archibald swiftly draped into courtroom in his favourite well ironed black robe as he loped to the bench instructing everyone to have a seat. He greeted the jurors, he then asked them about what had happened or didn't happen since yesterday's adjournment.
He looked at Howard Sullivan and then Nigel Stanley before asking: ''Is Keith Bradford here this morning?''
''Yes he is your honour.'' replied Nigel.
''Call your witness,'' Archibald ordered Nigel.
Nigel put me on the stand. This is something that I would do to a witness being a prosecutor, but today I'm standing as a witness in the trial of my own son. My own colleague Nigel about to question me. I just feel very, very sad. The look on my face was glaringly gut-wrenching and nerve-wracking.
The court reporter glared at me before Nigel started throwing his questions at me, it was an awkward feeling, I have never in

my life been put in such an uneasy embarrassment and very inconvenience awkward position.
''Mr Keith Bradford, could you explain to this honourable court the circumstances that led to your investigating the murder of the late Steve Claxton.'' Nigel asked.
''I am a prosecutor and I was on the team of prosecutors for the murder of the late Steve Claxton alongside Inspector Kelvin Armstrong, Colonel Peter Blacksmith and Inspector Jasper Willard. After the arrest of the accused person I stepped down from the investigation when we found out that the accused person is my biological son.''
''Thank you Keith. The accused person, Tom your son, could you explain to the jury when last you saw this young man before the allegation brought against him came to your knowledge?.''
''The last time I saw Tom was when he was eighteen months old before his mother and I separated and later got divorced.''
''What led to the breakdown of your marriage to Tom's mother?''
''She was battling with drug abuse for many years. When we divorced I left town and did not know that our son Tom had been taken into social care and fostered by various families and homes.''
''In your opinion would you say that going by the information you gathered on the past record of your son and what he had been through as he was growing up, that he is capable of carrying out the allegations that has been put to him by the state?''
''Tom is a child who has found himself in unfortunate circumstances. His mother Teresa I heard later died but had re-married about five years after Tom had been taken into foster care. Teresa was not well enough to look after Tom or herself.''
''So in your opinion would you say that Tom was a mentally unstable child?''
''With the circumstances surrounding his up-bringing it is possible that he could be mentally unstable.''

''Mr Keith Bradford, if the deceased late Steven Claxton was your son who had been murdered would you say the same thing about Tom.''
''Yes I would.''
''But he is not your biological son and so you would rather testify in the interest of your son rather than your stepson, is that correct?''
''But I was on the prosecution team in the first instance to find justice for the family of the late Steven Claxton.''
''Indeed you were Mr Keith Bradford; you were an integral part of the prosecution team in this case until it came to your knowledge that your biological son was the accused person in this case. Is that correct?''
''Yes.''
''And how does that make you feel?''
''It's very devastating.''
''Mr Bradford do you have any regrets for having abandoned your son when he needed you the most making him end up as a notorious criminal that you later on in life found to be embarrassing and disgraceful to associate with?''
''Objection! Objection! Your honour my client is presumed innocent until he is proven guilty. My learned colleague is out of order referring to Tom as a notorious criminal. The allegation of murder has not been proven, my client is not a notorious criminal.'' Howard said shaking profusely.
''I ask that the last question by Mr Stanley be stricken from the record and the jury be instructed to disregard it.'' Archibald said.
''I'll withdraw the question.'' Stanley said to Howard with a smile as his face skittered.
''Please disregard the last question from Mr Stanley.'' Archibald instructed the jury.
''No further questions.'' said Stanley.
''Any redirect examination, Mr Howard Sullivan?''
''Yes Milord.''
''Very well you may proceed Mr Howard Sullivan.''
''Mr Keith Bradford when you commenced the investigation of the case of your son along with the prosecution team, you

did not have the faintest idea that the 1st defendant was your son. Is that correct?''
''Yes I did not know.''
''And when you found out the position of the 1st defendant you opted out of the prosecution team, you stepped down so that justice will not only be done, but so that justice will undoubtedly be seen to have been done. Is that true?''
''Yes that is correct.''
''From the information you know so far, how would you describe the character of your son?''
''I feel regret today that I am not able to tell you all the stages of growth that Tom has had from the tender age that I walked out on his mother. Tom from the record is a troubled child who have been battling with drug abuse and substance abuse.''
''Would you be able to tell this court what Tom's mother went through and whether Tom had inherited some traits from his mother.''
''The late Teresa was a drug addict, she battled with mental health issues as a result, and she got into trouble sniffing cocaine at her place of work when she worked as a nurse. She was given several warnings before she went through disciplinary proceedings and later was struck off as a nursing practitioner.''
''Going by Tom's mother's health do you think that she would have been able to bring up Tom?''
''No, I don't think she would have.''
''Do you think that Tom had been let down by both his parents and that he had been a victim of circumstances himself.''
''Yes I think so.''
''Could you tell the jury why you thought leaving an eighteen-month-old son with a woman who was battling with drug abuse was the right thing for you to do 27 years ago?''
''I am not proud of my action. I was a very young prosecuting attorney. After marriage I could not cope with the pressure I was facing in my home with Teresa. The marriage broke down irretrievably and Teresa and I parted. I have not married since my divorcing of Teresa. I concentrated on my career. I did not know that the state had taken Tom into care.''

''And how does that make you feel today seeing what the young man had been through?''
''I am not proud of the choices that I made as a young lawyer. If I could turn back the hand of the clock, then I would make difference choices.''
''And now that you cannot turn back the hand of the clock, what would you like the jury to know concerning the allegations against the 1st defendant?''
''Tom due to his up-bringing suffered from depression, low self-esteem, anxiety, and panic attacks in a dark and lonely place. He suffers from comparing himself with others and he is seriously addicted to drugs and substance abuse. Unfortunately, Teresa battled with these conditions too and she did not have a neglected upbringing, but rather her parents Mathew and Phoebe lived in Pennsylvania. She was just unfortunate to be battling with these demons in her life before she eventually died.''
''Mr Bradford, in all your 30 years of practicing as a prosecuting attorney, would you ever have thought that you would be today standing in the witness stand to testify in a case involving serious allegation of a capital offence against your own biological son?''
''No.''
''If you have one sentence to say to the jury, what would it be Mr Bradford?''
''I will say that, it is not over until it is over. Tom was in the wrong place at the wrong time. I think he is not criminally responsible for any act or omission that occurs independent of the exercise of his will. I think he should be acquitted. I'm not saying so because he is my son, I'm saying so because he is a young man who is a victim of the circumstances that he found himself in and...''
''That was more than one sentence Mr Bradford.''
''I'm so sorry.'' Keith replied.
''That is all for the witness Milord.''

Looking at the jurors, Judge Archibald Magnusson addressed the jury.

''Ladies and gentlemen, this trial is almost over. There will be no more witnesses. It is now time for me to meet with the attorneys to iron out some technical areas of the law after which they will be given the opportunity to make their final arguments to you. We will go on recess now and we will reconvene at 1:45pm. I will ensure that you get the case around four-thirty and I will allow you to deliberate until five-forty-five. Should you not reach a verdict today, then you will be taken back to your rooms until tomorrow. The time is not 11:15am, and we'll recess until 1:45pm like I said. I will now need to see the prosecuting and defence attorneys in my chambers.''
Keith Bradford became very shaky and Howard Sullivan gathered his files while staring at Keith. Keith fidgeted and grinned awkwardly at the jurors, nerves caught the better part of him, for a moment he was scared like he had never been before, he now knew how it feel to be in the witness stand, if he had his way he would never have taken the chance, he then turned back to Howard who remained quiet at this time, waiting to hear what Keith have got to say:
''Howard, I think Dr Cassandra has really messed things up, don't you?''
''How do you mean?''
''I mean her testimony.''
''No one is going to believe that Tom is legally insane after Cassandra's messed things up.''
''Howard I am worried for my son.''
''Why worry when you can plead?''
''Are you thinking what I am thinking?''
''And what are you thinking as Keith the prosecutor?'' Howard said smiling at him.
''It is not a smiling matter; I have been doing some thinking.''
''What?''
''Do you think it might be a good idea to throw in the towel as in explore the possibilities of a plea bargain?''
''No way, not on my watch are we going to write off that boy by agreeing to what he did not do.''

'I' am thinking of us getting him a lesser sentence than life sentence.''
''Forget it, we are sticking to the fact that he did not do it. Is that clear?''
''Yeah.''
''Look, Keith you are a prosecutor and you are about to give up that easily in a trial of your only child. Are you thinking he actually poisoned Steven after the conflicting expert witnesses: I have to fight this case to the end. The consultant pathologist said that the poison that killed Steve is cyanide while the forensic medical expert says it is strychnine, their only common ground is that the dose used from the two poisonous substances could either determine whether Steve died instantly or died 1.5 hours after he had taken the substance. We don't know which of the two evidence is accurate, which means the mode of operation of the murderer is not yet unveiled. Yes he killed Steve with poison but there is a lot of variance in the mode of his operation in this case.''
''You can say that, but what about Cassandra messing things up with her evidence?''
''Let's leave that for a minute.'' He demurred, then fidgeted and grinned awkwardly at Keith.
''Keith I just cannot stand Nigel Stanley.''
''Do you want me to help you to put together an effective closing argument? You really need to play on the jury, look them in the eye, talk into their ears, you know it takes one to hang the jury.''
''Yes you are right Keith.''
''You have to make them cry, if you can, then that is what you must do.''
''It is not a screen or stage drama you know.''
''That is what it is Howard; you have to make the jury cry, real tears in the jury box. It is always effective. I have done it for 30 years, so just take it from me. I have seen so many defence attorneys on the other side do it. The jury still have a lot to do. See they still have to work through the exhibits, photographs, fingerprints, and all the ballistics reports and laboratory pathology tests and results.''

''Don't worry Keith, I know how you feel, standing there helpless in your only son's trial. You wish you could represent him yourself, but you can't. I have to do that for you. All I need to get through it is a spell-binding performance on final summation. I will put together the greatest closing argument in the history of jurisprudence. It has to be done and that is what it is going to take to save the Prosecutor's son. Isn't that what you want?''
''Yes that is what I want. Howard, you will win this case. I can picture a compilation of your greatest closing argument.''

Chapter 27

The Address

The court recess was over and court resumed at 1:45pm, the prosecuting attorney was ready to give his address:

''Ladies and gentlemen of the jury, cast your mind back to the events that brought this case about. The very incident that occurred mysteriously making this case not an ordinary case but one that will leave an indelible history in our case law. The crime that was committed in this case must not go unpunished. An innocent chatered accountant was murdered in cold blood under tragic circumstances, the weapon of his murder was cyanide, the perpetrator of the murder poisoned his victim to death. The allegation that the prosecution has brought against the accused person is founded with evidence. The court must exercise its discretion judicially and judiciously and not arbitrarily, taking into consideration relevant evidence before it, in the resolution of questions arising from the case which calls for the exercise of discretion.

The court must take all relevant evidence into account in the resolution of all questions arising from application; the court must also take into account all relevant provisions of the evidence act and other statutes which have bearing on the proper determination of the matter. As you are aware this is a capital offence, the seriousness of these allegations speaks for itself, we should be guided by the nature of the charge, the severity of punishment, the character of evidence, the criminal record of the accused person, the likelihood of repetition of the offence, the burden of displacing the fact that an accused person is innocent of the allegation against him is on his accuser who must adduce the evidence of guilt, this burden is on my team and I today, at this moment and in this hour. The court must always bear in mind the evidence of the prosecution against the accused, and if the said evidence is strong and direct, the chances of being set free are remote, the defendant has pleaded not guilty to the charge, following his plea of not guilty to the charge, his application for bail was filed on his behalf by his learned counsel. You honour after hearing both parties during the preliminary hearing delivered your ruling refusing the application for bail but your right honourable lordship made an order for accelerated hearing that brought us to where we are today. Up till now the accused person has enjoyed the constitutional right to be presumed innocent of the alleged offence until he is found guilty by a competent court. A capital offence is a notorious offence which I would like the jury not to take lightly. The court must bear in mind the evidence of the prosecution against the accused, and if the said evidence is strong and direct, the chances of being set free are remote, the constitution of this country does not imply an exemption of a wrong doer from prosecution, rather it means that in a criminal trial, the burden of displacing the fact that an accused person is innocent of the allegation against him is on his accuser who must adduce the evidence of guilt. The factors that are being worthy of consideration in the determination of this case is the key vital evidence put to this honourable court by the prosecution witnesses. The consultant pathologist and the forensic medical practitioners. This honourable court must also take into account all relevant provisions of the evidence act and other statutes which have bearing on the proper determination of this matter. The decision reached by the jury and this court must flow from a thorough appraisal of the material presented before this court, and where it appears that the court failed to take into account relevant factors, then the appellate court may be justified in interfering with the decision.

He stared at his notepad, then he walked passed the podium moving around staring at the Judge and then he made eye contact with the jurors then he continued:

Ladies and gentlemen, justice has been acknowledged to be neither a partisan watchdog nor a malleable actor that takes care of the interest of an accused person alone. We must consider the nature of the charge, the strength of the evidence that the prosecution have put to this honourable court which supports the charge, we must consider the gravity of the punishment in the event of conviction, we must consider the previous criminal record of the accused person which is so glaring in the criminal records of the accused person. The defendant is not a first time offender and we have to be mindful of the fact that he could strike again if proper care is not taken…''

''Objection Milord! Objection!'' shouted Howard Sullivan.

''Sustained. The state cannot refer to facts not in evidence. The jury will disregard the last statement by Mr Nigel Stanley.''

Nigel ignored Archibald and Howard and stared painfully at the jury. He then continued making his point when the shouting died down.

''Ladies and Gentlemen of the Jury what Lawyers do is to make a fortune using the law. The rule of law is not money, the rule of law is the law. The jury and indeed the court are not politicians as to sell the law to special interests for money. It is a known fact that in the world of today people sue each other for money. The world is intoxicated with an insatiable want for money, but let it be known gentlemen of the jury that even though everywhere in the law, is all about money but there is one place that is an exception to that and where is that exceptional place?. It is right there where you are sitting right now, inside the jury box you are not here for money or fame or fortune. You are here twelve in number to uphold and deliver a truthful verdict. You are here today to stand for the truth, you are here today to stand for what is the right thing to do in this case. There is only one way you can stand up for that truth. It is through the verdict you deliver today. What is the truth in this matter? The truth in this matter is that Steve

Claxton was murdered by someone who knew him, someone he trusted, someone that he chose to wine and dine with, someone who decided to kill in cold blooded murder, Steven Claxton was a victim of a violent crime that took his life. His killer is a serial killer, well experienced murderer who is not a first-time offender, experienced enough in the ways of murder investigations to know how not to leave incriminating evidence or traces of incriminating evidence behind for anyone to detect. His killer is a smooth operator.

The truth therefore is that Tom Blackstone murdered Steve Claxton by administering poison inside the drink that Steve drank on the night they went out for a meal and a drink. It was the drink that Steven drank that killed him. The consultant pathologist tendered his evidence as post-mortem result and laboratory test results which we marked as exhibit A. The forensic medical expert also confirmed that the cause of death is cyanide, the probability that the accused died after one hour of having his drink is irrelevant because even strychnine poison would still have killed Steven depending on the dose that found its way into Steven's body. The truth is that Steven's killer is a notorious criminal who knows what he was doing and smart at his game of killing people.

Nigel again walked back to the podium stared at his notepad, looked at the jurors in the eye again, this time making eye contact with each and everyone of them - one after the other, then stared at the big photo frame sitting on the wall above Archibald's chair, the magnificent photo was the picture of the royal coat of arms which usually appeared in courtrooms in England and Wales. The crest depicts justice coming from Her Majesty the Queen and shows that the law court is part of the Royal Court. Nigel stuck his eyes on the large photo frame as it stood magnificently on the wall, he then took a long breadth and then continued:

...Tom Blackstone is not a first-time offender; he was normal and of sound mind...legally sane when he raped Evelyn

(Steve's girlfriend). He was in his right frame of mind when he committed theft in the London riots, this man has a criminal history that cannot be overlooked. He premeditated and calculated murdering the deceased, he had a motive, his motive was vengeance, he was not happy about the content of letter that Steven shared and showed him on the day. The letter was written by their mother Teresa, and was given to Steven by his grand-parents Matthew and Phoebe, In that letter Teresa did not mention Tom as a beneficiary to her will, and she did not even know whether Tom was alive or still in a foster home. These are the facts that Tom bottled inside of him. Let me cast your mind back to the day that Tom was arrested after the London riots, he tried to call Steven, but he could not get through, and he instantly developed hatred for Steve when Steve did not answer his phone before Tom was arrested for his shop lifting at the London riots. Tom had resented Steve ever since the day of arrest. It was on his release that he found out that Steve had changed his phone number and that was why Tom could not reach Steve on the day of Tom's arrest. Steve never intended to snub or ignore Tom in his time of trouble but that was what Tom thought, he was convinced that Steve chose to ignore him when he was in trouble and he resented Steve for that. Let us remember that it was Steve that called Tom after a long time after he was released from jail to check on him and to ask him out for a meal. Tom never at any point in time intended to reach out to his long lost brother! It was Steve who reached out in love. Tom revenged and killed Steven at their re-union dinner. This man named Tom had a motive to take his half-brother's life, a motive to inherit their grandparents' house in Pennsylvania. Phoebe witnessed to this possibility in her testimony. Every hand is pointing to the fact that the allegations that the prosecution had made against the defendant is true and founded. Let me also cast your mind back to the work experience that Tom has had in his life, he's worked in a chemical factory, he knows about chemical weapons. This man planned to murder the deceased. He is a notorious gang star from his group of friends, the saying goes, show me your friends and I will tell you who you are! The

likes of Gary, Neil and his girlfriend; all Tom's friends are dodgy characters like himself, he would always get into trouble.
Nigel again stared at the picture of the Royal Coat of Arms on the wall above the Judges very high chair where Archibald sat, as if Nigel was seeking a form of affirmation from the picture on the wall, he then looked at Archibald and his eyes back to the jurors… He continued:

Gentlemen and Ladies Tom Blackstone is the killer that we are looking for and he must be brought to book. We want him to tell us what he did, how he did it and to reverse his 'no guilty' plea to 'guilty' which is the right thing to do in this matter. This is not a suicide case, it is a murder case. The truth is that Steven was up till the time of his death, a happy man, in his prime, enjoying what life has to offer him, getting ready to get married, and as he was doing it his wicked half-brother whom he trusted cut short his life for one single motive………..JEALOUSY AND ENVY!.''

''Objection Milord! Objection!'' Howard said without even shouting.

''Sustained,'' Archibald said in a calm tone.

Nigel continued ignoring the commotion that was in the air but not in people's voices. He then paused to have a drink of water before shifting gears. Stared at his notepad for longer than he normally would, then he looked at the jurors again. He was happy with what he saw on some of their faces. He then continued:

''Ladies and gentlemen of the jury you will agree with me that the testimony of the defendant's neuro-psychiatrist cannot be admissible. She is not a credible witness. Her medical examination is nothing but a speculation. Dr Cassandra Guideville testifying for the defence claimed to be a highly trained specialist who treats many for all sorts of mental illnesses, yet when crimes are involved she cannot recognize insanity. Her testimony should be carefully weighed. She has in the past witnessed that an accused person is legally sane and yet she admits such defendants to her hospital. She had done so many times. In fact she has contradicted the evidence given by between two to three of her colleagues, which was later on found to be a serious mis-judgement on her part. She knows deep down in her heart that Tom Blackstone is not insane. He was in his right frame of mind when he murdered his half-brother in cold blood. The question now is: Is the jury going to follow the truth in this court today?. I pray the jury to deliver a guilty verdict, to make sure that justice is not only done, but that justice is manifestly and undoubtedly be seen to have been done in the case of The State versus Tom Blackstone.''

Looking directly into the eyes of all twelve jurors, Nigel finally said, ''The State rests.''

The court room watched him, they listened to every word that the lead prosecuting attorney had to say. He was a clear courtroom preacher. He's done his speech so many times before in the past. The spectators held their seats and chatted quietly.

Howard Sullivan explained to the jury how the most important thing for them to concentrate on is that 'if it does not fit, then they must acquit his client.' He was a witty counsel who knew his stuff. He was clever and even if his client was guilty of murder, that was not what he was in court to admit. He was in court to be that Lawyer that he was. To do good.
''Ladies and Gentlemen, if you cast your mind back to the characters in Julius Caesar written by William Shakespeare, you might have read it or maybe seen the movie. It is the story of how Caesar, a Roman leader was betrayed by Brutus who was a close ally, Caesar recognised that Brutus was one of the murderers who had conspired to have him murdered or have him assassinated if you like to use that word. Julius Caesar trusted Brutus and that was why he was surprised seeing him

his enemies and so he said ''Et tu Brut.'' (and you Brutus?). This case is not like what Caesar was thinking. Tom Blackstone is not a betrayer like Brutus; he did not kill Steve Claxton. I am here to convince this honourable court that If the late Steven Claxton did not commit suicide, then what we have just began is the search for his killer because it was not Tom Blackstone that committed this murder. The allegations put against the defendant are untrue. The evidence and exhibits tendered by the prosecution are inadmissible. Well, everyone in this courtroom knew that the two expert witnesses that the prosecution attorney asked to testify in this case have conflicting evidence. Dr Jeremy McWhinney the consultant pathologist reported cyanide as the cause of death, while Dr Bartholomew De La Pole who is the forensic medicine expert reported that the cause of death is more likely to be strychnine giving that the deceased died about an hour after drinking the poison. Both experts are confused about the report, the balance of probabilities cannot be based on evidence that are based on fake laboratory results, preponderance of evidence is a challenge in this case. We cannot rely on the facts that has been put before this honourable court by these two experts. Both of them admitted that the cause of death of the deceased is the dose of poison that he had taken, by that I mean, if he took a lethal dose he should have died instantly in the restaurant where he dined with the defendant, but if he took a non-lethal dose then his death would have been delayed in which case he collapsed in the train, one of the experts even said that the cause of death is more likely to be strychnine than cyanide. The only thing they have in common in their evidence is that it was poison that killed the deceased. That is the truth. What we now need to know is that this poison was taken by the deceased to end his own life, by his own hands on the day in question. My client was a troubled young man from childhood. We have heard from his father Keith Bradford that his son had a turbulent childhood, he battled drug abuse and substance abuse: this was a trait he inherited from his mother, Teresa. And yes he's had a troubled past but that is not an excuse for the wrong person to be punished in this case. Dr

Cassandra Guideville has given a very credible evidence. Tom is not capable of killing a fly, let alone his half-brother. The late Steve was brought up by his grand-parents. He was an orphan. He was lonely. Lonely throughout his life. He was sick and tired of being alone and that is why he ventured into travelling from the US to the UK for his University education, he needed a change. Underneath he was already dying. It was when he met Tom that he began to get his identity. Tom came to fill the gap and played the role of a sibling in Steven's life. He did not kill Steven.

The judgement of this court cannot be based on conflicting expert witness evidence. The case is about suicide and not murder. The coroner's report made it clear that the cause of death was poison, but the report did not rule out the fact that the poison could have been administered by the deceased. This is the jig-saw puzzle that we have to unravel and until we do so, we stand the danger of convicting and sending to jail the wrong man. Doing so defeats the purpose of the judiciary. We must be sure. The jury must be surer than sure itself before a verdict of 'guilty' is reached.

I want you to write a story and deliver a verdict where truth and justice prevail even if the defendant is poor and has had a troubled past criminal record, that is not licence for him to go to jail for an offence that he has not committed. He may be a drug addict but he is not a murderer, there is a clear difference between the two states, you define what we are seeing and not mix-match the facts. We must not forget the basic principles of criminal law, unless an allegation made against my client is proven, then we cannot rely on it. *Mens rea* means intention to commit the crime while *Actus reus* is the actual action of carrying out those crimes. The prosecution in this case has not proven my client as directly involved with the use of cyanide or strychnine, these poisons were not found on his hands, or in his pocket, either was any record found tracing my client to the crime. Unless we establish that the crime committed in this case has the two elements of actus Reus and mens rea, then

we cannot convict Tom Blackstone. If it does not fit, we must acquit. The defendant should be acquitted and sent home to his father a free man.''
Howard paused and glanced over at judge Archibald for a long moment, then he turned back to the jurors. And repeated:

''Ladies and gentlemen, before I was appointed to represent the defendant, I thought I was a winner in the game of law – and that's how I viewed the law, as just a game. Like any other lawyer, when I tried a case, I wanted to win. I wanted to beat the other lawyer. In some cases, it wasn't about truth or justice; it was just about winning and money. But that was not right, I was wrong. The law isn't a game. It's not about winning or money. It's about truth and justice....and life. Today your verdict will determine whether the defendant is jailed for life or that he walks home a free man back to the father that he never knew. Back to the man who would have brought him up away from exposure to street gangs, as you already know Tom is a son of a prosecutor, a prosecutor dad that he never grew up with, if he did, he would not be here today, he would be an elite or graduate from Harvard or Cambridge or Oxford University, but that is not the case for Tom.

Tom needs Keith now, as much as he needed his father 27 years ago. Please don't take him away from his father. A prosecutor waits on the front row for his son to come home.

You decide with your verdict today whether or not you will let him go home to his dad for a second chance at life!''

The courtroom was silent as Howard sat next to his client Tom. He then glanced at the jury again, he felt a flicker and a ray of hope even though no one had promised his client freedom!

Looking directly at the jury, Judge Archibald Magnusson addressed the twelve. He explained that the trial is now almost over and that there will be no more witnesses. He went further to make them aware that they will get the case and he will allow them to deliberate until around 5:45pm when he expected them to have reached a verdict, however if they do not reach a verdict today, then they will be taken back to their rooms until tomorrow.

At 3:45pm, Archibald bid farewell to his jury, they were admonished to elect a foreman amongst them, told them to get organized and to do what they have to do. He reiterated how very important their deliberations were, and that they should not worry if they do not reach a verdict as it is not the end of the world, but that he will be left with no choice than to order a recess until nine o'clock on the 9th of May. They then stood up and filed slowly from the courtroom. Archibald made sure they were out of sight, he then recessed until 5:45pm, he instructed Howard and Nigel to remain close to the courtroom or make sure that they leave their telephone number with the court clerk.
There was murmuring going on among the spectators, they held their seats as they chatted quietly.

No one expected a quick verdict in this case, the bailiff locked them in the jury room. Audolf Crow was elected the foreman by acclamation. Audolf laid the jury instructions and exhibits that had been tendered during the trial on a small rounded mahogany table in the middle of the room where they could all see the instructions and exhibits clearly. They sat down around the table with anxiety written all over their faces.
With a bold face he asked: ''Can I suggest that we should take an informal vote so we know where we are in this matter. Do we all agree to that?'' There were no objections from any of the twelve, they all agreed for them to take an informal vote. Audolf had a list of twelve names, he then instructed that they should Vote guilty, not guilty, or undecided. He also told them that they can choose to pass for now.

And one after the other:
1.

''Eleanor Gomez.''
''Guilty.''

2.
''Yvonne Cox.''
''Guilty.''

3.
''David Anderson.''
''Undecided.''
4.
''Cornelius Lafayette.''
''Guilty.''

5.
''Stella Brook.''
''Not Guilty.''

6.
''Craig Hernandez.''
''Undecided.''

7.
''Alison Bailey.''
''Pass.''

8.
''Elizabeth Richardson.''
''Undecided at the moment, I need time to think and to talk it through please.''
''It's very important for all of us to do the thinking and talking it through.'' Audolf confirmed.

9.
''Michael Reed.''
''Not Guilty.''

10.

''George Williams.''
''Guilty.''

11.
''Grace Spencer.''
''Not Guilty.''
''That is eleven. And I am Audolf Crow that makes it twelve of us who have voted, and I vote ''Not Guilty.''

12.
''Audolf Crow.''
''Not Guilty.''

He took a deep breath for a long one minute or so and then said, We have 4 not guilties, 4 guilties, 1 pass and 3 Undecideds. It is clear that we'll need more time to reach a verdict in this case.''

They all looked at one another, then they once again looked through all the exhibits in front of them on the table: the X-rays, photographs, forensic laboratory reports, images of body organs taken during post-mortem examination, autopsy results, coroners and inquest reports. It was 5:40pm and at 5:45 Audolf Crow informed the judge they had not reached a verdict. They needed more time to reach a consensus and to deliberate, it had been a very long day, they were thirsty and ravenous, they just wanted to go to their rooms to rest for the day. Judge Archibald Magnusson recessed until 9th of May.

Chapter 28

Monday, 9th May 2016

Reuben Gibbs called the packed courtroom to order, and Archibald welcomed his jury. He ordered them to retire to the jury room and commence their deliberations. He would meet with them just before 11:45am before noon. The jury filed out and went into the jury room.

''Well here we are for the big day, how should we proceed with this?'' Audolf asked with anxiety swirled around him.

''I'll go first,'' said Alison Bailey.

''I don't see any reason why you can't, let's hear it.'' replied Audolf.

''See, I passed yesterday, and could just not make up my mind, there's a lot of issues with this case, like – how can an ex-convict just go scot free like that, but the expert witnesses are crap, and I don't think the boy is legally insane as the mental health doctor is making us believe. So I am going to go for a guilty. Why should he go unpunished? Everyone's going to think that we let him go because his dad is a prosecuting attorney, innit?'' she said in cockney English. I am not passing this time, I am voting Tom guilty.''

''This is the whole idea of this deliberations, we have to spit out what we are thinking to make us reach our decisions." Audolf remarked.

'Yes – I voted undecided yesterday, but I am going to vote not guilty today. My gut instinct tells me that boy Tom may have been in trouble with the state so many times, and yeah he's been down for rape, theft, you name it, and his criminal record is nothing to write home about, but the prosecution has not convinced me that they caught cyanide or strychnine on his hands or in his pocket. So why should he go down for a crime that we are not sure he's done, simply because he's offended before? And what if it is true that Steven took his own life. What if? We cannot overlook that possibility. That's my take and you see even if Tom actually did it, I believe he is legally insane, he is a troubled young man, with drug abuse and substance abuse; and you don't know what you'll get from such a person.'' said David Anderson.

''You think he is legally insane?'' asked Craig Hernandez.

'Yes, I think he did not do it and even if he did he is legally insane to know what he was doing.''

''I see what you mean, that was what I was thinking when I voted undecided yesterday. I think Tom is not guilty. I have made my mind up now, he is not guilty.'' Said Craig Hernandez.

''That means you actually believe Mrs Cassandra?'' asked Audolf.

''Yes I do,'' replied Craig.

''Elizabeth Richardson what do you think?'' asked the foreman.
''I think he is not guilty, the prosecuting attorney has not yet found the victim's killer, there must be more to it than meets the eye. The most obvious thing is not necessarily the main thing in this case. We have to be careful not to punish the wrong person and that is my main fear. I'd rather play it safe with that young man, than to send him to life imprisonment for what he has not actually or in fact done, just because the prosecution is looking for someone to go down for doing the crime, when they still actually have not done a lot of proving or convincing, if you see what I mean.'' Elizabeth Richardson said as worry gnawed her.

''David Anderson what is your vote, you were undecided yesterday?''

''I am going to vote not guilty. I am not sure whether the deceased poisoned himself or not. I just don't know. We must avoid any form of miscarriage of justice. If it does not fit we must acquit the boy. My main worry is that there is no evidence directly linking or tying Tom's hands to the crime of murder even if he had the intention to murder, there is no evidence to suggest his being involved with 'actus reus', we cannot rely on speculation,'' David was so sure of his not guilty vote.

''I don't see why anybody would believe Dr Cassandra Guideville or whatever she's named. She goes around saying stuff just to make it work for her, she is not a credible witness. Just like when Nigel said that there was a case that she was the only one who had a different opinion to her colleagues when she said the victim had mental health problems and the court agreed with her colleagues and not her. She is like a chameleon who changes colours to suit the occasion. Can't you see it?'' asked Alison Bailey.

''No, I don't see it. How can I? The story of that boy's life is sad. I know he has criminal record but I don't think he could commit murder, not from the evidence in front of us. I mean if he poisoned Steve in that restaurant with cyanide, then why didn't Steve collapse and die on the spot, that is what I am puzzled about. If someone drinks a lethal dose of poison, then he should have slumped and died immediately, but Steve did not slump in the restaurant, he convulsed inside the train, how then did Tom poison him on the train. I am puzzled by the facts in this case. There is a mystery that is yet to be unravelled and we have to maybe kind of go to the court of appeal to iron this case out maybe. That is what I think?''

After the deliberations the jury went around the table, one at a time, expressing opinions and answering questions from one another. It became cut clear in the open that all the undecideds and the only pass have all leaned toward not guilty, it seemed.

At 11:40am the jury had reached their verdict. Mr Reuben Gibbs made the attorneys aware that the jury were now ready to deliver their verdict. Reuben brought the courtroom to order, the spectators were doubled in number to what it was in the morning, there was murmuring, chatting going on and when it all was quiet, the jurors filed into their seats. There were no sentiments nor smiles, everyone looked serious. The press were more than a dozen outside the court premises, the case has attracted the media, and Archibald felt it was the right thing to do getting the jury to go and have their lunch at 12pm, knowing that they are not allowed to leave the court premises under any circumstances before the verdict was read, he also would like them to rest a bit as the afternoon is going to be down to business. He then ordered them to make sure they finish their lunch by 1:15pm after which the court will reconvene.

As early as noon as the jury were having their lunch the court surroundings were crowded with so many people in their hundreds. Cars from hundreds of miles away were parked on the shoulders of the highways outside the city limits. The courtroom was packed to the brim as if it was hosting a congregational festival. A crew of TV people were hanging everywhere. The jurors having started the day nice and early were not getting tired, haggard and strained as they could sense tension in the air. It has not been easy for them, and they felt like hostages. It was intimidating when you are sitting on a jury in a case like this. The poison being the weapon of murder in this case even made it more popular.

The court clerk called at 1:30pm. The jury had a verdict.

At 1:30pm Archibald assumed the bench and an electrified silence engulfed the courtroom. There was no sound from the outside. There was perfect stillness inside the courtroom and out. The court felt as if it was echoing Michael Jackson's song 'This is it!' Then Archibald asked ''I have been advised that the jury has reached a verdict, is that correct, Mr Bailiff? Very well. We will soon seat the jury, but before we do so, could I make you aware that this court will not tolerate any outbursts or unnecessary displays of emotion. I will direct the sheriff to remove any person who creates a disturbance during the trial. If need be, I will clear the courtroom. Mr Bailiff, will you seat the jury for me please.''

The jury awkwardly filled the jury box. They appeared jittery, tense and scared. Audolf Crow the foreman held a piece of paper in his hands, it felt like it was someone's life that was being held in the hands of another. The piece of paper attracted the attention of everyone.

''Ladies and gentlemen, have you reached a verdict?''

''Yes sir, we have,'' answered the foreman in a high-pitched, nervous voice.
''Hand it to the clerk, please.''

Reuben Gibbs took it and handed it to His Honour, who studied it forever. ''Ok, it is ok, it is in order,'' Archibald said. He has done this so many times in his career and nothing was new either way when it comes to the court verdict and judgment.

''Mr Tom Blackstone,'' Judge Archibald Magnusson said, ''please rise.''

Tom and Howard his defence attorney stood and turned to the jury. Several jurors, black, had tears in their eyes, as Tom did in his, his body literally shaking like jelly, while his hands was trembling like a tsunami. Howard then put his arm around his shoulders and pulled him close. Keith Bradford was looking at his son and tears rolled down his eyes, for the first time in his life he felt what defendants felt while he was prosecuting them, this time it was his son, his blood who was in trouble. What if he goes to jail for life, what was he going to do. There were so many questions going through Keith's head. At this point, Howard closed his eyes and held his breath. His hands shook and his stomach ached, both happening at the same time.

After the foreman of the jury had handed the verdict to the bailiff who had in turn handed it to Archibald. Judge Archibald first rubbed his reading glasses, gazed again at the piece of paper, then for the second time he raised his eyes to the defendant again before he finally handed the verdict back to Reuben Gibbs, he then said. "Please read the verdict." He unfolded it and faced the defendant.

"In the matter of **R versus Tom Blackstone**, as to each count of the indictment, we the jury find the defendant not guilty."

Keith Bradford needed to hear these words from Archibald more than anyone else, throughout the trial he's been an emotional wreck, yet he could not really show his inner feelings for a son that he hardly knew. It was a huge relief hearing Archibald utter those words 'not guilty', this was the first time that they will mean something to him, as a prosecutor he's been jubilant many times over when the judge pronounced the defendant 'guilty' when he was prosecuting. But this case was different, he is happy with a 'not guilty' verdict. It is the irony of life. He faced a lawyer's dilemma through the trial of his only child, his only son. Tom buried his face in Howard's chest and embraced him, they both had tears rolling down their faces. Keith sprang from the front pew where he had sat and grabbed Tom, then hugged Howard. The court room erupted in cheers and shouts and applause. Howard stood shaking his head in bewilderment and wonderment at the turn of events 'just like that?' he asked himself in his thoughts. He whispered into Keith's ears, "I bet it is all over!" "Really?" Keith replied. "Yes really, it's all over." Howard turned to the bench and his eyes met Judge

Archibald Magnusson's eyes. The judge nodded at Howard and Howard nodded back.

Phoebe and Evelyn screamed and burst into tears ''How could anyone set Tom free?'' Phoebe shouted out loud, in her thin voice at her old age. Evelyn continue to sob like a baby. Evelyn buried her head in Phoebe's arms. This verdict is not what Phoebe, Evelyn and Nigel Stanley would have liked to hear. Tom Blackstone was free. 'How can he be free?' Nigel thought, he then began to remove his files, legal pads and all other important-criminal procedure books he had brought with him, and throwing them all into his briefcase. What a dilemma, he whispered to himself.

One of the spectators, a male voice, with excitement shouted inside the court, ''Not guilty! Not guilty! Tom is not guilty!" he continued to shout through the doors. His voice stood out from the sea of other screaming faces. Tom will soon find out that, the loud voice is that of his friend Gary, who was making such loud noise. As if that was not enough, Neil who was also Tom's friend ran to a small balcony over the front steps and screamed to the masses below ''Not guilty'', ''Not guilty''. There was a loud noise from the crowd outside.
''Order, Order in court,'' Archibald was saying when the delayed reaction from the outside came thundering through the windows. He rapped the gavel. Archibald was almost inaudible in midst of the roar. Again, he repeated: ''Order, Order in the court,'' he shouted when the delayed reaction from the outside came thundering through the windows. The youth who knew Tom very well on the street and from the hostel where he lived were all excited and there was no doubt that the jubilation uproar was coming from them outside the court, the judge asked the sheriff to restore order after which the noise coming from outside died a natural death.

The Judge smiled at Tom. ''Tom Blackstone, you have been tried by a jury of your peers and found not guilty. I do not recall any expert testimony that you are now dangerous or in need of further psychiatric treatment. You are a free man from today.'' Looking at Howard Sullivan and Nigel Stanley he said: ''If there is nothing further, this court will stand adjourned until 10 May.''

The jurors hugged each other; they were locked in the jury room to await the last bus ride to the guest house. Reporters crowded Howard, Keith and Tom. They pushed their way through the crowd and out of the courtroom. About fourty-five minutes later, they finally made their way through the mob of reporters and cameras and to the sidewalk fronting the court-house building, it was crowded with reporters and the press. There was yelling and whooping voices from the crowd. The journalists pressed against the railing and began firing questions at Howard. With the microphone held in front of Howard, one of the reporters managed to push through his microphone into his face.

''Attorney Howard the jury reached a verdict of not guilty by a majority of seven to five, how does that make you feel now that your client is free?''

For a minute Howard was numb, lifeless, paralysed. Anything you could to describe his overwhelming state of shock, he could not help his eyes watering, with a weak smile in front of the press he knew he ought to be brave and pull himself together by snapping out of showing emotions. He knew everyone was watching him and was not going to make a spectacle of himself.

''Well as you can see it is all on record that my client is not guilty. It is the right to do. The court's verdict is right. This young man did not murder anyone, why would he do such a thing? The prosecutors have not found who they are looking for and they have to continue to look for the murderer of the late Steven, whoever committed the gruesome murder is still out there. The expert witness testimony is conflicting.''

''Do you think the State might appeal to a higher court for redress?''
Howard inched forward through the crowd, and he stopped on the top step under the pillars where the plywood platform held a thousand microphones. The shouting from the army of reporters was completely inaudible.

''The prosecution is in a dilemma, they are free to do whatever they want to do, but one thing that we are all clear about is that a jury made up of 12 people have reached a verdict after considering all the facts and evidence and they have found my client not guilty as charged. All the allegations that had been brought against my client have now been dropped. Tom Blackstone is now a free man.''
''But this young man is not a first-time offender Mr Howard, he's been convicted for rape in the past, is that correct?''

''I am not going to stand here to answer your questions on my client's history, the trial today is not about rape, it is a capital offence trial of which the jurors have found my client not guilty. You will agree with me that today, justice has not only been done, but that justice have been manifestly and undoubtedly been seen to have been done. None of the evidence relied upon by the prosecution attorney in this case is admissible, there was conflicting evidence by forensic medical experts and the consultant pathologist over the dosage of poison. There was no consensus as to whether cyanide or strychnine caused the death of the late Steven.''

''But the deceased died of poison and that was agreed by both expert witnesses.''

''Well you are not the judge, neither are you a member of the jury…the press cannot try a case or reach verdict on it, that is the job of the judiciary, if you are finding any of the facts raised today confusing, then I will admonish you to go and read the full report of the facts of this case and the determination in the law reports which should be published anytime from now.''

Howard then held up his hands, and said he would have no further comments and that if the press had any further questions, then he would have them in his office at 3pm for a full-blown press conference.

Keith Bradford knew most of the reporters. He had seen them before when he prosecuted and had been interviewed on several occasions, but this time it was different because he was not on the prosecution side but on the defence side which has put him in an awkward position with the press.

As he inched forward to push through the mob down the hall and out of the rear door, he was met by a swarm of reporters.

''Mr Keith Bradford as prosecutor, it must be difficult for you to be standing on the side of the defence team today for obvious reasons, how does that make you feel?''

''A man has got to do what a man has got to do, is all I can say.''

''Has it ever crossed your mind in your three decades of practice as a prosecutor that you will one day be on the defence team representing a member of your family?''

''No.''

''Why?''

''Because you would expect your family to be law abiding and not get into any form of trouble with the law.''

''You must be pleased that your son is walking away from the court room today as a free man, would it not have been very devastating for you and your career as prosecutor if it was otherwise, Mr Keith Bradford?''

''I am pleased that justice have been served today in the best possible way.''

''Are you saying that because the verdict is in favour of your son?''

''The prosecution team did a pretty good job and I am proud of them, but the defence attorney put up a good defence.''

''Would you have said something different if the verdict was guilty?''

''That is the point I am making, the boy has been found not guilty.''

''How does it make you feel that the little boy you left with your former wife when he was barely two years old has brought you so much embarrassment after over two decades.''

''I don't wish my story on my worst foe. I am not proud of what has happened in the past. Like I said before there is a lesson for everyone in my story. My advice to young professionals is that they should take their family seriously if they have one. Marriage is not a bed of roses. You must stick with it when it is rough. Take your role as a father seriously because if you don't, it may come back to haunt you.''

''Do you think that the mistake you made in the past has now come back to haunt you through your son, Tom?''

''You have just said so, why do you want to hear it again from my mouth?''
''Is Tom going to move in to live with you from now on?''

''Yes, we have a lot to catch up on…and I am glad that he is a free man.''

Keith, Tom and Howard clutched hands and smiled at each other, both searching for words, they embraced each other, then walked away from the reporters until they disappeared to the side road where their car was parked. Outside the court building side road a hundred cars lined both shoulders east and west of court Road Avenue; the long front yard was packed with vehicles.

When they got back to the office, there were dozens of reporters packed inside Howard's office conference room, they took pictures of Howard, Keith and Tom. Howard answered some of their questions again before he bid them farewell.

''Tracey!'' Howard called.

''Yep!'' replied Tracey, his office manager and legal secretary.

''Winning this case calls for celebration, could you pour out margaritas into four glasses please, one for yourself if you like!'' Howard said as joy blossomed within him infecting everyone around him.
Tracey poured out the margaritas into four glasses, and they gulped it down. After the press conference, Tracey booked a taxi-cab to take all four to their respective homes as they were all tipsy and would dare not drive any of their cars home.

Chapter 29

Tom, 1st of June 2016

The trial was now over and today marks twenty-one days since I walked out of court a free man. My dad embraced me. He's given me a second chance. He's decided to raise me up all over again, may be from where he stopped when I was only two years old. If only he could turn back the hand of the clock, he would. But that is not exactly possible. I am now an adult and nothing can erase the mistakes that I have made in the past. I have been to jail and then released after serving my jail terms mostly for misdemeanours, my record is not quite straight forward. I have lived with various foster carers and families. I guess the greatest challenge for my dad is trying to change my adoptive name 'Blackstone' back to his own name 'Bradford'. After I moved in with my dad, he sorted out all the papers for my name to change. He paid a couple of hundreds of pounds to file for my name change petition in court. It also costs a small amount of money to get forms notarized.

My dad and I travelled to Pennsylvania to my late mother's grave to lay a wreath and to say prayers. Going to her grave side is the closest I could ever get to her. The last time my dad saw her was when he walked away from their marriage. My grand-mother (Phoebe) helped us to locate my late mum's graveside, initially after the court trial, she did not want to have anything to do with my dad and I, but after about six month's she began to pick up my dad's phone call, all my dad wanted to do was to make up for what had gone wrong in the past. He wanted to make peace, to let go of all grudges, to move on and if possible to take care of my granny. She told us all about how my mother met Brian Claxton, fell in love with him and they gave birth to Steven, it was during Steve's birth that my mother died, she was buried at Easton Philadelphia, Philadelphia County, Pennsylvania.

We departed from London, Gatwick on the 23rd of December, our flight took a good nine hours and twenty minutes. We arrived at Philadelphia at just after midnight and my dad had pre-booked an on suite hotel for us to stay for a week. The last time I travelled to Pennsylvania was when the late Steve took me to the US, that was the very first time I travelled on a plane and that was when I met Phoebe for the first time. I have never in my life been treated or enjoyed long distance travel like this, travelling again this time with dad brings the memory of Steve back to me.

When we phoned Phoebe on Christmas Eve, we were not turned away, she welcomed us and even though her voice was frail, she was able to describe where my mother's graveside was in Eaton, and gave us a good description of how we could get there. She told us the exact words written on her tomb stone. The only thing Phoebe did not do was to invite us over to where she lived. Unlike when Steve and I visited her, she accommodated us, but this time she did not and we understood and respected her decision.

We set out early at around 11am on Christmas Eve, and brought wreath with us all the way from London, as well as shopping for flowers at the florist shop about five miles away from Eaton. I saw Keith wipe his eyes about once or twice, it was emotional for him. I guess the only way for him to properly move on was to say good bye to the late Teresa. One thing is, he knows her in person. The only thing was that their marriage did not work. That was not the case for me. I really did not get to know my mother. I was only two years old; I don't even have a recollection of any sort. I felt sad. I have been told the story of how she battled with addiction of drug abuse, alcohol addiction, depression and self-harm in a dark and lonely place. I was told how she had been rehabilitated in Arizona when she was pregnant with Steve. I was told she lost her licence to practice as a nurse in England because of substance abuse at work. Everything I know about my late mum were things I'd been told. I did not see any of it with my eyes. I have had to deal with it psychologically. It was not easy for me.

We arrived at the Ivy Hill Cemetery also known as Germantown and Chestnut Hill Cemetery. We followed the description that Phoebe had given us and after about fifteen minutes we were able to locate my mother's graveside. My dad was the first to lay his wreath; I laid my own flowers and a wreath with 'MUM' hand written on it. I saw dad wipe his eyes with his handkerchief, then he bent down to say a few words, it was loud enough for me to hear his voice clearly in the line of:

''Teresa may your soul continue to rest in peace. I am very sorry that things ended between us the way it did. When I moved out on that night, I never knew that social services was going to take Tommy away from you. I made a hasty decision as a young man; I could not cope with the pressure of my profession as a State Prosecutor and having a young family. I am sorry I walked away. I regret it and I am paying for it right now. If the late Steve is there beside you in the celestial, greet him for me. I never met him, but I feel sorry for the way he died too. It was tragic. Tom had been through a court trial that could have ended in him going to prison for life. I will have to live with the trauma for the rest of my life. If it would ever make you feel better in heaven where you are right now, I never got married or had any meaningful relationship after we separated and then divorced. All I ever did was practice as a prosecuting attorney. If it is ever going to make you feel better, Tommy now lives with me; I have had to pick up from where I stopped twenty seven years ago. He is now a grown man. I promise you that I will do everything and anything to make up for my mistake. I will look after him. I will nurture him like you would have. Teresa, I will come and visit your side at least once a year with Tommy. If it is ever possible, please find it in your heart to forgive me. Continue to rest in peace in the bosom of the Lord. Adieu!''

I saw my dad wipe his eyes again. It was my turn to say something, but I just did not know what to say at my late mum's graveside. I just summed up courage to say few words in the lines of:

''Mum, I won't stand here and pretend that I know you or that you know me because I do not have re-collection of either. What I know for sure is that your name is on my birth certificate and that the same name is the name that is engraved on your tombstone. I know you are my mum. I can feel it. I wish you were there for me mum. I have really been through thick and thin all because you've not been around. I have seen some of my friend's mothers and I know what she means to them. I can't say the same of my mum because I hardly ever knew her...but nonetheless I love you like a son should love his mother. Dying was not your fault after all. It was a necessary end that would come when it did. No one knows the time or the hour when death will come knocking on the door. The last time I travelled to Pennsylvania with the late Steve, I should have asked him to bring me here, but I am so sorry that it never occurred to me, please find it in your heart to forgive me.
Mum, if I could tell you, then I would, but you see, you are now in a better place, no more sorrow over there where you are, no court trials, no more pain for you, no more sorrow and you only die once, you don't have to do that again I think. Your battle with substance abuse is gone forever, you can't be depressed where you are now, you are free from all of it and I wish myself such freedom from my addiction. Yeah, I hope you are listening, and I have said enough. Love you mum. Rest in Peace. One love mum. One love.''

I said my tribute to my late mum by kneeling by her graveside. I felt a big relief after my speech ended. A picture of her was still visible on the stone. I could not help but to cry. It was the saddest day of my life.

''Thanks dad for bringing me here.''

''We both need to be here son, it is therapeutic, and is the only way we can come to terms with the death of your mother.''

''Yes you are right dad. It feels very sad, I just did not know what to say.''

''But you said a lot.''

''Do you think she knows that we came here close to her side?'' Tom asked.

''Yes she does. In the celestial world she does.''

''Really?''

''Well that is one of the myths I was told by my own mum.'' Keith replied.
''Are we going to go and visit Phoebe before we go back to London?''

''I'll rather we don't, she really doesn't want to see us, at least not after your acquittal at the court trial after the death of Steve. In reality Steve is the only grandson she actually got to know properly.''

''Did you ask her whether she would like us to visit her tomorrow Christmas Day?''

''Yes I did ask her before we left London, but she declined, so I won't push it.'' He sneered.

''Ok dad, what are we going to do now?''

''We'll look for a good restaurant where we can have a decent lunch and we'll take it up from there.''

Dad and I went to a restaurant called Suzani on Welsh Road in Philadelphia. It was an awesome place. It was open from

11am to 11pm and so we spent a good number of hours relaxing and getting fed. The moment we walked in, there was a rich culture decoration, we sat on their cosy sofa spots and the moment of truth was when they brought the food. It was Mediterranean styled food just as we would find in Soho in London, I mean the Nopi restaurant in Warwick street in Soho or The Paloma restaurant on Rupert street, Chinatown or Berwick street in Soho.

We felt at home. The food was amazing. We had Samosa which was bread ball with minced meat and spices in it. My favourite was Kutab which was pretty much the same as Samsa but the dough that is used is different and the filling that can be chosen is either beef or feta-spinach. All the information about the food was presented to us on the menu sheet. We also had a Kebab platter which was a combination of Lamb, beef and Lula. I think everyone should try Lula when you visit a Mediterranean restaurant. The lula went down well with chicken kebab skewers. The chicken Tabaka was a whole chicken roasted and crisped to perfection served with homemade tomato sauce on the side. We requested for a bowl of rice with it.

Then we came to the dessert. We had Napoleon dessert, it was tasteful, and I was flat. My heart was won completely.

''This is lovely and tasty Mediterranean styled food. Are you enjoying it?''

''Thanks dad, it is amazing. We should visit here again before we go back to London.''

''I'm going to order tea or coffee now, which one would you like?''

''A strong coffee.''

''Ok I'll have the same.''

The waiter came round with two coffee pots, milk, sugar and the bill. Keith paid for the meal and left a tip in the tray on the table.

Dad and I did not leave the restaurant immediately after our meal. We went to the seating and relaxing corner and sat on a sofa, there was a basket-ball game on the television. We had a lengthy chat.

We did some sight - seeing since it was Christmas Eve. Everywhere was well lit! This was the first Christmas that I would spend outside London or Croydon. I have lived the whole of my life in England, and coming to America offered a change.

''What do you think of America?'' Keith asked.

''It is a beautiful place, but I'll rather stay in England where I am used to and come here for just holidays. Like you said, we will be coming every year to visit mum's grave side and maybe with time Phoebe will warm up to us. You never know dad. Things may change for the better.''

''Let's hope so, she is getting older by the day, she needs care and I am happy to support her in her old age, now that her husband Mathew had died and Steven is no longer here to look after her.''

''It looks like the only person she likes to relate with right now is Evelyn, Steve's girlfriend.''

''But Evelyn and her parents live in London.'' Keith replied.

''The question is how is Evelyn going to reach out to look after her when she is in England and Phoebe is in Pennsylvania?''

''We will play our own part by phoning her every now and again to check in with her.''

''Do you think she might need to be cared for in a residential home for the elderly at some point?''

''Yes she would, she cannot continue to live alone, although she said carers do come daily to help her with some house chores and cleaning, but as time goes by she will need to be bathed and properly cared for twenty-four seven.''

''Yeah.''

''I would have loved to contact Evelyn to find out more on how we can support Phoebe, that is something that your mother Teresa would have loved me to do and I want to do.''

''I don't think Evelyn would like to have anything to do with you.''

''Why do you think so?''

''Well it is because of what happened between me and her. I was very young and I was in care. I lived with her and her parents.'' Tom recalled.

''Tell me, did you do it?''

''You mean did I do what she said that I did to her?'' Tom said with his nose crinkling and his eyes glistening.

''Yes, did you actually rape her when you were a teenager; your secret is safe with me. I am your dad.''

''Do you promise not to tell anyone?'' Tom asked, his eyelids sagged and paused.'' Ok, I know the prosecuting attorney tried his best to send me down for maximum sentence but the defence attorney plead my case based on what I told them at the time, so I had a lesser sentence.''

''But that does not answer my question, son, did you do it, I mean did you rape Evelyn?''

Tom was quiet for about two minutes without any form of response to Keith.

''Look at it this way, the reason why I am asking you to tell me the truth is because that will determine whether Evelyn can help us to get closer to Phoebe, your Gran. Your late mum is looking down on us; we have just been to her graveside. If we look after her mother I know she will be happy with us.''

''Yes dad, you are right. OK I did. I raped Evelyn and I think that the last thing she will ever do is to want to have anything to do with me. Giving the evidence that Evelyn and Phoebe gave in court during the trial, they actually believe that I killed Steve by poisoning him, just because I had once raped someone!'' Tom said and his hands began to wobble, his body shaking as if there was something pushing him to spit it all out at once. His dad has been a prosecuting attorney for almost three decades. He is the best person to deal with likes of Tom.

''Do you have anything else that you would like to tell me apart from the rape?''

''How do you mean dad?''

''I mean you remember yesterday night when you told me that you had a bad dream in your sleep and that you were going to tell me all about your nightmare, what was all that about?''

''I think it was because of the 9 hours 20 minutes flight from London to Philadelphia, you know I am not used to flying by air.''

''Son, you were hallucinating when you woke up! What was that about?''

''Dad, are you sure that I can trust you with serious information?''

''When you say serious information, what do you mean?''

''What I mean is that if I tell you the truth, can you promise to keep it to yourself and not tell anyone or report it to the police?''

''You are my son and family is first. Why should I betray the trust you have in me?''

''I am glad you see it that way, dad.''

''See your profession has in the past stood between you and your family, by that I mean my late mum, you and I. I hope you can walk away from your profession for the sake of your family now dad. Can you?''
''It depends on what you mean Tom. I would still like to continue to work as an attorney.''

''But you can also work as a defence attorney couldn't you?''

''How does that change anything?''

''My point exactly. I cannot tell you any secret and I don't think you will be able to keep any promise not to disclose information to the police as long as you continue to be a prosecutor.'' Tom said.

''Listen to this, I don't have to be a prosecutor to report anyone to the police for doing something wrong. Anyone can do that. We prosecutors help to prosecute people who are arrested by the police for a crime. Do you see what I mean son?'' Keith explained.

''Yeah I see what you mean. Is my secret safe with you then?''

''Yes Tom, your secret is safe with me. Please share your fears with me, it has taken 27 odd years for us to get to where we are right now. I promise I won't tell anyone.''

''Dad I think you will be in a dilemma, something like a lawyer's dilemma because if I tell you something that is not in line with the law, you will be in a dilemma as to whether to protect your son from getting arrested or whether to hand your son over to face the consequences of his actions by facing the wrath of the law.'' Tom said as his eyes narrowed.

''Listen, it is either you trust me or you don't.'' replied Keith.

''Ok.''

''What you should know about hallucinations is that whatever you see, hear, smell, tastes or feel are things that don't exist outside your mind. It may be you hearing voices that just don't exist and this may be due to your mental health condition. Hallucination is common in people with schizophrenia.'' Keith explained.

''Yeah.''

''Were you frightened? What did you hear or see? There should be an identifiable cause for you to experience the apparent perception of something not present.''

''Yesterday night was not the first time that I have experienced horrific hallucinations...I had it on the night before the court trial.''

''Oh I see. Tell me what you heard, saw or felt when this happens?''

''Yesterday night I saw Steve.''

''Sorry, I don't get it...you saw Steve?''

''You heard me right. I saw the late Steve…''

''Sorry, when you said you saw Steve you mean you were hearing his voice or that you hallucinated seeing him?''

''Initially I saw him in my dream and that is when I shouted and woke up!''

''What did he say to you in the dream.''

''He told me to make sure that I tell mum by her graveside that I murdered him in cold blood.''

''And was that what you did?''

''Yes dad, that was what I did…Steve is following me everywhere I see him in my dream and when I am awake too…''

''You mean you see his ghost?''

''I don't know whether what I am seeing is his ghost, but I could hear his voice clearly last night and this morning before we visited mum's graveside.''

''Are you sure about what you are saying?''

''Yes dad it is true.''

''And did you actually do what he was asking you to tell your mum?''

''Yes I did.''

''You mean you did commit murder as you continued to suffer from horrific hallucinations in apparent perception of something you were not physically involved in?''

''No, that is not what I said dad. What I am saying is that I am confessing to you that I actually took Steve's life.''

''But how do you mean Tom.'' Keith looked horrified and astonished, choking on his words, and asked his son again. ''But what are you talking about, is this a dream or do you have a physical recollection of harming Steve?''

''I physically have a recollection of the event that occurred when Steve and I went out for a meal and drinks in West end.''

''So what actually happened?''

''I'm only going to confess what happened on that night to you because you have promised not to tell anyone as my dad, are you going to keep your promise?''

''Listen to this…I will not betray you…I have lost you once and will not allow that to happen again.''

''But you are a prosecutor…''

''Yes I know I am, you don't have to worry about that where family is concerned.''

''Are you sure about that dad?''

''Are you going to tell me your confession or not cause I am running out of patience.''

''Dad, you are a lawyer – no one who's been convicted before would ever trust a prosecutor, I need you to promise me that you will keep your lips sealed, and that you will not tell a soul the truth that I am about to tell you.''

''How many times will I tell you that your secret is safe with me? I know I am in a dilemma here, but I promise not to tell a soul. It stays here between us.''

''Give me just one reason why I should believe you?''

''Listen just spit out what you want to say, technically not every confession is admissible as evidence in court.''

''What do you mean by that?''

''What that means is that if a confession is obtained under duress it may not be admissible in evidence against the accused person.''

''Really?''

''Yes – if a confession is made by a someone who is legally insane, then, it may not be admissible; that is one bone of contention when we get to court, but it may not come to that if we keep it all here, so you really do not have anything to worry about son.''

''But I am not under duress dad.''

''Yes I know, but you said that you were hallucinating last night, and then you had a nightmare and bad dream, you said you hallucinated, that you were hearing Steve's voice, that he told you to spit out what you had done to him. Is that correct?''

''Yeah dad. You really are clever; you retain a lot of information in a short space of time.'' Tom said.

''Now to the secret you were going to tell me. What is it?''

''I am the only one that knows what killed Steve and how he died.''

''Say that again…''

''I said that I am the only one who knows what killed Steve and how he died.''

''Who killed Steve?''

''I did.''

''How did you go about doing that?''

''I poisoned him with cyanide, but not inside the restaurant when we were having a drink or meal.''

''You got me confused there, you mean the consultant pathologist laboratory report was accurate that the cause of death is cyanide.'' Keith paused. ''What then is the mystery behind the late Steve dying while on the train and not while you were both in the restaurant?''

''The mystery that I alone know is that when Steve and I got to the station, we both stood on the platform and I offered him a wrapped mint. I had two mints in my hand, I put one in my mouth and gave Steve a coated minted cyanide, I then bid him good-bye as he boarded his train. I later heard that he slumped on board the train.''
''Oh my God…tell me you didn't.''

''I hope you can handle our secret dad, I hope you can handle the shock.''

''Were you insane when you did it?''

''I don't know what came over me dad. Steve had everything going for him, I was the disadvantaged, he neglected me when I phoned him before I went to prison, he later told me that he had changed his phone number, and I resented him, I was jealous of the fact that he was going to inherit everything our grandparents had, that my childhood was more unfortunate than his own...we were born by the same mother but it doesn't feel so…life hasn't been fair on me… Steve had everything but I had nothing.''

''But you did not have to poison him, that was cruel.''

''Don't judge me dad, please don't you dare judge me.''

''Son, I am not proud of what you did, you committed a capital offence here.''

''That is the secret, dad, you have promised to keep it between us and the ball is now in your court.''

''I find this sad. I wish you never did. How can I live up to practice my profession among my colleagues if they get to know that my biological son had done something so terrible?''

''This is it, dad, you are better off keeping it between us and not utter it to a soul or your career will be ruined.'' Tom said as bitterness filled his mouth.

''We will keep it a secret. I promise not to tell a soul. You are the only child that I have. You have lost once under circumstances beyond my control. I will not allow that to happen again. It is one of the hardest decisions that I have had to make in my career.'' Keith said as he plunged into despair.

''Thank you for your understanding dad.''

''We've been in this restaurant since 11am, let us start making our way back to our hotel for an early night. There is a lot of thinking for me to do. But just before we go, could you tell me where you got the cyanide from?''
''What do you need that information for, since you promised not to tell anyone.''

''You look too innocent to know how to get a poison.''

''You know I used to work for a chemical company when I lived in that hostel in Croydon, I learnt from that job what various chemicals were used for.''

''Oh my God! Let us go, we have a lot to ponder upon.''

''So Steve did not commit suicide after all.''

''He never did. He could not do such a thing. Why would he?!''

Keith and Tom spent two more nights in Pennsylvania before they returned to England. Phoebe did not allow them to visit her at home. Keith phoned her again before they departed, she was delighted to hear that they located her daughter's grave to lay wreaths and flowers. After the discussion that Keith had with his son at the restaurant, he knew that he could never again face either Phoebe or Evelyn.

Chapter 30

Nemesis

I did not sleep for a good two days after Tom told me what he had done. What he said to me is something you watch in a horror film, not what you would expect to hear from a son where you have not been part of his life for almost three decades. My plan was to go back to work since Tom walked away from court a free man. I was in a dilemma. When my investigation team began gathering evidence to prosecute in the late Steven's case, I voluntarily pulled out from the team. It was the right thing to do. We found out that he was my son. I would rather be on the side of the defence team to help the son that I never knew very well. But things are different now after Tom confessed what he had done to me. I know that Tom had been in trouble so many times before and that he is not on the right side of the law for misdemeanours. He had served jail terms and has been released back into society. I can deal with that. What I cannot handle is the extent to which he could go and that he had already gone in the world of crime. How could he take Steve's life? How could he murder someone out of hatred and jealousy? Tom is a hardened criminal. I have to be very careful on how to handle him. If I give him the impression that I am going to hand him over to the cops. He may plan to harm me too. So I have to be careful. I have not been there for him when it really mattered and I will not be surprised if he harboured some form of resentment or ill-will toward me in the past at least to some extent. Although it doesn't appear to be so, but after hearing directly from him what he had done to Steve, I just cannot rule out the extent to which his anger can go.

My thirty year career as state prosecuting attorney has been without blemish. I have tried to be impartial, fair, objective and balanced. My prosecution team has been blind to prejudice and we have maintained the good shape of our criminal justice practice and the legal profession. I have always had at the back of my mind an uncanny knack of knowing exactly what the public was thinking – about crime, about what the defence attorney and his team were up to. I know about sentencing and much else. I am the shop steward who remembered their names, their hopes and their concerns. I'm always on the side of the state to ensure that justice is not only done, but that it is manifestly and undoubtedly seen to have been done.

As a state attorney I executed my office without fear or favour, affection or ill will. I have taken my continuous professional development seriously through learning. Over the years I have gathered and gained wisdom, compassion and eloquence, diligence and common sense with robust independence and impartiality, leadership and administrative skills too.

Agreeing with an estranged son, who has suddenly come into my life to conceal a capital offence that he had committed defeats the very essence of the profession that I cherish so much.

Not handing Tom over to the Police after his confession is not the right thing to do. I am in a dilemma. How could I continue to prosecute if my son goes to jail for life for a crime that he committed. If I choose to keep quiet, then I stand a chance of carrying on with my career with the hope that somehow the state will find out the truth about the case of Steve's death. But how can I continue to live with that?.

I came to a conclusion that I am going to carry on with my career as if nothing had happened, as if Tom had not confessed to me. I will take each day as it comes. I will go with the flow and if the truth is revealed I will face the consequences then.

And so on 1st August 2016, I returned to work as a prosecuting attorney, there was a large backlog of cases to be tried: capital offences and misdemeanours. I was busy continuously for three months making appearances in the Magistrate courts,

High courts and even the Court of Appeal. I did not utter a word about my son's confession to anyone. I just couldn't. I truly was in a dilemma – *The Lawyer's Dilemma.*

Chapter 31

Fate

Chief Inspector Kelvin Armstrong and Colonel Peter Blacksmith were very prominent during the investigation and gathering of evidence before the trial of Tom. They formed a formidable team throughout the investigation.

Inspector Jasper Willard – after Tom's case – was moved to take on a Duty Inspector post in Canterbury Police for six months. On his return to the London office, there had been some development and new evidence that may lead to the re-opening of the investigation of Steve Claxton's death.

''Welcome back Jasper, how was Canterbury Constabulary?'' Kelvin asked.

''It was ok, I missed London, but I survived working in Kent.''

Chief Inspector Armstrong turned into the doorway of New Scotland Yard. The two men were well acquainted. They worked together on Tom's case before Keith Bradford pulled out to kind of join the defence team because of his son.

''We shall want all the help we can get on this case.'' Kelvin said.

''You mean we are not yet done with investigation of Steve?'' Jasper asked.
''Some new evidence has emerged and we cannot disregard it or let it slip us by.''

''Really?''

''It looks like we are going for a retrial, that case is not over yet.''

''But how did we miss crucial facts?'' Jasper said, he had full belief in the impartiality of British justice.

''The weight of the new evidence is so phenomenon that it cannot be ignored.'' Kelvin said.

''What is the evidence about?''

''The death of Steve is an intriguing story of violent death in a public place, it was a calculated murder and we now know who his killer is and why.''

''Is it a confessional statement?''

''No, it is not a confessional statement that incriminated the accused person, it is evidence obtained from CCTV Control room of the British transport police office. The CCTV footage showed Tom handing over a kind of wrapped up sweet to Steve before he boarded his train, it was immediately after he put the sweet in his mouth that he convulsed and collapsed in the train. The accused person then walked briskly away from the train station platform and made his way to Croydon after the crime he committed.'' Kelvin explained.

''Do you have the CCTV footage here?''

''Yes we have marked it as Exhibit C. According to the footage Tom put a non-poisonous mint in his own mouth, while he wrapped up another mint lined with cyanide with the intention to finish off his victim having a violent death in a public place before he whisked away from the scene of his crime.'' Kelvin further explained.

''Which type of poison did he use?''

''It was cyanide which had instant effect on the late Steve the moment he put it in his mouth. Don't ask me how Tom got cyanide inside a coated mint. We have a hardened criminal in our hands in this case, whether he is legally insane or not is now for the Court of Appeal to determine.''

''And has Keith Bradford been informed of the latest development?'' Jasper asked.

''I will call the CPS tomorrow to speak to Keith.'' Kelvin said.

''That will be a very devastating news for him given that Tom walked free at the trial at the High Court.''
''We will wait and see where the whole case is heading to in the next few months.'' Kelvin said.

''We have to make an immediate arrest of Tom Bradford tonight.'' Jasper said.

''You mean Tom Blackstone?'' Kelvin said.

''No, his father had completed the procedure for his surname to be changed back to Bradford, so he is now Tom Bradford.'' Jasper explained.

''I wonder how Keith is going to take the latest news!'' Kelvin said.

''He will be convinced when the CCTV footage is played for him to see in court.'' Jasper concluded.

Chapter 32

Retribution, 4th August 2016

The doorbell rang at 6:30pm. Tom was home and he wondered who was at the door. Keith had not yet arrived from work. A loud knock on the door by Chief Inspector Kelvin Armstrong, Colonel Peter Blacksmith stood directly behind him while they both wait for an answer.

Tom ran downstairs wondering who was at the door. He opened the door and low and behold his eyes met Kelvin, whose face he's seen before when he was arrested at Mr and Mrs Blackstone's place.

''How may I help you?'' Tom asked the officers, who stared at them in their squeaky clean, admirable Police uniform.

''Young man there is certainly a lot you can do to help us, you are under arrest for the murder of Steven Claxton, you have the right to remain silent, you do not have to say anything, but it may harm your defence if you do not mention when questioned something which you later rely on in court. Anything you do say may be given in evidence against you in the court of law.''

Kelvin handcuffed him and thereafter whisked him to the Police van they came with, parked in front of the house.

''Is it my dad who told you that I did it, isn't it!''

''How do you mean?'' Peter asked.
''I know I should never have trusted him, how could I be so stupid to believe he would keep his mouth shut and not tell anyone.''

''What did you tell your dad?'' asked Kelvin.

''Why are you asking me what you already know, if my dad had not told you that I was guilty you will not be here to arrest me, would you?''

The two police officers pulled to the side to whisper to each other.

''Kelvin, is there something that we do not know?' Peter said quietly.

''Could it be that Keith was aware that his son did in fact murder Steve all along?'' Kelvin whispered.

''No. I doubt it. Why would a prosecutor do such a thing?''

''Why would he not do such a thing to protect his only son.''

''But why would he risk losing his career for obstructing the cause of justice?''

''We have a lot of investigation to do. The burden of proving the case is on the prosecution remember?''

''You are right saying that, just let us get this boy to the station to have him locked away before he absconds.''

They arrived at the station and the jailer took Tom's wallet, money, watch, key, ring, and pocketknife, he listed the items on an inventory form that Tom signed and dated. In a small room next to the jailer's station, he was photographed and fingerprinted. The court sheriff waited outside the door and led him down the hall to a small room where drunks were taken to blow into the Breathalyzer.

''Can I please call my dad?'' Tom asked.

''Of course you can.''

Peter handed him the station phone to make his phone call.

''Dad, where are you right now, I have been arrested. You told me that you will not tell a soul – you betrayed me, and I won't trust you again ever.''

''Calm down, I have not told anyone anything…'' Keith replied.

''But how did Police know and why did they come and arrest me?''

''I don't know what you are talking about, can you hand the phone over to the officer.''

Tom handed the phone to Kelvin.

''Keith, we've got Tom here with us, it may be a good idea for you to get an attorney for him, he will be interviewed in the next 15 minutes.''

''Gosh Kelvin – tell me it's not happening to me. Can I see you before the interview starts please?'' Keith asked.

''Do what you have to do quickly Keith and get here as soon as you can, you are going to need to get a defence attorney for your son sooner rather than later.''

''Ok then will see you soon.''

Keith arrived thirty minutes after the interview had already began. He had to wait for it to finish before he could stand a chance to speak to Kelvin.

The interview room was shut. Two tape recorders sat side by side near the edge of the sheriff's desk.

''We'd like to ask you some questions, okay?'' Kelvin asked.

''Before I start, I want to make sure you understand your rights. First of all, you have the right to remain silent. Understand?''

''Yeah.''

''Can you read and write?''

''Yeah.''

''Very good. Then read this and sign it. It says you've been advised of your rights.''

Tom signed the dotted lines on the paper. Kelvin pushed the red button on one of the tape recorders.

''You understand that tape recorder is on?''

''Yeah.''

''It's 4th August at 7:45pm in the evening.''

''Yeah.''

''What is your full name?''

''Tommy Bradford.''

''Any nickname?''

''People call me Tom.''

''Your address?''

''64 Phybil Phoenix road, South East London.''

''Who do you live with.''

''I live with my dad.''

''How long for have you lived with your dad?''

''Just about eight months.''

''Where did you live before moving in with your dad?''

''I was with my foster care parents before I went to prison, when I was released I lived in a hostel in Croydon.''

''You started to live with your dad after you walked out from court a free man after your trial for the murder of Steve Claxton. Is that correct?''

''Yeah.'' Tom said as he dropped his chin to his chest.

''Why do you think we came to arrest you?''

''I don't know you tell me.'' Tom replied sarcastically. He cringed, then threw his head back and breathed out heavily.

''Look, we are not here to waste your time or our time.'' Kelvin said dropping his head.

''Hmmm what did my dad tell you about me?''

''He is outside, I have not spoken to him yet.'' Kelvin said.

''Then why did you come and arrest me?'' Tom asked.

''Because we have received new evidence linking you to the death of Steve.''

''What new evidence?''

''Tell me Tom, did you murder Steve? Just spit it out, if you help us to get to the truth, I'll help you as much as I can, I am not promising you, but me and Colonel Peter work close together. Just tell us what happened on the night Steve died, we are trying to help you.''

''I can't speak to you now. I need to speak to my dad first.''

''Tell me, did you confess what you did to your dad?''

''No comment.''

''There is a good chance that you could get off with just few years here in this jail if you plead guilty, you may not be jailed for life if your lawyer agrees to plea bargain. The choice is yours Tom.'' Kelvin explained.

Tom dropped his head and rubbed his temples.

''Ok.''

''Let us start by you telling me what you told your dad?''

''I confessed to my dad the dream that I had…''

''Let's hear it – what was the dream about?''

''After we visited my mother's grave where we'd been to lay some wreaths and flowers in Pennsylvania I could not sleep, I was hearing voices.''

''Whose voice did you hear?''
''I was hallucinating – it was like Steve's voice but I heard it in my head.''

''So you heard Steve's voice – what did he say to you?''

''He asked me to tell my dad what had happened to him.''

''You mean Steve's ghost appeared to you, telling you to tell your dad how you killed him?''

''No I can't do this. I don't remember what he said. I swear I don't remember."
Kelvin pushed another button on the recorder. ''We'll type this up and get you to sign it.''

Tom shook his head, he asked to go out for fresh air and for a smoke, his hands had begun to shake, his eyes red.

"You can go for a smoke and freshen up with the help of Sheriff Clarke."

Clarke led Tom out. Keith walked in to have a conversation with Kelvin.

''Keith I have just interviewed Tom. He said that you betrayed him. What does he mean by that?''
''I should have told you when I returned from the US. I took him with me to visit his mother's grave in Pennsylvania and while we were staying in the hotel he told me of how he was hallucinating and hearing voices.''

''When he confessed to you why did you not report it immediately?''

''I don't know.''

''Did you promise him not to tell anyone? You are a prosecutor for goodness sake, Keith how could you promise such a thing? You know Tom hasn't got a clean criminal record history. Why did he not speak the truth before the first trial. The defence could have plea bargained that is if he pled guilty in the first instance.''

''Kelvin I don't know what to do right now.''

Detective Inspector Baron Gonzalez walked into the interview room. He was acting on instructions of Chief Inspector of Police to interview Keith. Kelvin and Keith worked together before Tom was arrested and prosecuted during the first trial. The two men are familiar with each other. It was the right thing to do for another Detective to interview Keith giving that new evidence and facts have now emerged in the case.

''Kelvin, sorry to bulge into the interview room. I am taking over this interview with Keith. You can continue with your interview with Tom when he returns with Sheriff Clarke."

''Keith, my name is Detective Inspector Baron Gonzalzez. I have been assigned to investigate this case by Scotland Yard. I know you know how it all works, you are an attorney yourself, none of these things should be new to you, but no one is above the law. The rule of law applies to everyone. Before I start I want to make sure you understand your rights. First of all, you have the right to remain silent. I believe you understand that sir?''

''I understand all of that.''

''And thanks for your co-operation. You don't have to talk if you don't want to but if you do, anything you say can and will be used against you in court. I believe you understand that too?''

''Yes I do.''

''You are an intelligent attorney. You can read and write fluently, efficiently and effectively.''

''Yes.''

''Good, then read this and sign it. It says you've been advised of your rights.''

Keith signed the dotted lines. Detective Inspector Gonzalzez pushed the red button on one of the tape recorders.

''Can I advise you that this tape recorder is now on?''

''Ok.'' Keith replied, his mood plummeted.

"It's the 4th of August at 9:00pm in the evening.''

''Yeah.''

''What is your full name?''

''Keith Bradford.''

''Any nickname?''

''People call me Keith.''

''Your address?''

''64 Phybil Phoenix road, South East London.''

''Who do you live with.''

''I have lived alone for many years until my son moved in with me after his court trial.''

''How long has your son been living with you for?''
''Just about eight months.''

''Where did your son live before his court trial?''

''He lived in a hostel somewhere in Croydon. I did not know anything about his whereabouts for almost three decades. It was before his criminal court trial that I found out that he is my biological son.''

''Keith, your son was arrested two hours ago because of new evidence that have come to our attention during further investigation. You may not know, but during Tom's interview with Inspector Kelvin Armstrong he told us that he confided in you not to reveal to the police something that he did. Could you tell me what this secret is? What did you agree with him not to tell anyone?''

''Like I was explaining to Kelvin earlier. After Tom's first trial, I travelled with him to US to lay wreath and flowers by his mother's grave. When we returned to the hotel where we stayed, he told me that he was hearing voices in his head.''

''Whose voice was he hearing?''

''He said he was hearing the late Steve's voices in his dream.''

''Sorry was he hearing voices in his dream or while hallucinating?''

''Both – he was hearing Steve's voices when he goes to sleep and while hallucinating.''
''What did he say Steve told him to do?''

''He said Steve told him to go and report to the Police what he had done.'' Keith said, his nose wrinkled.

''What did Tom tell you that he had done?''

''He said that he killed Steve.''

''Tom confessed to murdering Steve, is that correct?''

''I did not think it is fair to conclude that Tom murdered Steve because Tom had a mental health condition. His account of what he said he did was hallucination and in his dream.''

''Did Tom ask you to promise him not to tell anyone?''

''Yes he did.''

''And was that what you did Mr Keith Bradford?''

''It happened just few days ago.'' Keith replied as he fought back tears.

''Does it make any difference if Tom had asked you to promise him just yesterday, why did you agree to conceal the crime that Tom pled guilty to?''
''I am an attorney, I won't sit down here and have you insult me or accuse me of concealing a crime. Tom has a mental health crisis, his confession or statement is as a result of hallucination and dreams, his mere words cannot be admissible in the court under section 77 of the criminal evidence act of 1984. The law makes it clear that confession of a witness with mental health condition is not admissible.''

''Keith, I know you are an attorney, but it is not for you to sit down here and decide what evidence is admissible by the Jury or Judge, that is for the court to decide not you. The rule of Law will run its course, you cannot pre-empt the court trial before it takes place.''

''You can say that.''

''What I am asking you for the purposes of this interview is for you to tell me why you did not report to the police immediately that your son confessed to the violent crime that he had committed.''

''I am not going to continue to listen to your false accusations. Tom is legally insane that was the determination by the trial court. Tom was set free based on his mental health history.''

''Mr Keith Bradford you did not report to the police immediately the confession of your son over the crime that he said that he committed. You had the opportunity to inform the

law enforcement agents at the slightest opportunity that you had when you returned back to work as a prosecutor. Perverting the course of justice is an offence committed when a person prevents Justice from being served on himself/herself or another party. You and I know that in England and Wales, it is common law offence, carrying a maximum sentence of life imprisonment.'' Baron explained.
Keith was quiet.

''Keith it appears to me that you were not thinking deeply enough when you promised Tom that you would not tell anyone about what he had told you. You should know better that the right thing to do under the circumstances is for you to report it. You did not because of the emotional tie that you had for your son. Is that correct Keith?''

Keith continued to be silent. He had never been confronted or accused of any offence, his head dropped, he became numb, he was not worried for Tom at that moment. He was worried for himself and his career. He was petrified and wondered where and how these accusations coming from Baron is going to impact on his prosecuting career.

''I am arresting you for perverting the course of justice, you do not have to say anything. But it may harm your defence if you do not mention when questioned something which you later rely on in court. Anything you do or say may be given in evidence against you in the court of law.'' Baron recited an all too familiar caution statement to Keith. Keith was speechless. He shook his head, then breathed deeply at Baron.

''This interview ends at 10:25pm,'' Baron pushed another button on the recorder. ''We'll type this up and get you to sign it.'' Baron said to Keith.

Keith shook his head. Baron asked the cops to handcuff him after which he was taken to the cell where he passed the night.

Chapter 33

The Reckoning

The High Court Judge, Justice Tremaine Hernandez fidgeted nervously in the tall leather chair behind the huge, battered oak desk in the Judge's chambers behind the courtroom, a large crowd had gathered to see the outcome of the murder trial of the late Steve Claxton. The news was all over the press. Why is Tom Bradford being re-tried? Lawyers gathered around the coffee machine and gossiped about the murder trial.

The Judge's black robe hung in a corner by the window that looked north over the Old Bailey. Justice Tremaine Hernandez was the nervous type who worried about court hearings even though he had practiced as a Judge for fifteen years though each case was different with its technicalities. No two cases are exactly the same, every case is considered on its own merit, and with different peculiarities and characteristics, Hernandez never learned to relax. The case in front of him on that day was a big one so to say. Tom Bradford had already been tried but the crown have found new evidence and a retrial has been ordered.
As a High court Judge Hernandez had reached his pinnacle.

Senior court clerk Mr Tariq Dias who knocked on the door, had been loyal working with Hernandez for ten years.

''Come in!'' Hernandez demanded.

''Afternoon, Judge.''

''How many people are out there?''
''The courtroom is packed, not less than two hundred people are inside the court right now sir.''

''This trial has got the press all over it and the retrial has only just began. You mean two hundred people in court already? Tell me, what do they want?''
Mr Dias shook his head ''I guess they are concerned that justice be done for the late Steven, his death was a gruesome, violent murder in the city of London where he also went to University sir.''

Hernandez quieted and stared out the window. ''Do you know whether Steve's grand-mum and girl-friend are here from Pennsylvania?''

''Yes, Phoebe is here from Pennsylvania and Steve's girlfriend Evelyn and her parents are here too.''

''What about Keith and Tom?''

''They too are here, I recognise a few of them, but I don't know everyone out there sir.''

''How about the security out there?''

''Sheriff's got the court bailiffs on stand-by, they stood reserved close to the courtroom. Court security officer checked everybody at the door before they entered the courtroom.''

''Has security found anything suspicious?''

''No, sir nothing suspicious in court sir.''

''Where are the two defendants, Tom and Keith right now?''

''Sheriff's got them sir. They'll be here in a minute sir.''
Justice Hernandez seemed satisfied.

''Ok you may go.''

''One more thing sir!''

''What is it Dias?''
''I have got a note here addressed to you sir, it is hand-written sir.'' He put the note on the desk.

''Hand written note for me? From who?''

''It is a request from a TV crew from London to film the hearing sir.''

''What! What did you just say?''
Hernandez's face turned red, he became furious on his swivel chair, he rocked it. ''Cameras," he yelled ''In my court room!'' He ripped the note that Dias placed on his desk, threw the pieces in the direction of the dustbin without even reading the content of the note.

''Where are they now?''

''By the court corridor sir.''

''Can you please go and order them out of the courthouse.'' The Judge demanded.

Dias left quickly to carry out the instructions.

It was clear that there had to be a crowd in the courtroom because there was no empty parking spaces around the Old Bailey. A handful of reporters and photographers waited anxiously near the rear of the courthouse by the wooden door where Tom and Keith would enter. The jail was about one block of the square on the south side, down the highway. The court driver drove Keith and Tom in the back seat with a squad car in front and another behind, the procession turned off the road leading to the court into the short driveway leading under the veranda of the courthouse. About four sheriffs and two court bailiffs escorted the defendants past the reporters through the doors and up the backstairs to the small room just outside the court room. The prosecuting attorney Nigel Stanley grabbed his wig, gown and briefcase, raced across the street. He ran up the backstairs, through a small hall outside the jury room, and he entered the courtroom from adjacent side door just as the clerk Mr Dias led his honour Justice Hernandez to the bench.

''All rise for the Court,'' Mr Tariq Dias shouted. Everyone stood. Hernandez stepped to the bench and sat down.

''Be seated,'' he yelled "Where are the defendants?" He asked. ''Can you please bring them in.''

Tom and Keith were led handcuffed, into the courtroom from the small holding room. The court bailiff removed their handcuffs and seated them next to Mr Howard Sullivan, the defence attorney, at the long table where the defence sat. Next to it was another long table where the crown prosecutor Nigel Stanley sat taking notes and looking all important and serious. In the front row just behind the prosecuting attorney was Phoebe and Evelyn being the only family Steve had left behind, who both looked at Keith and Tom disdainfully.

The proceedings commenced at 10am. ''Mr Nigel Stanley you may call your first witness.'' The judge said.

''Your Lordship, the crown calls Inspector Kelvin Armstrong. After him the state shall call Senior Detective Inspector Baron Gonzalez.''

Kelvin was sworn and sat in the witness chair to the left of Justice Hernandez a few feet from the podium.

Defence Attorney Howard Sullivan sat down along with several other attorneys, all of whom pretended to be busy reading important materials staring intermittently at their legal note pads.

''Would you please state your name?''
''Inspector Kelvin Armstrong.''

''Can you tell this honourable court what led to your going to arrest Tom Bradford on 4th of August?''

''We received intelligent advice from the CCTV Control Room to suggest that new evidence have emerged for the murder of
Steve Claxton.''

''When you say we, you mean the Metropolitan Police.''

''Yes sir but what I actually mean is the London Transport Police CCTV control room department.''

''Ok I see. Can you tell the court what the new evidence is and how you came about it?''

''The London Transport CCTV control room discovered one of their cameras had recorded a moving image and video clip revealing Tom handing a sweet or mint over to the deceased just before he jumped on the train on the night that he was murdered.''
''Do you have the camera video coverage of the moving images of the deceased and Tom here with you in court?''

''Yes I do sir.'' Said Inspector Kelvin Armstrong.

''Very well can you give the video camera footage tape to the court clerk for his Lordship to sight and then mark it as Exhibit 1.''

Kelvin handed the camera footage video clip to the court Sheriff, the Judge sighted it after which it was marked Exhibit 1.

''Milord might I ask that the camera video footage be played by the Sheriff to the hearing of the jury and court?'' asked Nigel Stanley.

''You may very well do so. Sheriff you can play the camera footage of the moving images for the court to see.''

The CCTV camera footage of moving images was played for the jury, the judge and court to see. It lasted six minutes before it reached the point where the images of the late Steve Claxton and Tom Bradford was starting to show their movement on the train station platform. The footage clearly showed Tom on the clip handing a wrapped sweet, looked like a mint, to Steve just before the deceased stepped inside the train. Steven then put the sweet in his mouth few seconds before he convulsed and collapsed on the train as the train moved off. By this time Tom had turned back to go and get his own train back to Croydon and therefore could not be linked to the crime at the time.

''You can end the video footage, mark it Exhibit 1 and hand it to Mr Tariq Dias.'' The Judge Instructed.
''You may proceed with your examination Mr Nigel Stanley.'' The Judge said.
''As it pleases your Lordship.'' Stanley said.
''Inspector Kelvin Armstrong, what did you do after viewing the footage in the video clip.''

''Senior Detective Inspector Baron Gonzalzez ordered that we visit Tom at home to have him arrested.''

''What time did you arrive at his home, can you remember at all?''

''Yes I do remember: it was at around 6:30 in the evening.''

Nigel paused and reviewed his legal note pad.

''Inspector what other evidence do you have against these defendants?''

''We interviewed Tom yesterday at the jail. He signed a confession.''

Mr Sullivan jumped up to his feet. ''Objection Milord! Objection! I know a confession is admissible in a hearing like this but there is no mention of any confession in the affidavit. My client during the 1st trial was proven to be legally insane; his confession is therefore not admissible. Section 77 of the Police and Criminal Evidence Act 1984 sir.''

''Overruled!. Sit down. Continue Stanley." The Judge ruled.

''May it please Milord.'' Stanley said.
''Inspector Kelvin when you took down the confessional statement from the 1st defendant during the course of your interview with the 1st defendant, did you advise him of his rights?'' asked the Judge.

''Yes sir.'' replied Kelvin.
''Stanley you may continue with your examination.'' The judge instructed.

''Did he understand them, by that I mean did Tom understand his rights following on your advising him?'' Stanley asked.

''Yes sir, he did, he said he understood.''

''Did he sign a statement to that effect.'' Stanley clarified.

''Yes he did.''

''Who was present when Tom made his confessional statement?''

''Myself, Senior Detective Inspector Baron Gonzalzez and Colonel Peter Blacksmith.''
''Do you have the confessional statement here?''

''Yes.''
''Please read it out to the hearing of the court.'' The Judge commanded.

The courtroom was still and silent as Kelvin read the short statement. Phoebe and Evelyn looked at each other with a sigh of relief written on their faces, they stared blankly at both Tom and Keith.

''Did Tom sign the confessions?''

''Yes in front of three witnesses.''
''Thank you Inspector.'' Stanley said when Kelvin finished his last sentence.

''Your Lordship, the state has nothing further.''

''You may cross-examine the first prosecution witness Mr Howard Sullivan."

''I have nothing at this time your Lordship.'' Said Sullivan.

''Call your next witness.'' demanded Justice Hernandez.

''The state calls Detective Inspector Baron Gonzalzez.''

''Can you tell this honourable court your name?''

''I am Detective Inspector Baron Gonzalzez. I work for the CPS.''

''When you say the CPS, do you mean the Crown Prosecution service?''

''Yes sir.''
''Good. On the day that you arrested Keith Bradford what information led you to arrest him?''

''The second defendant, Keith told me that his son had confessed to him that he (Tom) murdered Steven. Keith said Tom told him this while they were in US where they had been to visit Tom's mother's graveside.''

''Detective, what was your response to Keith?'' Stanley asked.

''I asked him if his son had asked him to keep his confession as a secret and not tell anyone?''
''And what did he say?''

''He said yes.''

''And was that what he did?''
''Yes he kept his son's confession a secret.''

''Why would he do such a thing, he is an attorney, he should know the right thing to do under the circumstances.'' Stanley pointed out.

''I confronted him on why he did not report the first defendant to the police before he returned to work in August.''

''When you confronted Keith with this allegation what did he tell you?''

''He said his son's confession was not admissible in court because he is mentally and legally insane. He also quoted section 77 of the Criminal Evidence Act 1984.''

''And what did you tell him.''

''I told him that even though he is an attorney, it is not for him to say what evidence is admissible in the court of law. That is for the Judge to decide on, whether a confession is admissible or not based on the mental health of the accused person.'' Explained Detective Gonzalzez.

''And what did he say?''

''He relayed the story of how he took his son to US to lay wreaths and flowers by his late mother's grave. When they got to the restaurant, his son began to tell him that he was hallucinating and dreaming of the late Steve. Tom said he was hearing voices in his sleep and the voices were that of Steve.''

''And what was it that Steve was saying to Tom while Tom was hallucinating or in his dreams?''

''Keith said that Tom confessed that he heard voices in his dream from Steve telling him to say what he had done to Steve.''

''And what was it that Tom said that he had done to Steve.''

''Tom said that he had murdered Steve in cold blood by poisoning him.''

''When Tom said this to his dad, what did Keith do?''

''Keith said he was surprised that Tom did such a thing.''

''What was Tom's response to Keith?''

''Keith was asked by Tom to promise him to keep his confession a secret.''

''Is that what Keith did?''

''Keith agreed and he decided not to report his son's confession to the Police.''

''Inspector did you explain to Keith the implication of his action?''

''Yes sir. I explained to him that he erred with regard to the law. That he had perverted the course of justice which is an offence committed when a person prevents justice from being served on him or herself or on another party. In England and Wales it is a common law offence, carrying a maximum sentence of life imprisonment.'' said Detective Inspector Gonzalzez.

''Did Keith understand the allegation you put to him?''

''Yes but he said that his son was not in the right frame of mind and that he did not know what he was doing or saying. That Tom was experiencing apparent perception of something not present due to his suffering from horrific hallucinations, delusion, illusions and figment of imagination which made whatever he says not believable or admissible in court.''

''Detective what did you do after hearing him say that to you.''

''I arrested him for perverting the course of justice by concealing the crime of his son and not reporting his son's confession to the Police for immediate action and consequent arrest.''

''What was his reaction to your arrest, did he show remorse?''

''He said he was a lawyer and an attorney and that he would not do anything contrary to the law. He also explained that he found himself in a difficult situation in that he had for almost thirty years lost the opportunity to bring up and be there for his long lost only son, the last time that he saw Tom was when he was only eighteen months old, Keith lamented that he was petrified by the mere thought of losing the opportunity to be there for the young man. Keith was in a dilemma.'' ''Objection! Objection!'' Shouted Howard as he jumped out of his chair. ''Your Lordship I know hearsay is admissible in a hearing like this, but this is triple hearsay. Keith has not said those words to this honourable court by himself. This is hearsay, the inspector is speaking for him. He was not there when the conversation transpired between father and son. I pray the court to dismiss this third-party hearsay. It is inadmissible in evidence.''

''Objection overruled. Sit down Howard, you may continue with your examination Nigel Stanley.''

''Call your next witness Nigel.'' The Judge demanded.

''We have nothing further your Lordship.''

''Good. Sit down Nigel. Mr Sullivan do you have any witnesses?"

''No your Lordship.'' Said Stanley.

''Good, Stanley. The court finds that there is 'prima facie' evidence that numerous crimes have been committed by Tom Bradford and Keith Bradford, the court orders these defendants to be held in custody throughout the duration of the trial."

Howard rose gently, ''Yes Milord the defence would like to request the court for bail of Keith Bradford and to set a reasonable bond for the defendants."

''Forget it!'' snapped Justice Hernandez. ''Bail will be denied as you know. Keith Bradford is an attorney who has practiced law enough to know the right thing to do. He should know the rule of law and abide by it. Steve would have been alive today if not for a senseless act and premeditated murder. A life has been lost in this case. Steve was murdered in a calculated attack, his life has been wasted and cut short as a result of a brutal attack. Application for bail of the two defendants is denied. The defendants will remain in the custody of the old bailey sheriff. Court is adjourned."

Justice Hernandez banged and rapped his gavel and disappeared. Mr Dias shouted ''Cooooourt! he then paused before saying…''case is adjourned till the morning." The court security, sheriff and bailiffs came around Tom and Keith, handcuffed them, and they too disappeared from the courtroom, into the holding room, down the backstairs, past the reporters and into the squad car.

Howard stayed behind after the court session to have a discussion with his defence team. It was obvious that the prosecution had a field day. The lawyers watched the crowd file silently through the enormous wooden doors at the rear of the courtroom. The prosecution team discussed in the rotunda. Sullivan spent the rest of the day seeing his clients Tom and Keith.

Chapter 34

The Lawyer's Dilemma

It was the 2nd day of the trial. The Judge sat high and lordly behind the elevated bench, his back to the wall under the magnificent portrait on the wall, it was the huge photo portrait of The Royal Coat of Arms looking straight at everyone in the room. It was common for it to appear in courtrooms in England and Wales. The Royal Coat of Arms came into being in 1399 under King Henry IV and is used by the reigning Monarch. The motto on it is in French – Dieu et mon droit – which means 'God and my right', referring to the divine right of the Monarch to govern.

The two attorneys representing the State and the defence respectively and court officials traditionally bow to the Judges' bench when they enter the court room to show respect for the Queen's justice. Judges and Justices of the Peace are officially representatives of the Crown.

The jury box was against the wall to the right. To the Judge's left were yellow portraits of other
forgotten heroes. The witness stand was next to the bench, but lower of course, and in front of the jury. On the left stood a long enclosed work bench covered with large red dockets books. Clerks and lawyers usually milled around behind it during a trial. Behind the work bench through the wall, was the holding room.

Sullivan in the 1st trial had convinced the court that Tom was legally insane. The defence team was planning to mitigate for Keith by establishing that he is an unfortunate lawyer who found himself in a dilemma. He was a dad who had lost touch with a son that he neglected while he was a toddler, who was now left to pick up the pieces of neglect of that boy by his mother and father. They would hear that Keith stumbled onto a child by accident; the boy had grown up to become a hardened criminal over the years. Keith had just begun to bond with this 'stranger' son of his, and in the process he implicated himself trying to cover up for the crime that he had committed.

On the morning of the 1st of October 2016 at 9am, the High Court clerk read out the names of the two accused persons who were to stand for trial, it was in the case of:

R
Versus
Mr Tommy Graham Bradford – 1st Defendant
Mr Keith Crawford Bradford – 2nd Defendant

Justice Tremaine Hernandez was filled with mixed feelings. He had not seen anything like the case he was about to preside upon. In his almost twenty years on the bench, nothing like this. An attorney who comes to his court to uphold the law and to bring criminals to face the wrath of the law is now himself facing the wrath of the law. Some journalists were already speculating what the outcome of the case was going to be. Lawyers were already discussing or gossiping about this murder trial. This case was different; there had already been a past trial where the first defendant had been acquitted due to insufficient evidence to convict him of the allegation. His father hardly knew his son when Tom was prosecuted, but he supported the defence team. He stepped down as the prosecutor.

Senior court clerk Mr Tariq Dias walked into Hernandez's chambers to see him and to let him know the atmosphere of the courtroom. Dias knocked on Hernandez's door.
''Yes come right in Dias.'' The Judge said.
''Good morning sir.''

''Good morning Dias, tell me what is the courtroom atmosphere like out there?''

''It is packed sir.''

''Packed with who?''

''Everybody, it feels like the whole country is here today.''

''What do you mean?''

''So many lawyers standing along the courtroom corridors, I can recognise some of the journalists and the press.'' Dias said.

''How is the security inside and all around the courtroom and outside area?''

''People have been checked properly before entering the courtroom. Court sheriffs and bailiffs are all around both inside and outside the courtroom.''

''Has the Sheriff got Keith and Tom with them?''

''Yes the Sheriff has got the defendants with him and they'll be here in a minute before the hearing starts.''
''If I can have my way again, I don't want any press in my court today, let them go and do their show off outside the court after the trial. I don't want any distractions; I simply haven't got time for that in this trial today. This is a very important trial involving a lawyer and his son. I know the world is watching out for the outcome of this trial. Can you go outside and order the press out of my court, is that ok, do you think you can do that for me?''

''Okay Judge,'' replied Dias as he rushed out to carry out the instructions and command.

Nigel Stanley felt awkward coming to court today. This case involved a fellow prosecutor where they have both worked together for almost twenty years. Keith should not be in this mess. Tom on the other hand is not new to going in and out of court. He's been in trouble so many times. But his dad had never before been prosecuted. Nigel, on his way into the court noticed that the car park was full, he was not surprised to see the court packed full. So many lawyers and Queens counsel, a group of reporters and photographers that were earlier ordered out of the courtroom were now waiting anxiously near the rear of the courthouse by the wooden doors where the accused persons usually come in through. Before the court sitting converged, three Sheriffs escorted the defendants past the reporters, through the doors and up the back stairs to the small room. Queens' counsels, defence lawyers and some other spectators watched the parking lot and quietly cursed the mob of reporters and cameramen.

Howard Sullivan was never nervous in any trial, but this case was different. Tom was acquitted in the first trial, the case was being retried with the same allegation and to make it more complicated his dad was the second defendant and Howard is defending them both. The outcome of this case will mark a turning point in his career with no shadow of a doubt. Earlier in the morning he went to the courthouse and hid in the law library to research all relevant case authorities that were similar to this case. He did not sleep at all in the night. He was well read and did his homework. Last night he constantly flipped the channels on a small colour television he had in his law office to catch up on the news and what the latest gossip regarding the trial was going around. This trial was going to be a defining moment in his law office practice. How to convince the court to acquit his client in this case is his biggest concern at the moment. It was going to be a defining moment in his legal practice as defence counsel. The court security guarded the front door, about ten other people sat on the rear steps. The court securities were set to stand awkwardly behind Keith Bradford and Tom Bradford and their lawyers, microphones were clustered in front of Howard Sullivan as they walked through the corridors. Reporters crammed into the room, which overflowed and trailed down the court corridor area.

At 9:45am the prisoners: Keith and Tom were transported to court. A squad of bailiffs escorted the prisoners down the sidewalk. One in front, two behind, and one on each side of Keith and Tom, both had handcuffs on their hand unfastened. The reporters, cameras rolled and clicked as the journalists flew their questions at Keith.

''Prosecutor, are you going to plead guilty to the allegation that has been brought against you?''

''Why did you try to cover up for your son, did you not know that perverting the course of justice was a criminal offence punishable with life imprisonment?''

''Sir, how will you plead?'' Keith was quiet, he ignored all the questions looking away from the cameras.

''Tom, is your QC going to plead insanity again, like he did at your last trial?''
Tom ignored the questions. Howard had told him previously not to say a word to the press before the trial.

''Was your hallucinations caused by trauma?''

''What do you see in your imagination?'' ''Was it Steve Claxton?'' ''Was he tormenting you in your dreams?''

''Say something to me Tom.'' The reporters asked like a menace.

The two defendants ignored the press, but proceeded walking to waiting patrol cars. The court sheriff ignored the mob. Howard ignored the mob. The photographers and paparazzi's scrambled trying to get the perfect shot of the most famous case re-trial at the Old Bailey in London.

This is not going to be a very easy case at all. All press conferences so far have been a hit. Segments of it ran on the networks and local stations, both on the evening and late news. The morning newspaper ran front page on pictures of Mr Keith Bradford and his crown prosecution counsel Nigel Stanley. Justice Hernandez knew that this was not going to be a quiet case.

Hernandez assumed the bench as the rear door was locked by Dias. Nigel Stanley knew that the circumstances surrounding Keith's case was pathetic and unfortunate, however the onus is for the prosecution to prove its case beyond all reasonable doubt, an accused person is presumed innocent until he or she is proven guilty. Keith's job is to bring criminals to book. He was a prosecutor. He was unfortunate to be in the current dilemma. Maybe if his path never crossed that of his son in life, he would never have been in this situation, but retribution and providence are inevitable.

The prosecuting attorney opened the case by asking Tom some questions, Stanley knew that as he stood most spectators in the court and people in the community are expecting and looking out for his examination of the accused persons and for the outcome of this case. It was the talk of the town.

Before Nigel Stanley commenced his questioning, an Oath was sworn to by the 1st defendant – Tom Bradford. He stood in the witness box and the court registrar handed him a Bible which he held. The registrar then asked Tom to repeat the oath after him. Tom had no problem doing so, it was not new to him, he had repeated the oath after several court registrars in the past.

Tom then stood to his feet to answer the prosecutor's questions when he commenced questioning:

''Tom Bradford, can you please tell this honourable court how you first met Steve Claxton?''

''When I first met Steve, I did not know that we were half-brothers. It was a miracle that we met.''

''What do you mean by that?'' Stanley asked.

''I was out in London and was involved in a car crash, as far as I can remember I woke up in the hospital because people had called the ambulance to take me to there. After I regained consciousness I saw a young man that I later got to know as Steve standing by my hospital bed.''

''Then what happened?''

''He introduced himself to me and said he was passing by when he saw two cars had collided on the road, he was moved with pity and helped others to call an ambulance. When the ambulance arrived he followed them with me to the accident and emergency department at St Thomas's hospital in London.''

''So he was a stranger at the time you saw him by your hospital bedside.''

''Yes he was.''

''Tell us what happened after that.''

''Steve went home and then came back the next day to the hospital to follow me up. It was then that I told him that I did not have any family and that I lived in a residential hostel in Croydon. When the nurses came round to give me my medicine, Steve saw my name on my records.''

''What was it on your records that got Steve interested?''

''My record showed that my surname is Bradford but was changed to Blackstone when I was adopted.''

''Why would such information interest Steve?''

''Steve and I later found out that we were related to one another.''

''How did you and Steve arrive at that discovery?''

''Steve told me that his grandmother Phoebe had told him in Pennsylvania that his mother had a son in her first marriage whose name is Tom and he saw the name was Bradford.''

''I see. That is an amazing way to meet your half-brother.'' He paused. ''Would you say that Steve was more fascinated that he had met you in this sojourn in life.''

''I think we were both fascinated and excited.''

''I understand you did not see one another for quite some time afterwards because you were convicted for a misdemeanor. Can you tell us the circumstances that led to a break in your communication with Steve?.''

''On the day that I was arrested by the Police, just before I was taken away, I tried to call Steve but he did not answer his phone, I later got to know when I was released that Steve had changed his number from the number I had and that explains why I could not reach him.''

''Is it true to say that you resented Steve for not picking up your phone call just before the police arrested you few days after the London riots?''

''I did not resent Steve. I am ok with his explanation that he had changed his phone number and that was why I could not reach him.''

''Is it fair to say that Steve was the one who came looking for you when you were released because he tried to call your number with his new number?''

''Yes he did.''

''What circumstances led to your arrest by the Police?''

''Objection Milord! Objection!" Howard jumped out of his seat. ''The criminal record of the victim is inadmissible!"

''Objection overruled,'' shouted Justice Hernandez affirmatively. ''Mr Tom Bradford you may continue with your answers to Mr Stanley's questions regarding your involvement and conviction for the London riots.''

''May it please your Lordship.'' Nigel said.

''Tom what circumstances led to your arrest by the Police.''

''I was with my friends on the day of the London riots, we went out to Croydon, when we got to Reeves corner, we saw everyone running around because the furniture shop was set ablaze. We then went to the high street to get few things.''

''Was that when you got arrested along with your friends?''

''Yes.''

''What items did the Police find in your possession when you were arrested along with your friends?''

''Objection Milord! Objection!" Roared Howard. ''Your Lordship this case is not about the London riots, my clients record is not relevant to the facts of this murder trial Milord.''

''Objection overruled. The character of the 1st defendant can be ascertained by his past conviction, you should bear it in mind that this is a re-trial Mr Sullivan.''

''As your Lordship pleases.'' Nigel said.

''Tom, let us leave the London riots for a moment, we may come back to it. Did you ever bother to find out where Steve was and why you could not get him on the phone when you tried to ask him for help before your arrest?''

''At the time of my arrest and release from inside I did not know that Steve was out of the UK on a world tour, it was later on that I found out that he was in trouble in one of the cities in Nigeria where he had visited while on tour.''

''Before you found out what happened to Steve, you had resented him, you thought he did not want to help you and that is why you thought he refused to pick up his phone, but you were wrong in your thinking Tom. You are a selfish young man who never ever considers what other people are going through, the only thing you care about is yourself. Is it not the truth that you purposed in your heart to end your half-brother's life out of jealousy, hatred and lack of compassion.''

''Sir I don't understand what you are talking about, how could I have helped Steve?.''

''You are not here to question me, I am here to question you. What I am asking is after you had been released from prison, you were not the one who went looking for Steve, or were you?''

''No I did not go looking for Steve.''

''Absolutely correct, you could not care less about the deceased and even when he told you that he almost lost his life in the hands of his abductors and kidnappers in Africa, you felt no sympathy for your half-brother, you proceeded to eliminate the deceased. Is that not what happened?''

''No comment.''

''Can you tell this honourable court what happened when you were released from prison, where did you go.''

''Like I said before I started to live in a residential hostel in Croydon.''

''Ok. Whose idea was it for you and late Steve to go out for a meal in London West End?''

''It was Steve's idea, he could afford to take us out for a meal in London, I could not afford that, like I said I was just getting back on my feet looking for a full-time job.''

''Is it right to say that Steve was always the one looking out for you isn't it?''

''No comment.''

''Why did you hate his guts, can you tell this honourable court why you did what you did?''

''No comment.''

''When Steve told you that he was kidnapped in Nigeria while he was on world tour and that he almost lost his life, what did you do?''

''I felt sorry for him.''

''Were you? We'll soon find out whether you really did feel sorry for your half-brother before he died. What else did Steve tell you about his kidnap and release.''

''He told me the circumstances that led to his being kidnapped.''

''And what did Steve say happened at the incident.''

''He landed safely in Abuja from a flight he took from Ghana, he then visited The Dome on Airport Road, he told me that the Dome is new to town with bowling alleys which is the only bowling in West Africa and he had read about it in London, it had pool tables, video games and several restaurants.''

''Then what happened when he left the Dome with other tourists?''

''They spent the night at Sheraton Hotel in Abuja before they went to Yankari National Park, he said the Park was a good seven to eight hours drive to the East of Abuja, they had set out nice and early. they then stopped in Jos to see the National

Museum, he told me that they had lunch at a place named Ceder Tree restaurant.''

''Then what happened?''

''His tourist car convoy was ambushed by gun men outside the town area. After their meal they drove for an hour and suddenly unknown gunmen from nowhere attacked their convoy, putting a gun over to the driver's throat asking him to stop the car.''

''Then what did he tell you happened?''

''He said they were ambushed, that the driver was thrown to the back of the car where he sat and they were driven for another hour into a bush, two men had pointed guns to their heads in the car asking them to remain silent or else their heads would be blown off their necks.''

''Is that all that happened?''

''No, when they got to a big bush, the gunmen asked them to make phone calls to people they knew because they wanted a ransom of four million Nigerian Naira, Steve did not know anyone in Nigeria, but one of the tourists just called the British Consular Office in Abuja but there was no response to the call as it was a Saturday.''

''Oh dear, then what did Steve do?''

''He was helpless. He told me that he tried my phone number and some other UK numbers from Abuja, Nigeria but he could not get through to anyone. I was in jail and I didn't have access to my mobile phone, we were not allowed.''

''And would you have responded differently to the late Steve's call for help if you were a free man and not in prison?''

''I would have helped him.''

''But you still did not look out for your half-brother even after you came out of prison, he was the one that actually came looking for you. Is that correct?''

''But he had a good job so he could afford to take the trains and to book flights to wherever he wished.''

''Is it fair to say that you resent the late Steve?''

''I did not resent Steve.''

''I put it to you that you resented Steve and that is why you cut his life short. You never wished him well, you never wished him to return safely from his world tour, the predicament and unfortunate kidnapping ordeal that he went through in Nigeria was a thing of joy for you, when he relayed his experience to you, you did not feel sorry for him. I put it to you that you are a wicked man, Tom, you have taken your jealousy too far and you have taken someone's life for which you shall never again walk free. For your information Steve alongside the two other tourists suffered a terrible ordeal in Jos, Nigeria, Steve finally was able to reach Phoebe on the phone and so were other tourists and among them raised the sum of money demanded by the kidnappers otherwise they would have been killed after they've been held hostage for 2 weeks in the bush with no food to eat or drink. All three tourists were at the mercy of the British consular officer who flew them back to England when they got stranded in the hands of kidnappers during their holiday in Northern Nigeria. It was a shame. An experience that no one would ever wish on their foe if I can put it that way?''

''No comment.''

''Can you tell this court what was going on in your mind when you took the late Steve's life in cold blood?''

''No comment.''

''You are the face of core evil and you are here today to face the wrath of the law in its full force, you have no escape route in this trial. Your malicious intent towards your half-brother is now in the open for everyone to see. You do not have a hiding place.''

''No comment.''

''I put it to you that there is nothing wrong with you, you are legally sane to answer for your actions. You are responsible for your own actions. You have both mens rea (intent) and actus reus (action) actively present in the crime that you have committed. You carefully planned out your crime. Your murder was premeditated, you have no reason to do what you did. You are nothing but an ingrate for doing what you did to the late Steve. He used his money to pay for the food you ate and drink that you drank. What the late Steve did not know was that he was wining and dining with the devil. Your meal with him on that night turned out to be his last meal. I put it to you that you are a heartless person and a risk and menace to anyone that comes in contact with you. You said something about your job, if I hear you correctly earlier, what job did you say you were doing on a part-time basis.''

''I worked in a chemical factory.''

''Where is this company located?''

''Somewhere around Beddington farm along Therapia Lane.''

''So you know a lot about chemicals and poisons.''

''I don't work directly with chemicals; I just help with loading vans and cleaning the storage rooms.''

''What sort of items are stored in the storage rooms that you are employed to clean?''

''Many different types of chemicals and substances.''

''When you say substances, did you mean poisons like Cyanide and Strychnine?''

''I am not sure what substances are in the carriages.''

''Are there no labels on the carriages or inside the storage that you could visibly see to identify the substances.''

''Yes there are labels on the carriages.''

''And did you not read the labels and get yourself familiar with what the substances are used for?''

''They belong to my employer not me, we are not allowed to touch them.''

''Tom Bradford of course you know the contents of the storage room that you cleaned daily, you know the items and you are very familiar with the poisons, I put it to you that you got the poison that you used to murder the late Steve from one of the carriages. You stole the poison and you premeditated the murder of your half-brother on the night that he took you out for a meal at West-End. I put it to you that you resented Steve. You were jealous of him. The more he liked you, the more you hated him. You know nothing but to commit crimes. You have raped before, you have stolen before, your name is not new to the criminal justice system. Most prosecutors in this town know you as Tom Blackstone which is your adopted name. It was only recently that your dad changed your surname back to his own. Your father actually thought you had genuinely repented, what he did not know is that you are a hardened criminal who will always commit crimes unless the court locks you up away somewhere. Is that not the truth, the whole truth and nothing but the truth?''

''No comment.''

''It will all become clearer to you as we proceed.'' He paused. ''Can you tell this honourable court what happened on the evening that you and Steve arrived at the restaurant?''

''What do you mean by what happened, we went to the restaurant to have a meal.''

''So the late Steve took you out for a treat and you decided to end his life, why did you do such a thing. What had he done wrong, that has made you do what you did. Did you hate Steve?''

''I did not hate Steve.''

''If you did not hate Steve, why then did you poison him?''

''I only had a dream and I shared the dream with my dad.''

''Before we come to your dream and your confession to your dad, can you please watch the video clip of photo images that I am about to play to this court and tell me if you recognise yourself and what you were trying to do or what you actually did?''
Nigel looked in the direction of the Judge and said, ''Milord the prosecution asks for leave to play Exhibit A – CCTV

footage of moving photo images of the deceased and the 1st defendant before the deceased convulsed and collapse inside the train he boarded."

''Very well so you may proceed to air the photo image evidence.''

Exhibit A photo image recording device began to play…after a long silence

''Mr Tom Bradford can you identify the persons on the CCTV footage that you have just watched?''

''No comment.''

''What was the small wrapped minted sweet in your hands, you just handed it to the late Steve in the footage?''

''No comment.''

''Is that the poison you presented to Steve and he took it from you because you had put the first one in your own mouth, Steve thinking you had the same mint for him and so he took it from you, without him knowing that you planned to take his life by offering him a mint which had poison inside of it?''

''No comment.''

''Was the content of this CCTV footage the dream you had when you said to your dad that Steve told you to spit out the truth about what had happened on the night that he was murdered in cold blood?''

''No comment.''

''What was your motive for poisoning Steve with Cyanide?''

''No comment.''

''Where did you get the cyanide from?''

''No comment.''

''Was it from your work place?''

''No comment.''

''Did you find it in one of the carriages inside the rooms you were employed to clean every day?''

''No comment.''

''What was the content of the letter that the late Steve brought with him to the restaurant for you to read?''

''No comment.''

''Was it a letter that your mum had written to your grandparents explaining that she had a property in London for the late Steve and yourself?''

''But she did not mention my name in the letter. It was only Steve's name in the letter.''

''I see. Was that the reason why you got jealous and you decided to end Steve's life so that you can inherit the real estate of Phoebe and Mathew and your late mum Teresa.''

''No comment.''

''Did you take Steve's life because you resented him and you were jealous of him?''

''No comment.''

''Steve was an accomplished accountant, he had a girlfriend, he was planning to get married to before he found out his girlfriend had been through serious sexual assault in the past. He did not know that you were the same 'Tommy' that Evelyn was talking about as the rapist.''

''No comment.''

''Is it fair to say that the late Steve would never have taken you out for a meal if he knew that you were the notorious person that got his girlfriend raped while you lived with the Blackstone family." He paused. "You said earlier that Steve helped you when you had an accident. You said he was the only one there by your bed-side at the hospital. You said that Steve was thrilled to have found the half-brother that his grand-parents had talked about. He loved you. He treated you well. Why did you pay him back with cutting his life short for no reason? Can you tell this honourable court why you did what you did Mr Tom Bradford?''

''No comment.''

Nigel looked in the direction of the Judge and said, ''Milord the prosecution ask for leave to tender **Exhibit B – Confessional statement of Tom Bradford.''**

''Very well you may so proceed to tender the confessional statement as evidence marked **Exhibit B.''**

Exhibit B was taken by the court Sheriff over to where Tom was standing. He was made to see the document.

''Mr Tom Bradford can you recognise **Exhibit B** - This is a statement you signed as a confessional statement when you were interviewed at the Police station by Detective Chief Inspector Baron Gonzalzez and Chief Inspector Kelvin Armstrong.''

''No comment.''

''Can you recognise your signature on the statement?''

''No comment.''

''No more questions for the accused person your Lordship.''

The court went on recess as the case was adjourned for 2 hours. It reconvened at 11:45am to continue with the hearing before Justice Tremaine Hernandez.

Chapter 35

Kismet

When the court re-convened at 11:45am, the defence attorney began a cross examination of Tom.

''Tom Bradford, can you tell this honourable court a brief account of your background as a child and could you tell us what happened when you travelled to Pennsylvania to visit your mother's grave.''

''I lived most of my childhood hopping from one family to another.''

''When you say hopping from one family to another, did you mean foster parents?''

''Yes, I lived in so many places since the age of 2 years old; I became a drug addict by the age of thirteen. I remember celebrating my first teenage year with my friends on the streets.''

''And how does that make you feel.''

''Not good.''

''When you say not good, what do you mean?''

''I really wanted to come clean and give up taking drugs but I find it very hard. I was told that my late mother had the same problem before she died.''

''Where did you get the information about your mother from?''

''Social workers have the files with them, they have all the information about the circumstances that led me to being taken into care. My mother was a drug addict, she lost her license to practice as a nurse because she had depression after which she began self-harming. My dad walked out on both of us, I was only eighteen months old at the time. I was told that my mother was over-weight and that made her have a low self-esteem, she suffered from obesity and she had a mental health condition, she suffered from anxiety, panic attacks and addiction to substance misuse. These were the things my dad could not cope with, that was why he walked away from us.''

''When you say that your dad walked away from 'us', you mean from you and your mum?''

''Yes, he walked away from my mum and I when we needed him the most.''

Just as Tom finished the last sentence a loud outburst of someone crying out loud came from where Keith was sitting. He sobbed bitterly, everyone looked in the direction of the first row where he sat. It all turned dramatic inside the court as the bailiff and security men all walked briskly towards Keith, Howard passed his handkerchief to the Bailiff to give to Keith, he sobbed again, wiped his eyes of tears, mumbled few words out in the lines of, ''oh my God! Oh my God! Can't believe this is happening to me, Teresa and I have let down my boy…we truly have…it should not be this bad on him…oh my God,'' Keith cried out, he wept and sobbed in front of the court.

The Judge then asked for a few hours of adjournment to enable Tom's dad to recover from his emotions.

''As it pleases your Lordship,'' was chorused by Howard and Stanley simultaneously.

The court clerk announced a short recess. The Judge went into his chambers. Everyone sat where they were. Keith was taken to the waiting room adjacent to the Judge's chambers. A glass of water was brought for Keith. Even though he was the 2nd defendant in this case, he was known to the court as a prosecutor. He was in an unfortunate situation. A dilemma that no lawyer would wish on their worst enemy.

Howard Sullivan continued his examination on Tom…

''When you met the late Steve for the first time after your car crash, what effect did it have on you?''

''It messed with my head because I did not know all these years that I had any family,'' Tom replied.

''Did you feel like revenging or taking your feeling out on anyone?''

''I don't know. I attend my mental health care treatment in Roehampton regularly.''

''Was the late Steve aware that you had mental health issues?''

''I did not tell him anything about that.''

''When you re-united with your dad after the first trial, how did that make you feel?''

''I felt good.''

''Tell us what happened when you and your dad visited your mother's graveside in Pennsylvania?''

''On the day before we visited the Ivy Hill Cemetery, I was having hallucinations.''

''How often do you suffer from horrific hallucinations?''

''Objection! Objection Milord, defence counsel is asking a leading question from the defendant.'' Nigel shouted.

''Objection sustained Nigel. Howard can you stop leading the accused, rephrase your question without leading, you should know the right thing to ask with your years of practice at the bar.''

''Apologies your honour.'' He paused then put the question across to Tom again, this time without the word horrific.''

''How often do you suffer from hallucinations?'' Howard asked.

''Very often, I get it all the time.''

''Are you on any medications?''

''Yes, I am on a lot of medications.''

''If you don't take your medications, do you know what the consequences may be?''

''I may do something that I am not aware of.''

''What do you mean by doing something that you are not aware of.''

''I mean I don't have control over what I do.''

''Would you say that you were in control of your actions when you were arrested and subsequently interviewed?''

''I can't remember what I did before I got arrested.'' ''Ok, can you remember making any decision or doing
anything before you got arrested?''

''No. I cannot remember making any decision.''

''Why is that?''

''I don't know why, sometimes I am ok and sometimes I am not – I just say stuff.''

''You were not mentally sane to carry out the actions that you have been alleged to have done in Exhibit A and Exhibit B. Is that correct?''

''No, I am not.''

''No more questions for the 1st defendant Milord.'' Howard said.

Chapter 36

Karma

Prosecuting attorney Nigel Stanley again commenced questioning but before he began an Oath was sworn to by Keith Bradford. The 2nd defendant took a stand in the witness box and the court registrar handed him a Bible, which he held. The registrar then asked the defendant to repeat the Oath after him before he proceeded to take a seat.

It was awkward for Nigel to be asking a colleague questions in the same trial as his only son. Keith was well composed though, he stood on his feet to answer the prosecuting attorney's questions.
''Mr Keith Bradford can you tell this honourable court what happened when you first heard that your biological son was going to face his first trial for the allegation of murder?''

''It was devastating and shocking at the same time.''

''I understand that when you say it is devastating, no one would wish such on his or her own child, but can you explain why it is a shock to you?''

''Inspector Kelvin Armstrong made the arrest and he told me that the boy they arrested was my look alike.''

''And what did you do when you heard that?''

''I was curious to see the boy.''

''When you saw the boy did you connect to him as your child?''

''I don't understand what you mean?''

''I mean did you see the resemblance that Inspector Kelvin Armstrong saw?''

''Yes I did.''

''As a prosecutor at the time, what then did you do.''

''I looked for help to team us with the defence counsel.''

''You wanted your son to walk out of court a free man, is that it?''

''Well, yes.''

''But why would you do such a thing?''

''Such as what?''

''I mean as a prosecutor you bring accused persons here to face the wrath of the law, isn't that what you do?''

''Yes, that is what I do for a living.''

''Ok, so why were you seeking defence for a child that is facing an allegation for murder?''

''I cared for him as a long-lost child.''

''When you say a long-lost child, what do you mean?''

''I felt I have not been there for Tom all his life.''

''Would you say that you felt that you had neglected and failed your only child?''

''Yes I did.''

''Was it because of this same feeling that made you to connive with your son to conceal his confession?''

''I did not connive with Tom to conceal his crime or confessional statement.''

''Why then didn't you report the incident to CPS – after all you work there?''

''Tom was not in the right frame of mind when he made his confessional statements, he told me at his mother's grave when I took him to the US.''

''What did he tell you?''

''He said he hallucinated and heard a lot of noises and voices in his head.''

''And what were the voices saying to Tom?''

''He said the voices told him to tell me that he was responsible for Steve's death.''

''And why would you not believe what Tom said?''

''Because under section 77 of the Police and Criminal Evidence Act 1984 a confession made by a mentally handicapped person is not admissible.''

''Mr Keith Bradford that is not for you to decide in this case, why not leave that decision for the court to reach.''

''He did not know what he was doing.''

''Of course he knew what he was doing when he poisoned Steve.''

''He said that he did not know what was going on.''

''And you believe him?''

''Yes I do, I have no reason not to.''

''As a prosecutor, try to imagine that this case is not about your child and that it is about someone else, would you have reported the confession?''

''Well it depends.''

''It depends on what?'' Nigel asked.

''I mean it depends on the individual case.''

Nigel stared at his notepad, then he walked passed the podium moving around staring at the Judge and then he made eye contact with the jurors then he continued:

''Keith I put it to you that if this case had not been related to your son, you would have reported it to the Police and have the first defendant arrested soon after he confessed to you. Mr Keith Bradford, you have allowed your emotional tie to your son to cloud your judgement in this matter. You were in a position to choose whether to uphold the law or to cover up for your son, you were in a dilemma, you chose to damn the consequences, you have not acted professionally under the circumstances that you found yourself. Your son committed an offence, he confided in you to keep it a secret and not to tell anyone, you knew that the right thing for you to do was to report it to the police. You failed to do so. I put it to you that you have failed the state, the crown, and you betrayed the very hands that feed you. You have breached your position of trust as a prosecutor.''

''Why would I do such a thing to the prosecution service that I have served for almost three decades, for God's sake, I have been qualified as an attorney way before Tom was born. I have worked as a State prosecutor for donkey's years, why would I betray the state?''

''That is the question I would like you to answer before this honourable court, it will make things easy in this case Mr Bradford. The reason why we are here today is for me to ask you these questions and not the other way round.''

Keith was quiet, he got emotional, wiped tears off his eyes with his handkerchief.

Nigel, then wiped his reading glasses, stared at his notepad, he stared at the Judge and then he made eye contact with the jurors then he continued:

'I put it to you that you are an intelligent prosecutor. You were involved in investigating the death of Steve whom you knew was murdered in cold blood. You were on the side of the prosecuting team when the investigation began. You wanted the perpetrators of the crime of the murder to be brought to book, you wanted justice to not only be seen, but to be manifestly and undoubtedly seen to have been done. Steve's life was cut short due to a senseless act of wickedness of the 1st defendant. Your son carried out a gruesome killing of his halfbrother out of selfishness and jealousy. Mr Bradford the law that you have practiced for three decades is about truth and justice, about the life of innocent Steve who was killed in cold blood in an unprovoked attack. Tom premeditated the murder of Steve. He poisoned Steve under the pretext that he was sharing a mint with him after they had a meal. As a prosecutor this type of case is not new to you. However, you choose to cover up for your child. Tom poisoned his half- brother in a premeditated murder and you know it. Tell this honourable court what you would have done if the perpetrator of this capital offence was not your son?'' Keith continued to remain quiet.

''Is it correct to say that Tom asked you to promise him that you will not divulge his confession to anyone else?''
There was no response from Keith as he chose to remain quiet.
''By keeping quiet and not reporting your son's confession to the police you have perverted the course of justice, an offence committed when a person prevents justice from being served on himself or on another party. You obstructed the course of justice. A common law offence, carrying a maximum sentence of life imprisonment.''

''No comment.'' Keith said as he quivered with indignation.

''Can you explain in one sentence what was going through your mind when you walked away from your late wife and an eighteen-month old son almost three decades ago?''

''No comment.''

''Did you part ways with your late wife because she was battling drug addiction or is it because she was suffering from obesity?''

''No comment.''

''Was there too much pressure going on in your marriage because your wife lost her license to practice nursing due to her drug addiction?''
''No comment.''

''As a young prosecuting attorney did you find it difficult to combine your profession with your marital life and obligations.''

''You can say that.'' Keith said with an emotional voice, his eyes fought back tears, but they soon flooded with tears. Keith wiped tears off his eyes with the handkerchief he brought out of his pocket…his head and eyes were looking directly on the ground, he was full of remorse as he sobbed and wiped his face again.
Some of the jurors made eye contact with one another, there was murmuring from the public sitting area. The courtroom went quiet, so quiet that if you dropped a needle on the floor, you could hear it drop!.

Nigel then broke the silence when he said…

''Your Lordship I have no further questions for the defendant Mr Keith Bradford. The prosecution rests Milord.''

"Any examination Mr Howard Sullivan?" Justice Tremaine Hernandez asked.

''Milord the defence calls Keith Bradford for crossexamination.'' Howard said.

''Very well you may proceed.'' Said the Judge.

''Can you tell the court your name?''

''Keith Crawford Bradford. I work for the Crown Prosecution Service; I am a prosecutor by profession but not in this case.''

''Obviously not in this case, you are behind bars due to the allegations that have been put across to you. Is that correct?''

''Yes I know. I was just telling you my background because you asked.''

''I asked you for your name and not for what you do to earn a living.''

''I'm sorry.''

''That is ok Keith, this court is familiar with you and there is no point denying that very fact, your contribution to the bar is remarkable. I understand you and I understand what you mean and the dilemma that you are in.'' He paused. ''Keith, why did you try to cover your son's crime up, when he clearly confessed to murdering his half-brother Steve.''

''I am not proud of what I have done. When Tom told me that he hallucinated and that he saw Steve in his dream, I was shocked. I doubted him, I felt his hallucination was caused by trauma, I was not sure whether he was mentally deranged, suffering from phantasmagoria, or having a figment of delirium or imagination. He has a poor history of mental health baggage in his life.''
''Did Tom ask you not to tell anyone about his confession?''

''Yes he did.''

''Did he also ask you to keep his crime of brutal murder of Steve a secret?''

''Yes he did.''

''And what did you do?''

''I was in a dilemma, was confused and I did not report it.''

''Why did you do such a thing.''

''I was due to return to work after my vacation, when the information came from Tom.''

''Your reporting for duty as prosecutor is the more reason why you stand a better chance to report the gruesome crime to one of your colleagues.''

''Yes I know. I panicked. I was confused.''

''Was that the right thing to do considering your wealth of experience as a lawyer and an attorney?''
''I was emotionally moved by the thought that the only child I have only just re-united with has constantly been in so much trouble in his life. I felt that I have failed him.''

''Would you say that you were in a serious dilemma, the kind of dilemma that you did not know how to handle or what to say to a child you hardly ever know anything about?. You were moved with pity for your only biological son. You promised to protect him at the expense of a profession that you love so much and that you have practiced for thirty years of your life. Is that correct?''

''Yes.''

''You knew that you should not have done such a thing either knowingly or unknowingly, you chose to obstruct the course of justice, you perverted the course of justice. You knew the right thing to do, but you refused to do it because of the blood tie you had with your son, you damned all the consequences and you are now facing the consequences of your actions. Is that correct?''

''Yes I am.''

''You knew the right thing to do, but you did not do it. Why is that?''

''Yes I regret my actions and I have remorse for letting myself and the state down on this occasion.''

''It does not matter whether the accused person is related to you by blood, you owe the CPS a duty to report an alleged crime to the crown and failing that which you have – breached the trust that has been placed on you in your job as a prosecutor. You cannot cover up a crime. You agreed to keep Tom's confession secret. That was not the right thing to do and you know it.''

''I am not proud of what I have done and I agree that I erred.''

''Milord that is all for the second defendant, the defence rests.''
Justice Tremaine Hernandez adjourned the case at 5:15pm to the next morning.

Howard Sullivan was met outside the court by a group of paparazzi camera men and news reporters as they questioned him about what he had to say about the fact that his client Tom was freed at the first trial; they wanted to know what the speculations are on the outcome of the re-trial. One of the news reporters said:

''Mr Sullivan, is it fair to say that with the evidence before the court your client will most likely not walk home free in this retrial?''

''Well what has happened has happened, Tom is a vulnerable adult with demons of addictions and mental health conditions, this case will be considered by the Judge based on the factual evidence. My two clients are presumed innocent until they are proven guilty and the burden of proof is on the prosecution to prove their case beyond all reasonable doubt.''

''What happened to the mental health expert witness, is she going to appear again to give evidence?''

''The judge will have to decide on that, the court may issue a subpoena to invite an independent medical expert, we have tendered my client's medical record.''

The news reporter moved the microphone away from Sullivan placing it directly in front of Keith Bradford:

''Mr Keith Bradford this must be a difficult trial for you to face isn't it?''

''You can say that.''

''How does it feel standing in court as a second defendant and not a prosecutor, it must be horrendous for you.''
''I don't wish what I am going through right now in my life on my worst enemy.''

''As a lawyer, has it ever crossed your mind in your entire career that you will find yourself in this situation?''

''No, why would I?''

''Throughout your career and up until now, you have always stood on the side of the prosecution team, you are a senior prosecutor at that. Can you tell us what went wrong?''

''That is a difficult question for me to answer, what has happened has happened.''

''Why did you put yourself in such a difficult situation, were you trying to protect your son from being convicted for a capital offence?''

''It is a dilemma that I do not wish any lawyer to experience in their career. Not even on my foe, that is if I have one.''

''Tell us what happened before you separated from your wife when Tom was only two years old?''

''My late wife suffered from drug abuse, mental health conditions, anxiety, panic attacks, self-harm, low self-esteem, and she was addicted to substance and drug abuse, Teresa was vulnerable.''

''Why then did you walk away from her and your son?''

''I was a young professional, my job as a prosecutor is not an easy one, at the time my wife was an addict, my son was young, I was confused, it was too much for me to bear. I hope other young professional would learn from my case.''

''What would you like young practitioners struggling with family life and their profession to learn from your own experience?''

''I urge them to be patient with a woman with a young child. It does not make sense if you walk away from an innocent child whose mother is vulnerable. That was what I naively did. The consequences of my actions thirty years ago are heavy, drastic, and this is what I am suffering from today. I should have stayed with the late Teresa to sort things out.''

''Oh dear!'' proclaimed the reporter.

''This is the true story.'' Keith said with his face reddened.

''Was it too late to help your son Tom when you met him again after thirty years.''

Wiping tears off his eyes before he responded.

''Yes it was too late. Tom had lived in so many foster care homes and hostels in his life. Both parents were not there for him, the training he had in life were from friends and on the streets. I don't think I can ever forgive myself seeing the kind of adult that Tom has turned out to become.''

''Did it not occur to you at any point to look back and go and look for your son and your late wife?''

''I once heard that Teresa had remarried so that news put me off going to look for her and our son.''

''What about looking back to go and find your son?''

''He was in social care. I lost track completely.''

''That is a shame.'' Said the reporter with his face flushed.

''It is a shame indeed.''
''Did you ever meet Steve Claxton before he was murdered?''

''No I have never met him, I only know that Teresa re-married, I never knew she had another son.''

''Do you have any word of advice for parents who find themselves in the same dilemma as you during the early days of your career?''

''I admonish them to not start having a family until they are ready. Having time for your partner and your children is important. It is a lot of responsibility and you can only handle it when you are ready. When I got married, I had a lot to contend with as a practising attorney. I know there are so many professionals out there in similar circumstances as the one I faced. You have to put your family first. You don't have to work full-time, you can do flexible hours, you can sometimes work from home if you can. You can take a career break to look after your family. You can consider job sharing with some of your colleagues or you can choose to just be a stay at home dad, if I had done the latter, then Tom would not have turned out the way he did. Perhaps Teresa would not have re-married, maybe she would be alive today. But the case with me now is different. I did not do my due diligence as a young lawyer, I loved my profession and I neglected other things going on in my life, in fact I neglected the most important thing in my life and that is my wife and my son. Here I am today paying the price with a conviction and possible jail term. I have messed things up and it is now hunting me at a time in my life when I least expect this sort of thing to happen to me. If you are in my kind of situation, please learn from my story. Thank you.''

Keith wiped tears off his eyes again, he fought back tears, his jaw tightened with a hangdog expression.

The reporter pointed the microphone in front of Howard Sullivan: ''Do you have anything to add to what the second defendant has just told the press?''

''No I don't; this case has not yet been determined. The prosecution and defence team are yet to give their final addresses to the judge and jury. Let us go and do the job that we've got to do.''

Howard moved close to comfort Keith who is sobbing profusely then again wiped off his eyes with his handkerchief.

Chapter 37

The Speech

On the morning of the hearing, Justice Tremaine Hernandez fidgeted in his chair where he sat on his black leather high chair, behind a posh mahogany table right there inside the judge's chambers behind the courtroom, a lot of people had gathered to see that justice was done in the Tom Bradford case. He walked out of court a free man in the first trial, but the case had been reopened following the new evidence. Some lawyers were already discussing or gossiping about this murder trial. Hernandez knew that this was not just another routine hearing, this case was different, with new evidence emerging with the CCTV footage at the train station showing Tom handing over the sweet wrapped with cyanide. The CCTV footage corroborates the confession statement that Tom made at his interview at the station and the confession he made to his dad Keith.

Hernandez has spent a good twenty-years on the bench, he knew what he was doing, he knew the running's, it was not the first time his court was hearing sensitive matters, as a High court Judge who had reached his own pinnacle on the bench was now ready to do Justice again to this case, this was a job he would have to do. Why was the CCTV evidence not brought up during the first trial by the prosecuting attorney and the prosecution team in the first trial, they did not prove their case beyond all reasonable doubt and that was why they lost the case and Tom was freed.

Hernandez would have to read the facts put before him by the prosecutors and the defence team. In Tom's confession to Keith, he said Steve's ghost appeared to him in the dream, the defence would argue that the confession was inadmissible due to Tom's mental health in the light of section 77 of Police and Criminal Evidence act 1984.

The Judge would have to consider and weigh the evidence in front of him, there were conflicting expert witness testimonies; the two forensic medical experts and the consultant pathologist, both experts should have emphasised and elaborated on the fact that the dose of poison that killed Steve was what determines when he dies and not just the type of poison itself being cyanide or Strychnine. It was irrelevant that it was either of the two because the dosage determines when the victim dies. Also, the two experts had conflicting evidence in their reports; the consultant pathologist's report said it was cyanide while the forensic medical expert report said strychnine was the cause of Steven's death? The evidence of the expert witnesses was not admissible as they conflicted.

This case was coloured with controversy over admissibility of a confessional statement as in evidence during criminal trial. This was the sort of problems and dilemmas that lawyers usually faced when expert witness testimonies conflict and therefore leaving the judge to decide.

This case showed how very difficult it was to prove poison as cause of death and how hard it was to pin the allegation of murder on the perpetrator; it was sometimes a puzzle to find the killer of a poisoned victim.

In the present case before Justice Tremaine Hernandez, it was Tom's confession and the evidence of the CCTV photo and video footage from the camera that guided the court to ruling out suicide which was one of the contentious arguments raised by the defence in the first trial leading to Tom's acquittal.

The Judge was to consider whether Tom was mentally handicapped, in relation to his person, was he in a state of incomplete development of mind which includes significant impairment of intelligence and social functioning.

It was very visible to everyone who Tom Bradford was, people stared at him and his father Keith Bradford where they sat, on the row next to the back, there were so many of Tom's friends: Neil, Gary and residents of the hostel where he lived in Croydon. They all surrounded him in the rows of padded benches on the right side of the courtroom. The court sheriffs roamed about the court, all armed, apprehensive, their eyes keeping a nervous watch on the group of people sitting behind Tom and Keith who was sitting with his body bending over nervously, he had his elbows on his knees as he stared blankly at the floor to avoid eye contact with either the Judge whom Keith had appeared in his court a couple of times in the past when he represented the state and in fact was the lead prosecutor. The courtroom was tense with glooms and dooms, emotions and nerves became raw among dozens of lawyers and prosecutors who sat in the courtroom to support one of their own who was facing nothing but a lawyer's dilemma.

Nigel Stanley, on his way into the court noticed that the car park was full, and was not surprised to see the court packed full. A group of reporters and photographers that were earlier ordered out of the courtroom were now waiting anxiously near the rear of the courthouse by the wooden doors where the accused persons usually come in through. Earlier on before the court sitting converged were four sheriffs who escorted the defendants past the reporters, through the doors and up the back stairs to the small room. Keith soon began to look very weak, initially he had his back against the wall, not knowing what to think of himself and how he managed to get himself in the current predicament that he's found himself. Within twenty four hours he's become an emotional wreck, the court sheriffs kept an eye on him, it was difficult to predict what could happen to a man in this situation. He could collapse or burst into tears and heavy sobbing in the courtroom. He'd done that before in a subtle manner.

Opening the address was the **prosecuting attorney; looking at the jury, he started his summary**:

''Ladies and Gentlemen of the jury, it is unfortunate that another life of a prominent young man who has worked very hard during his life to become a chartered accountant has been lost. An error of judgement based on insufficient evidence occurred in the first trial, with the failure of the state to bring the killer of Steven Claxton to book and to face the wrath of the law for the offence that has been committed. This honourable court will not allow that to happen again while you are sitting down in this court to make a final decision. This case is a re-trial. The facts of this case are very clear, there is nothing to confuse this honourable court in believing that Tom Bradford murdered Steven Claxton in cold blood, the previous trial did not have enough evidence which was why Tom walked free. We cannot allow that to happen again. The consequences of Tom's actions are clear, the law is clear on this and that is that he is heading for life imprisonment. Let us look at the facts of this case again and again, we owe our conscience and the law that duty to uphold the truth, we must ensure that justice is not denied again as it was denied in the first trial. We must see to it that justice is not only done but that justice is manifestly and undoubtedly be seen to have been done beyond all reasonable doubt that it can ever be…'' Nigel stared at his notepad, made a slow walk as he passed the podium moving around with roaming eyes, he stared at the Judge and then made direct eye contact with the jurors then he continued:

''…Ladies and gentlemen, two elements are necessary to and should be established in order for anyone to be found guilty of the crime of murder: and these two things are *'mens rea'* and *'actus reus'* that is ***'intention'*** and ***'physical action'*** respectively. Both are present in this case; the first defendant could not control his deep-seated jealousy for the late Steven. All Steven wanted to do was to unite with a brother he never knew for most of his life. He did not know that he was inviting the devil to dine with him. The deceased was a very hard working soul; he came to England with the help of his grandparents who are aged. He struggled it out to gain admission at the London School of Economics, he qualified as an accountant and finance practitioner. He even studied to be admitted into the Institute of Chartered Accountants in this country. He was comfortable and just as he began to prepare himself for marriage, having met the love of his life Evelyn at the University and they had developed their relationship to a level where they had agreed to spend the rest of their lives together, that life was cut short by the first accused person. He confessed to doing so. He had no reason to take his half-brother's life. What he did, he did out of jealousy. I am sure that if Tom had asked Steve for all the inheritance that Phoebe and Mathew had left in their Will and Last Testament, Steve would have let go of all the assets, he wouldn't have argued or fought over real estate. So why, despite his kind heartedness would anyone think of cutting his life short. The question that I admonish this honourable court to ask the accused person is why did he do what he did? Why did he poison Steven, why did he attack the deceased violently in the crime that he committed on the night that they went out for a meal together in West End. Why? From the evidence before this court we could see the trend on positivity in the character of the deceased, this is an American who came to study in England, he was a tax payer, he had grandparents whom were dependent on him to look after them after all they had done for him to bring him up. Ladies and gentlemen, could I juggle your memory on the history of the deceased, his mother died during his birth, Mathew and Phoebe began to look after him from birth as their own child. At the age of eleven years, Steve's dad Brian Claxton died in the 9/11 Twin Tower attack. The late Steven was an orphan who was brought up by his

grandparents; his life was violently taken away from him in cold blood murder by the first accused person who knew what he was doing. He was in his right frame of mind. He admitted to it. He confessed to it.''
(Nigel Stanley asked the jury to close their eyes for one minute and they all did for
as long as one minute...):

Stanley then continued: ''You can now open your eyes ladies and gentlemen…''

''What we can see is premeditated murder and not suicide as argued in the first trial. This man Tom premeditated to silence the deceased, this murder was calculated and premeditated, the accused person was in the right frame of mind. It was not a hallucination. He was mentally sane when he did what he did. An error of judgement has occurred once and we cannot allow that to happen again. We cannot take that chance again. This time we must get it right for the records and for the sake of history. For the legal legacy that we are about to leave behind for the future generation coming to inherit the criminal justice system that we shall be leaving behind down the line, we must wash our hands clean from anybody's guilt or fault in this criminal case as a matter of fact. We are in the 21st century court of law where justice can be served and served fairly, freely, justly without fear or favour regardless of race, gender, creed, sex or religion. Given all the circumstances surrounding, this case needs to be put into consideration.

Given the past life of the first defendant, we should be guided on the present and the future capability of the defendant, you will agree with me that this young man cannot be pitied. He is not a first time offender. He is known to the law enforcement agents, he has been to prison before and he has returned home. But this time we have to do one thing, the right thing, and that is to put the first accused person behind bars where he belongs for the rest of his life. He does not have a hiding place.

You will agree with me that going by the two major exhibits tendered as evidence in this case: the first evidence being proven technology of a CCTV photo image footage, we saw how the accused deceitfully handed the poison to the deceased under the pretext that he was giving him a sweet or mint from the sweets he had in his hand, he put one sweet in his own mouth which evidently did not make him to convulse or slump, after that he handed the poisoned sweet to the deceased, the deceased did not have any reason to doubt that the sweet handed to him could be a poison. Why would he? He had just seen his so-called 'half-brother' put one of the sweets in his own mouth, and so there was no need to be suspicious or just not trusting his brother. He accepted the sweet from Tom and that was how Steven met his death. He reacted badly the moment he stepped on the train, he began to convulse inside the train…ladies and gentlemen, as the train moved forward the door of the train slid to close. Steven's killer was standing on the platform ready to run away back to Croydon where he lived, thinking that we would not find out. Thanks to technology, thanks to CCTV, thanks to the new evidence that has been brought before us today. But the big question is: is this evidence going to be admitted or not?. Will you admit the CCTV footage as proof?, will you send the accused person to where he belongs?, will you unanimously decide to call a spade a spade?. Will the court determine not to rob the grandparents of Steven of the justice that they once have been denied by the error of judgment and insufficient evidence in the first trial?

The facts of this case is the same as the facts in the previous trial, the issues are substantially similar but the difference is that a new evidence emerged from the CCTV footage linking the accused person directly to the crime that he committed.

The first trial was marked with errors, such errors are also perceived as leading to failure of justice. We cannot allow this to happen again today. What is going to be the verdict in this trial? Is the killer of Steve going to spend the rest of his life in prison behind bars where he belongs or is he going to be set free the second time? We cannot take this chance again. This time we must get it right for the records and for the sake of history. For the legal legacy that we are about to leave behind for the future generation, we must wash our hands clean from anybody's guilt or omission in this criminal trial as a matter of fact.

Ladies and gentlemen of the jury the life of a twenty-eight year-old a chartered accountant with a promising future had been senselessly cut short. He left behind his dependant aged grandparent and a fiancée whom he was preparing to getting married to. It is the duty of this honourable court to ensure that Steven's killer is brought to book. This is the precedent that we are gathered here today to set. For us, for our future, for the future of our children, for the sake of administering justice, the question that we now have to ask one another is, Is this honourable court going to deliver a fearless verdict? Would we be seen today to carry out justice that could be seen by everyone as being done? Or are we going to sweep the truth under the carpet a second time?. During the first trial, there was an omission, it did not occur to anyone that CCTV footage existed, there was no confessional statement. All the focus was on the conflicting evidence of the expert witnesses, the mental health of the accused person and the preponderance of evidence as to whether the deceased was capable of taking his own life. But today we are very clear that this case is not about suicide, Steve did not take his own life, his life was cut short by the 1st defendant, he was poisoned in a violent attack, an attack that was premeditated and calculated with the intention to murder, backed by a brutal attack. Jealousy and envy was the underlying factor, wickedness from a wicked mind without remorse. There was no hallucination in this case, there was no mental health disorder in this case, this case was not about suicide. The only reason for the re-trial of this case is so that justice can be done and manifestly and undoubtedly be seen to be done.

Ladies and Gentlemen, if the deceased was your brother, your cousin, your son or your friend, what would you do? If you cast your mind back to the facts of this case, if you are able to close your eyes in order to retain focus, please do. Cast your mind back to the night in question when the deceased died of cyanide poison under the pretext that he was being given a minted sweet after the meal he had in the restaurant with the accused person. Steven convulsed, choking to meet his sudden brutal death."

The courtroom went very quiet.

"The second defendant Keith Bradford had no excuse for perverting the course of justice, as a prosecutor he ought to know the law better than anyone else. He failed himself when he refused to uphold the law. He compromised himself to conceal the crime of his son even after his son confessed the crime to him. Perverting the course of justice is an offence committed when a person prevents justice from being served on him/herself or on another party.

Ladies and Gentleman, the above case shows the seriousness of the offence of perverting the course of justice.

In this case in front of us, Mr Keith Bradford agreed to keep his son's confession a secret, he refused to report his son's crime to the Police. He even mentioned that the confession was not admissible on grounds of his son's mental health disorder quoting Section 77 of the Police and Criminal Evidence Act. But it is not for the 2nd defendant to suggest to this honourable court that a confessional statement is admissible in evidence or not.

The confessional statement of Mr Tom Bradford was signed by him and the confession was made voluntarily by him without duress during the course of investigations and prosecution. Section 76 (2)(a) of the Police and Criminal Evidence Act 1984.

The court should be mindful of the rationale for applying trial within a trial and procedure in conducting trial within trial and its essence generally in criminal proceedings. Tom admitted and accepted expressly and even by clear implication that he committed the offence alleged against him. It was not a hallucination or dream. The offence of murder was carefully perpetrated on the deceased.

According to the Black's Law Dictionary, 9th Edition at page 338: 'A confession is an acknowledgement in express words, by the accused in a criminal case of the truth of the main fact charged or of some essential part of it.''

The confession made by the 1st defendant grounds conviction: it is direct, positive and unequivocal as far as the charge is concerned. The confession by Tom was made after Keith took him to visit his mother's graveside in Pennsylvania, the confession was free and voluntary and it proceeded from remorse, and a desire to make reparation for the crime. Tom confided in Keith and this was why he confessed his crime. The confession is admissible against Tom only and not against any other person, meaning the first defendant's confession cannot be used to convict an accomplice.

The accused cannot call evidence of a third party's out of court admission of guilt in order to establish his own innocence. The justification for this rule is based, said Lord Bridge, on the principle stated by Lord Normand in *Tepper v. The Queen* [1952] A.C. 480, 486 viz:

"The rule against the admission of hearsay evidence is fundamental. It is not the best evidence and it is not delivered on oath. The truthfulness and accuracy of the person whose words are spoken to by another witness cannot be tested by cross-examination, and the light which his demeanour would throw on his testimony is lost."

In the case of *Turner (Bryan)* 61 Cr.App.R. 67, where it was sought to produce evidence of a statement by one person that he, rather than one of the defendants, had taken part in the robbery, it was said, at p. 87: "This court is of opinion that the ruling of the learned judge in refusing to admit in evidence the statement made to a third party by a person not himself called as a witness in the trial was clearly correct."

Your Lordship the confession made by the accused person in this case contains both the *actus reus* and *mens rea* (where it is required) of the offence charged. The confessional statement has not in any way been challenged by the first defendant by retraction, he hasn't denied or said that he did not make the statement. My learned colleague; the defence has not objected to the admissibility of the confessional statement on grounds that the defendant never made the statement being proposed by the prosecution for tendering, my argument therefore is that if all the conditions for admissibility of the statement are met; the court will admit the statement in evidence and then later determine what weight to ascribe to it.

The confessional statement in this case was made voluntarily, the defendant has not resiled from his confessional statement, and even if he did resile on his statement that does not ipso facto render that statement inadmissible. The test of admissibility of a confessional statement is not whether the confession is true but the question of how the statement was obtained. It is clear in this case that the confessional statement made by Tom is one obtained without fear of prejudice or hope of advantage exercised over him by the prosecution or someone in a position of authority.

Ladies and Gentlemen we have not in this case reached a case of trial within a trial. Trial within a trial is a mini trial within the substantive or main trial as it were to determine the veracity of the account of the defendant as to whether his statement to the investigator was voluntarily made or not. In some instances, as it were, a trial within a trial would result in the temporary suspension of the main trial. This case does not warrant a trial within a trial because with the defendant the process of obtaining the statement from the defendant has not been challenged, the defendant was not coerced, induced, threatened, deceived or forced by means of any unnatural intervening factors which would have influenced the making of the statement in question. The test for the admissibility of a confessional statement is its voluntariness and once the issue is raised, it must be resolved before its admission.

Milord, The Court of Appeal echoed, determined and held in the case of **John v State (2013) LPELR-22197 (CA) that:** and I quote ''*Certainly, it is the law that in criminal trial, no statement by an accused person can be admitted against him unless it is shown to have been voluntarily made. That being so, where the admissibility of a confessional statement is challenged on the ground that it was not voluntarily made. In practice, that is done by way of a trial within trial, where evidence is led about the circumstances under which such a statement was made. It is therefore only when the accused has raised the issue that he did not make the statement voluntarily, that he need for trial within trial will arise.''* Milord, it is for this honourable court to determine whether the defendant's statement was not made in violation of the provisions of the Police and Criminal Evidence Act of 1984. That is, it is a trial within the main trial. It is to determine an interlocutory point of admissibility of a piece of evidence that is the confessional statement of the accused person allegedly made involuntarily.

Ladies and Gentlemen, this young man named Tom committed murder, premeditated murder, he confessed it to his father, the CCTV camera footage would not lie as the crime was recorded and on record, otherwise the truth about this case would never have come to light. If we can all close our eyes and cast our mind back to the night in question when the deceased died of cyanide poison. There was no provocation, I mean the deceased did not provoke the accused person, there was no argument over anything, the motive for this murder is pure jealousy, hatred and complex by the 1st defendant for the deceased."

The court room went very quiet.

"The second defendant on the other hand cannot get away from the wrath of the law for his offence of perverting the course of justice. Keith Bradford is a man who knows the law, practises the law, he's full of the bar, filled with the bench, saturated by the law, he has practised as a prosecutor for almost three decades, he eats with the law, drinks with the law, breathes the law, and is in a better position to know that the right thing for him to do was for him to report his son's confession to the Police, but he did not. Keith has let himself and the prosecution team down. This honourable court should be mindful of the precedence that we set today. Should a lawyer in dilemma be set free and made to walk away from his crime? Or should he be punished for what he has done as a deterrent to others who may find themselves in similar situation in the future, perhaps this case will serve as a lesson. Or are we going to allow the rule of law for some members of the public and not for others? The big question is for this honourable court to decide. I say no more. If justice is going to be done, it is in your hands to do and now is the time and moment to do so. Let us lay the precedent now that no one should get away with any form of murder. Tom murdered the late Steve in cold blood and it is the duty of the law to do justice without fear or favour. Now is the time to do justice and to allow the law to rule. Thank you.

Here is my submission, I rest my case."

Howard Sullivan stood to his feet, the learned defence counsel was ready to summarise his side of the case before the jury and the judge.
He stared at his notepad, he stared at the Judge and then made direct eye contact with the jurors then he continued:

"Ladies and gentlemen, it remains a fundamental principle in our Criminal Justice system that an accused person is presumed innocent until he or she is proven guilty. My client is going through trauma from a deep seated mental depression arising from neglect by his parents in his childhood, his mother suffered from drug addiction while she was married to the second defendant, when they divorced, Teresa's addiction became worse and she could not cope with nurturing the first defendant, this was the reason why the social services took Tom away from her, she then continued to battle with drug abuse until her second marriage when she gave birth to the late Steve. All along Tom was hopping from one foster carer to another, he did not have a stable home that he could call his own, all the up-bringing that he's had was from friends on the street and that has got him into so much trouble. Here is a young man that I implore this court to feel sorry for, he had no control over the circumstances and challenges that life has thrown at him. What my client needs is not to be sent to jail, what he needs is rehabilitation, counselling and a stable environment. The social system has failed in providing all these essential necessities to my client while he was in care. He has for many years suffered from distress, anxiety and even panic attacks. Tom, according to what Keith told us, was suffering from hallucinations, and heard unknown voices in his head after visiting his mother's graveside in Pennsylvania. This young man standing before this court is a victim and not a murderer, he should be sent to a rehabilitation centre and not into a prison. The verdict of this honourable court and the jury must not be based on pressure or just because the accused person previously walked free from the first trial. What you saw in that CCTV video coverage is not premeditated murder, it is a man suffering from a confused mind, his state of mind and head is not that of a normal mind, he is legally insane, this court cannot rely on his confessional statement because he is not mentally sound. Let us think deeply, the mitigating factors in this case cannot be overlooked. Tom did not intend to murder Steve, why would he do such a thing? Tom does not have a motive for wanting to murder Steve. Tom has been suffering from emotional trauma and drug addiction ever since his mother lost custody of looking after him. Gentlemen and Ladies, let us listen and read through every word and every line in the evidence and exhibits that have been tendered in this case. I implore this honourable court to see the vulnerability of a troubled man from infancy to adolescence and then adulthood in an unfortunate dark hour. With our eyes widely open let us look beyond all the letters without sentiments, let us do justice beyond all reasonable doubt as we write history in the judicial books today.

My second client did not intend to pervert the cause of justice, he is a dad who has only just re-connected with a son that he hardly ever knew. He erred in his judgment when he thought that Section 77 of the Police and Criminal Evidence Act 1984 will exonerate his son, Keith erred in that it was not for him to decide what confession is and what is not admissible by this honourable court, it remains solely the discretion of this honourable court to determine what confessional statement is admissible in evidence and which is not admissible.

Ladies and Gentlemen, with all due respect, permit me to refer the court to the provisions of section 77 of the Police and Criminal Evidence Act 1984 - Confessions by mentally handicapped persons.

(1) Without prejudice to the general duty of the court at a trial on indictment to direct the jury on any matter on which it appears to the court appropriate to do so, where at such a trial—

(a) the case against the accused depends wholly or substantially on a confession by him; and
(b) the court is satisfied—
(i) that he is mentally handicapped; and
(ii) that the confession was not made in the presence of an independent person.

The court shall warn the jury that there is special need for caution before convicting the accused in reliance on the confession, and shall explain that the need arises because of the circumstances mentioned in paragraphs (a) and (b) above.

(2) In any case where at the summary trial of a person for an offence it appears to the court that a warning under subsection (1) above would be required if the trial were on indictment, the court shall treat the case as one in which there is a special need for caution before convicting the accused on his confession.

(3) In this section—
"independent person" does not include a police officer or a person employed for, or engaged on, police purposes. The fact that this honourable court will need to address is whether the confessional statement that the first defendant made to his dad the second defendant is admissible or not. Let me remind this honourable court that the first defendant is a product of a dysfunctional childhood, he was not left with a choice on which family he lived with, and had lived in so many hostels, foster homes and along the line he picked up bad friends, and bad habits, he was mostly found on the wrong side of the law because he had no parental guidance, yet his father practiced as a prosecutor for almost thirty years before he reunited with his son. It was too late for Keith to prevent nemesis from

catching up with him and with his career. Ladies and Gentlemen the facts of this case is a very sorry one. To call it 'The Lawyer's Dilemma' can only but be the right thing to do under these circumstances Milord!

The court will have to ascertain whether the confessional statement made by Tom is admissible. There are certain procedural conditions that must be present for a trial within trial to be conducted as the same is not conducted simply for the asking. The preliminary steps to invoking the power for it are:

- That it is a court of competent jurisdiction that is conducting the main trial
- That the first defendant must be in court and in the dock for his trial
- That prosecution must seek to tender the defendant's confessional statement as an exhibit.
- That defendant (or his counsel) must object to the admissibility of the said statement that it was not freely and voluntarily made.
- After satisfying the above steps, the stage is set for a trial within a trial to be ordered by the court.
- The onus of proof is on the prosecution and in this case to prove that the confessional statement made by Tom in this contention was made under caution
- The word of caution must be in the language understood by the defendant
- The confessional statement must be signed
- And that the maker of the statement, in this case the first defendant understood the statement after the same was made to read over to him in a language he understands. The court on the other hand uses this test for determining the veracity or otherwise of a confessional statement by attempting to see whether there was any circumstantial evidence, which makes

it probable that, the confession is true. The tests consist of the following:

- Whether there is anything outside the confession to show that it is true,
- Whether the statement is corroborated, no matter how slightly;
- Whether the facts contained therein so far as can be tested, are true;
- Whether the defendant had the opportunity of committing the offence;
- Whether the confession of the defendant is possible;
- Whether the confession was consistent with the other facts which have been ascertained and proved in the matter.
- Most importantly, that the statement was made voluntarily.

Trial within a trial connotes a process in court where an accused facing a criminal trial in court protests to the admission of a confessional statement allegedly made by him to the police on the ground that the said statement was not and could not have been voluntarily made by him having been obtained under duress or some threat or actual physical torture to his person.

Ladies and gentlemen, there is cause for this honourable court to ascertain the steps for a trial within trial before the confessional statement made by the accused person can be admissible. The evidence in this case must be led by both parties, their counsel should address the court which we have done. The next step is that the court should deliver its ruling on the admissibility vel non of the disputed confession. Where there is more than one retracted confession made on different days and at different occasions, their admissibility must be tested in the voire dire one after the other. The normal procedure in all cases is for the prosecution to lead evidence first and be cross-examined after which the defendant will also lead evidence and be cross-examined. The next step is that after counsel's address, a ruling will then be delivered by the court either admitting or rejecting the disputed confession and marking it accordingly. A trial within a trial must not be lumped with the substantive trial as the same will lead to a verdict of acquittal. The onus is static and on the prosecution to prove that the disputed confessional statement was made freely and voluntarily. There is no better way or words to explain the rationale for trial within trial than to rely and adopt the words of the court in precedence when it was stated that "*The rationale behind instituting the procedure of trial within trial is to protect an accused person (particularly an illiterate person) from the overbearance of some overzealous investigating police officers bent on securing convictions in their matters at all costs by using all manner of inducements, threats or promises to obtain confessional statements in prosecution of their cases. The principle of trial within trial is one aspect of dispensing equal justice and fairness under the Rule of Law. By this simple procedure, its assured that statements of a person charged with a criminal offence obtained by a police officer or anyone in authority, otherwise afflicted by any inducement, threats or promises, being illegal at law, are expunged from the mainstream of the prosecution's case at the trial of his cause or matter; and the court is precluded from acting upon it in dealing with the case. The procedure of trial-within-trial is so much used to exclude involuntary statements of an accused person that is contrary to the law and it was stuck on for good reason.*" – See words of Chukwuma-Eneh, JSC in Ibeme v State (Supra) @357

Rhodes-Vivour, JSC added the following words in the said case when he echoed the following: *"A trial-within-trial, a mini trial ensures that an accused person is treated fairly in a criminal trial. The procedure guarantees equality in the criminal justice system thereby keeping the streams of justice pure. Where the prosecution seeks to tender an extra judicial confessional statement of an accused person and it is challenged on the ground that it was not made voluntarily, a trial within trial is conducted for the sole purpose of finding out if the statement was made voluntarily or whether the confessions were beaten out of the accused person. At the end of a trial within trial, if the trial judge is satisfied that the confessional statement was not voluntary, such a statement is not admissible in evidence. If on one hand the statement was made voluntarily, it is admitted in evidence. In both cases, the judge should rule accordingly and bring the trial within trial to an end. The main trial then continues.''* The matter for this honourable court to consider is the application of practice of trial within trial in order to ensure fairness and to promote the cause of justice and it is one of the measures through which the streams of justice can be kept clean and available for all and sundry to assess. In the light of my submission there are unanswered questions on the admissibility of the confessional statement allegedly made by the 1st defendant to the 2nd defendant. The 2nd defendant made it clear to this court that his son was hallucinating and was hearing voices in his head making his confession questionable. We have also heard evidence of mental health experts which suggests from their report that the 1st defendant is legally insane. All the facts of this case make it difficult to rely on the confessional statement as admissible in evidence under section 77 of the Police and Criminal Evidence Act 1984."

The defence attorney stared at his notepad, made a slow walk as he passed the podium moving around with roaming eyes, he stared at the Judge and then made direct eye contact with the jurors then he continued. Howard Sullivan mitigated for Mr Keith Bradford:

''Ladies and gentlemen, the 2nd defendant knows the law and would not ordinarily carry out the offence of perverting the course of justice as alleged. Perverting the course of justice is an offence committed when a person prevents justice from being served on him/herself or on another party in England and Wales. It is a common law offence. As a father Keith knows that his son was vulnerable with mental instability, he believed that he hallucinated, heard his confession but he was inconclusive on the admissibility of his son's statement. Let us cast our mind back to the relationship between this father and son, until the time of Tom's trial, Keith had not set his eyes on Tom for close to thirty years at the least. He was full of disappointment at the kind of person Tom has turned out to become, he wished he could turn back the hand of the clock to fill in the gaps in his son's life. When he travelled with Tom to the United States to visit the late Teresa's graveside, Tom got emotional and made a confessional statement that was difficult for a father who was a lawyer and prosecutor to believe! Keith was a lawyer in a dilemma, he did not intend to conceal a crime or to pervert the course of justice. Why would he do such a thing? Keith knows that his son is a product of a dysfunctional childhood, he was not left with a choice on whether he chose a good family to live with, and he was raised and fostered by gangsters on the street even before he lived with the Blackstone's family. Tom was a troubled child. I am not asking this honourable court to use the circumstances of Tom's childhood to exonerate him, we cannot use his childhood as an excuse to set him free from what he did but the important fact that we ought to base the reality on is that if this man was not influenced at a young age by the negative foster parents and several hostels where he lived and where he picked up all the bad habits of drug abuse and substance abuse, he will not be on the other side of the law. I urge the court to consider the circumstances that led to his growth as a child, let us temper justice with mercy as we judge him. Let us see him, yes; as a man who is troubled but not a gunned armed robber or murderer ready to take another person's life with a poisonous substance.

It is the duty of the court to investigate the truth or admissibility of evidence, held during this trial. And what is the truth in this story? It is the pure truth that Tom did not intend to murder the late Steve. Keith did not pervert the course of justice. He was a prosecuting attorney in confusion. Let us do justice beyond all reasonable doubt as we write history in the judicial books today. Tom and Keith should be free men.

Here is my submission. I rest my case.

Thank you."

Chapter 38

The Sentencing Remarks, 14 August 2016

R.

v

1. **Mr. Tommy Graham Bradford** (1st defendant)
2. **Mr. Keith Crawford Bradford** (2nd defendant)

The case heard in the criminal court on the 14th of August 2016; these are the sentencing remarks by Honourable Justice Tremaine Hernandez.

Tommy Bradford

1. I am left with no choice but to convict you for murder of Stephen Claxton that was done in a calculated cold blooded murder through the administration of a dangerous poisonous substance named cyanide. I must now sentence you for murder, you walked away a free man in your first trial and that was because there was insufficient evidence to substantiate the prosecution's assertion that you murdered the deceased in a brutal and violent attack by the use of poison on a train platform barely 15 minutes after you both had a meal and drink together. Anyone who watches the breathtakingly shocking CCTV footage would struggle to understand how you thought you could claim to have acted legally insane against your half-brother Stephen who had just spent his money to host you to a sumptuous dinner, bought you expensive drinks under the innocent belief that he was re-uniting with you and giving you a treat, he spent his own money for you to travel up to London, West End for a brotherly re-union treat: a day out with his half-brother whom he was bonding with. What he did not know was that he was dining with the devil from the deep blue sea. You disguised your wickedness of the wicked by offering Stephen a minted sweet, you knew that the sweet you first put in your own mouth did not have the poison, you had one first so that Stephen would not suspect that he could be in danger, you then handed to him a poison version of the minted sweet with the intention to cut his life short. You used a dangerous weapon to send your victim to an early grave, he instantly convulsed, suffered respiratory failure compounded by lactic acidosis. Cyanide is rapidly lethal, according to the medical report from the coroner, the lethal dose of cyanide that you used worked as a mitochondrial toxin, inhibiting cytochrome c oxidase in the electron transport chain, it prevented cells from aerobically using adenosine triphosphate for energy, the high concentration of the minted sweet that Stephen put in his mouth lead to his death in minutes, he slumped as he stepped inside the train after which the doors slid to close, the train moved, passengers rushed towards Stephen's body on the floor but by the time the driver got to the next station to get the ambulance crew to take him to A&E he had lost his life. You, Tom; knew what you had done, you turned your back to walk away as that train drove your victim of crime away in front of you, you walked away, you never thought that you would ever be found out to have committed this gruesome murder, you were so confident that you would walk away from this crime. You were set free in your first trial but this will not happen again and never ever will it happen again.

2. What you have done was a planned and calculated murder, both 'mens-rea' (intention) and 'actus reus' (action) were present in your crime. You have previously worked in a chemical factory so you know the running about how to get the poison, you knew where to get your lethal weapon and you discreetly got it from your source. You then planned on how you could administer it on your victim without anyone knowing, that too you got away with in your first trial, until nemesis caught up with you with new evidence emerging through the CCTV footage. What you have done has nothing to do with you being a product of a dysfunctional childhood, you don't have any excuse for taking Stephen's life, your motive is pure jealousy, hatred and greed to inherit real estate of your mother through your grandparents. Stephen trusted you and he wanted to bond with you, but you did not have the same level of kindness for him like he had for you, the more he wished to bond with you, the more you wish to eliminate him in cold blood. You were not just a man who had a previous conviction for theft during the London riots, but you had in your criminal history been convicted for raping the daughter of your foster carers even though they had adopted you as their own child. The Blackstone family opened the door of their home to you in order to help you, they picked you up from the streets, adopted you, made you bear their family name, you lived under their roof as a child but you raped their only daughter because committing crime was a way of life for you. The only thing you think about is you and nobody else.

3. The murder that you have committed was not provoked by any incident, there was entirely no row between you and your victim, there was no abuse, no swearing at each other, no fight, no quarrel, you waited for a suitable time for you to perpetrate a malicious, deliberate, cruel and violent vicious attack. Stephen did not know about your violent history. He did not know that the same Tom that violated his girlfriend Evelyn in a sexual assault was you. Evelyn did not know that you were Stephen's half-brother, if she did, she would have warned her fiancé in advance.

4. Stephen did not know that you suffered from mood swings, horrific hallucinations caused by trauma and delusion, illusion and figment imagination and delirium. He has never dealt with anyone with special needs before and that is why he did not suspect you as a person that he could be at immediate danger from. You have suffered from dissocial personality disorder ever since you were a child, with addiction to substance abuse, your medical record shows that you often skip taking your antianxiety medication. Stephen saw you as family, but you treated him like an enemy out of envy, hatred and jealously. You pulled out a dangerous lethal weapon in form of a cyanide. You were not psychotic at the time you offered a lethal minted sweet to your victim. I have no shadow of doubt that you would rage your inferiority complex and hypersensitivity to anyone who is more successful than you, even if they have shown you kind gesture, you did it to your foster parents and now you've done it to your innocent half-brother. You have a subtle temper that could hair trigger at any time on anyone that comes your way even without any form of provocation thrown at you. You are a time bomb always ready to explode at the slightest opportunity. You are unstable and your culpability is nevertheless unreduced when you rage, in my judgement of your personality disorder and apparent perception of something not present.

5. You have a group of friends whom you move along with, some of them live in the same residential hostel with you in Croydon. You have a habit of not taking your medication, but you did take cannabis along with your friends which sometimes made you more paranoid than usual, making you unstable with fluctuating behavioural pattern. Your medical record suggests that you have a tendency to self-harm though you never have harmed your own body, the only people you've ever endangered are the people who love you the most. You could never meet up to the standard of elitism like Stephen, you became threatened by his confidence and success. You decided to end his life by poisoning him with a lethal dose of cyanide and you killed him. You cut off his life with that single lethal dose of cyanide, with a high concentration leading to death within minutes. The result of an autopsy carried out on Stephen's corpse shows his skin to remain pink in contrast to the cherry-red of carbonmonoxide poisoning, despite cellular hypoxia. His body suffered sudden convulsion, chronic ingestion causing a variety of symptoms ranging from generalised weakness, confusion and bizarre behaviour, through to paralysis and liver failure. You lunged a frenzied and fast attack on your victim, who was nothing but helpless at the time he was attacked. No passenger on that train, in that hour, at that moment could assuage the pain and agony that Stephen suffered in his last hour. There was only one attacker in this crime and that was you. You were the aggressor who had a field day in front of a helpless aggresse. You were not acting in any self-defence because no one was attacking you and you therefore had nothing to defend.

6. Dr Bartholomew De La Pole, the forensic medicine expert reported that the deceased died from cyanide poisoning which resulted in him convulsing with a blue face within minutes of putting the minted sweet in his mouth. Dr Jeremy McWhinney, the consultant pathologist confirmed in his autopsy that laboratory test result confirmed that a lethal dose of cyanide was the main cause of death of the deceased. Immediately after your crime you calmly walked away from the platform where Stephen had boarded the train, you simply left the scene quickly, you walked back to the other side of the station where you boarded your train back to Croydon as if nothing had happened. You left the deceased on a train that had just passed you by, to die in the hands of passengers who hardly ever knew him to be Stephen. You left him at the mercy of strangers who cradled his dying head inside a commuter train at a rush hour in the evening.

7. You showed no remorse because you had planned what you did, you put on your jacket, went home without any blood stain on your clothes, no murder weapon in your hands, and you carefully planned the aftermath of your crime to cover your tracks. What you did not know at the time of your crime was that your crime was going to catch up with you. The CCTV footage corroborated your confessional statement and it is now time for the law to take its course with you for your deliberate act. You did not look back to hand yourself in to the Police or call for help for your half-brother, Stephen – a man you must have known you had badly, if not fatally, poisoned and you did not once tell anyone what you have done until the Police appeared at your doorstep to have you arrested.

8. Stephen Claxton was a hardworking as well as an accomplished young man with a promising future ahead of him. He was well brought up by his grandparents in Pennsylvania, USA. He came to London to further his education which started well with his high school grades in the US. He lost his mother at his birth and his dad Brian Claxton died on 9/11 during the Twin Tower incident. He'd been an orphan since the age of eleven and his grandparents did a good job of financing his education. It was now time for Stephen's aged granny to start to look up to him to look after her when Tom cut his life short. Stephen was a successful practicing chartered accountant, he was engaged to his fiancée Evelyn, and they were planning to get married next year to the joy of his friends, Phoebe and other well-wishers.

9. The impact statement from Phoebe and Evelyn speaks volumes of the irrevocable change and damage that you have caused to their lives. You caused Evelyn and Phoebe misery and anguish of losing a future husband and a promising grandson respectively. That anguish of losing Stephen under such circumstances will remain with Evelyn and Phoebe. Very sincerely and truly this was a needless death, a senseless loss of life all because of what you had done.

10. You have previous convictions which have a statutory aggravating feature. You have convictions for theft during the London riots in August 2011, you have in the past been convicted for raping your 'sister' who was the only daughter of your foster carers who were gracious to you by adopting you. With that incident dealt with by a plea of guilty to sexual assault at the time you carried out the attack, a plea bargain was reached by your defence and prosecution team.

11. You have committed a series of assaults and some criminal damage too as a young offender which are serious offence against justice. But none of your past convictions is on the scale of what you have done to Stephen. You have just taken someone's life and you will never again be a free man. You have carried out an entirely irrational response to no provocation whatsoever. You carried out this killing on someone you knew as your 'half-brother' which makes it an aggravating feature. However, your constant failure to take your medication and continuing to use cannabis which sometimes made you more paranoid, are not aggravating features, but they mean that there is no scope for considering you to have any degree of reduced culpability on the basis of your mental ill health as established during your first trial. It was your mental health condition that persuaded the jury to reach a not guilty verdict during your first trial. Your attack on Stephen was a premeditated attack to a vulnerable man, you knew the impact that cyanide, a dangerous poison could have on anyone, yet you went ahead to carry out your plan and because of your previous convictions it indicates to me that you intended to kill Stephen.

12. You are a 30-year old man who knew what he was doing, you will spend the best years of the life left to you in prison, away from your dad, your friends and those you love. You have brought this upon yourself and you have no one else to blame but yourself in this matter. Killing Stephen was your undoing and you have to live with the consequences of your brutality.

Sentence

I am obliged by law to sentence you to imprisonment for life on the count of murder of which you now stand convicted and I do so. I then have regard to Schedule 21 of the Criminal Justice Act 2003 and the scheme within it. That scheme is a flexible one, with a just outcome in each case depending on the specific facts and circumstances of the offender. Detailed consideration of aggravating or mitigating factors not taken into account for the purpose of fixing the starting point can result in a minimum term of any length whatever the starting point. The examples given against each starting point are illustrative and not exhaustive. Each case will always turn on its own facts. There is a need to have regard to proportionality in the sense identified as in the case of *R v Smith* [2017] EWCA Crim 1174; [2017] 2 Cr App R (S) 42 at [85].

13. The aggravating features in your case outweigh the available mitigation and justify a material increase in this starting point. Having regard to all relevant factors, I consider the appropriate minimum term on the count of murder to be 18 years. The day that you have already spent in custody will count towards this minimum term.

14. Sentence for murder is life imprisonment. Following on and in accordance with Schedule 21 to the Criminal Justice Act 2003, I have to set a minimum term. The starting point must be 18 years, I have described aggravating features, your mitigating factors are very limited. I sentence you to life imprisonment with a minimum term of 18 years. This is the minimum term which you will serve in custody, before the Parole Board may consider your possible release. If you are released by the Board you will remain on licence and subject to recall to prison, for the rest of your life. Make sure to take your medication regularly and stay away from cannabis and any form of substance abuse so that you can remain well stable and remorseful while you are in prison. Please take him down.

Keith Bradford

You have worked very hard as a prosecuting attorney for almost three decades and I have no doubt that you are a lawyer of excellent reputation. The current situation you have found yourself in is a tricky one due to the emotional tie that you have with your only son, a child that you hardly ever knew. Your involvement with Tom during the first trial was to ensure that justice is done but for obvious reasons you were on the side of the defence team and not the state, you saw your son walk free from a crime that he committed, the reason being that there was not sufficient evidence to find him guilty. Tom is now facing a re-trial with you alongside for perverting the course of justice, you naturally assumed that it was all over and that you could pick up the pieces of your relationship with your son from where you left him thirty years ago. What you did not realise is that fate and the day of reckoning is beckoning on you. When you walked away from your wife; a young mother who was suffering from substance and drug abuse, you also neglected your only son at a tender age of two years old, you made a foolish decision by not putting your family first. You were a young prosecuting attorney with a busy work schedule but the choices you made concerning your family was irrational, selfish, childish and irresponsible.

I have no doubt in my mind that lawyers and other professionals around the world would learn a big lesson from your life story. If you stayed with Teresa at her darkest hour, you both would have raised Tom up in a way that you would be proud of today, perhaps he would have grown up to study law like you did, just like Stephen studied accountancy like his own dad Brian Claxton. But you have sharked your responsibility and you are now suffering the consequences of your immature behaviour three decades ago. Your wife was going through a difficult time, she had depression and possibly a prolonged post-natal traumatic disorder, you were meant to support her through that difficult stage of her life, she was with a young child, that child was yours. Looking at Tom in this court today shows a striking resemblance between you and him, if you had stayed behind to work things out with Teresa, your story would have been different today. You were a young lawyer who was irrational with his decision making. I wonder where your parents were when you made such an irrational decision to walk away from your young family. You will now have to live with the nemesis of your actions for the rest of your life, seeing your son go to prison for life.

I hope that young lawyers would learn from your case and never start a family when they are not ready for the responsibilities because they might end up with adverse consequences. Marriage is not an institution that you rush into when you are not ready. Bringing up children requires your time, dedication and devotion. Your presence in your home and in the life of your children is very important as much as your profession or career is. Your family should come first. By the time you chose to put Tom first, it was too late, in your absence he had grown up to be a problematic child and you are now facing the hardest task to put his life back together. This tragic story could have been otherwise if you had been more patient, careful and reasonable when it really mattered. I admonish you to seriously learn from your past life.

When your son told you that he suffered from horrific hallucinations which was caused by trauma, illusions, imagination, mirage and apparition, you should have taken his confessional statement seriously. You should have reported his confession to the police. You knew the right thing to do, but you did not do it. You were ashamed that your son had committed murder and tried to justify what he had done by making yourself to believe that section 77 of the criminal evidence act 1984 would avail the admissibility of your son's confessional statement. Could I make it clear to you that Tom was not legally insane when he murdered Stephen? He knew what he was doing when he did what he did. You should have turned him in the moment he told you the truth about what he had done, if you had done that, you would not be a second defendant in this matter, neither would you be answering to the allegation of perverting the course of justice.

Perverting the course of justice is an offence committed when a person prevents justice from being served on him/herself or on another party. It is an offence under the common law of England and Wales carrying a maximum sentence of life imprisonment. It is an offence to:

1. Conspire with another to pervert the course of justice, and
2. Intending to pervert the course of justice

This offence, and the subject matter of the related forms of criminal conspiracy, have been referred to as:

1. Perverting the course of justice
2. Interfering with the administration of justice
3. Obstructing the administration of justice
4. Obstructing the course of justice
5. Defeating the due course of justice
6. Defeating the ends of justice

Your son told you exactly what had happened. He then asked you to promise him not to tell anyone what he had done, you should have declined his request and reported his confessional statement to the police, that was the right thing for you to do, but you never did. This court has not found you to have fabricated or disposed of evidence. I am not convinced that you have some intellectual weaknesses or that there was anything that would limit your understanding of how serious a position Tom was in and how entirely wrong and unlawful it would be to conceal anything he had to tell you or confess to you. You remained quiet and did not tell anyone even when you went back to work after your annual leave ended in August. You helped your son to cover his crime. There was no sign that you tried to get Tom to turn himself in before he was re-arrested by the Inspector of Police.

I need to consider to what extent was the interest of justice damaged through your actions, the police would have arrested Tom on the day he made his confession to you, before you returned to work in August, your action impeded that arrest but did not prevent it.

Keith you put your integrity on the line by acting under misguided loyalty for your son, you were a lawyer in serious dilemma with emotional ties with the only son he had. These are not excuses, but they go to explain how humanly vulnerable any professional could be and this includes a lawyer of unquestionable character, your emotional weakness was brought to bear, you became helpless, you knew the right thing for you to do as a lawyer, you compromised your virtues, you damned all the consequences of what a professional so dear to your heart would ever stood for and you compromised your integrity with a criminal that you called your son. I will accept that you were emotionally confused with him and your closeness during your trip to Pennsylvania when you visited Teresa's grave side clouded your sense of judgement and reasonability. Your emotional bond with Tom has pushed you to break the law. This does not excuse what you did but it does have an impact on your culpability.

You have failed to act with integrity, you have failed to uphold the proper administration of justice, but I do not think that you have entirely behaved in a way that maintains the trust the public places in the provision of legal services. For this reason I have considered the guidelines in relation to suspended sentences and in light of the mitigation put forward by your counsel, Mr Howard Sullivan, in particular the vulnerability you have to emotional bonds with your only son that you have not had the opportunity of raising.

I find you guilty of perverting the course of justice, but I am delaying your serving of a sentence after I have found you to be guilty, this is in order to allow you to perform a period of probation. If you do not break the law during this period and fulfil the particular conditions of the probation, then your suspended sentence shall be dismissed. I sentence you to a potential course of suspended sentence of 24 months imprisonment, I have decided that this is the least sentence I can pass. If you are found guilty of another offence during the suspension period, both the original and new sentence will be served.

Up until now you have always been a man of integrity, you worked for the state as a prosecutor, you have no previous conviction, you've never been on the other side of the law. You are an attorney at law. Your case is unfortunate and what has happened to you is a nightmare that no lawyer should ever dream of going through in their life-time. I so hold.

The defence Counsel
Mr Howard Sullivan

The prosecutor
Mr Nigel Stanley

The Judge
Honourable Justice Tremaine Hernandez

Chapter 39

The Press

At the end of the trial, the court sheriffs directed the spectators to leave the courtroom in an orderly manner. The reporters were after the prosecuting counsel, but were instructed to meet him in the rotunda in a few minutes. The prosecutor made them wait by first going to the chambers and giving his regards to the judge. He then walked all the way taking the stairs to the second floor to check on some case authorities in the court library briefly. When the courtroom was empty and they had waited long enough, he walked through the rear door, into the rotunda and faced the camera. A microphone with green letters on it was thrust into his face.

As the legal team for the prosecution and the defence counsel stepped out in front of the court there was a barrage of press photographers, a swarm of reporters, paparazzi and cameramen who had throughout the court session had been waiting outside the court premises, one after the other they stood holding their microphones and waiting to ask questions.

Journalist: ''Prosecuting attorney, you must feel a huge relief seeing justice done in the re-trial of this case. Can you tell us what happened to the evidence during the first trial that led to the 1st defendant's acquittal?''

Prosecutor: ''There was an omission in the first trial, no one knew that the CCTV footage existed. There was no confessional statement from the accused person either, making it very difficult to pin him to the crime that he had committed.''

Journalist: ''Would you say that the investigation team erred under the circumstances, would you say that a thorough investigation was not conducted, because if you did, the accused person should never have walked free from the first trial.''

Prosecutor: ''Whichever way you choose to look at it today is a victorious day for the prosecuting team, we pressed charges for murder in the first trial, the defence raised the plea of insanity, the court got caught in between the probability and possibility of the deceased committing suicide, but we now know that is not true. Stephen was brutally murdered by the accused person and here we are today to witness a well calculated and planned out murder. This is not the first time that we will be witnessing murder through poison, it is one of the hardest crimes to unravel, unlike when an accused person uses a dangerous and offensive weapon like knife, that weapon is visible and the impact of the knife on the victim is clearly seen with the shedding of blood, thrusting of the knife would make profuse blood loss visible for everyone to see the blade pass through the muscle into the
jugular vein and into carotid artery, but this is not the case in a poison attack. Cyanide or strychnine is a lethal weapon, it is invisible, the victim could hardly ever witness it's being administered in their food or drink. In Stephen's case there was no argument or provocation, Tom was a smooth operating killer, an enemy never to dine with, he led his victim on as if everything was ok between them, no one could suspect such a vicious killer unless of cause the camera picks it up. The only other proof would be for him to confess what he had done through his confessional statement; otherwise he would have remained a free man.''

Journalist: ''You could say that, Mr Nigel Stanley, but the 'onus probandi' or the burden of proof is always on the prosecution to prove its case while the defence team has a presumption of innocence.''

Prosecutor: ''Yes you are right in saying that and we did prove our case beyond all reasonable doubt in the second trial, we did it so successfully that even the defence's mitigation with a plea of insanity or legal insanity could not see the light of day. We did what we had to do in the re-trial and there is one thing for us to celebrate upon today, he who asserts must prove and that is exactly what we have done, we were obligated to prove our assertion and proving it, we did today. The CCTV footage was a defining moment, videos and photographs cannot lie. Technology saved the day.''

Journalist: ''Is it then fair to say that technology saves the day and not the prosecution team.''

Prosecutor: ''You can put it this way; both the prosecuting team and technology room operatives saved the day, justice is meant for all and it should be delivered with the help of the law enforcement agent and the people in the country. The Judge has pronounced his judgment, the jury have made their decision and there is nothing we can do about it now. Justice has not only been done, but justice has manifestly and undoubtedly been seen to have been done without any shadow of doubt. The accused person is now going to jail for murder. You have heard the court verdict yourself. You are a journalist and you can read through the law reports when this case is officially reported in the pages of law reports. Justice has truly been served. Let us now learn from this trial that no one is above the law and if you can do the crime, you will certainly do the time. Thank you.''

Journalist: ''Mr Howard Sullivan did you at any point in time during the first trial of your client knew that he was responsible for the allegation that was put against him and if you did know, would you have still defended him in this matter and why would you do such a thing such as defending a murderer?''

Howard Sullivan: ''It is a fundamental principle of natural justice that an accused person is innocent of the allegations against him until he is proven guilty. The prosecution did not prove their assertion in the first trial and they lost their case. What you journalists do not often realise is that it really does not matter which side of the court a lawyer stands to represent a client, we owe our client a moral and legal duty to represent him or her. That is the training that we received as either a Barrister or Solicitor or both. We put mitigating factors across and it is left for the court to consider the facts of the case and the evidence in front of it as well as the mitigating factors.''

Another reporter turning to Howard stood very close to his face; he raised the microphone up close, and then asked:

Reporter: ''Are you saying that you are relieved that your client is going to serve an 18 year sentence, then why did you represent him all along in the first place?''

Howard Sullivan: ''What has happened should never have happened to the deceased but we cannot for the rest of our lives be crying over spilled milk. May Stephen's soul rest in peace and may his aged grand-mother Phoebe and fiancée Evelyn forever be comforted. What has happened has happened, we cannot turn back the hand of the clock, what we can now do is to learn lessons from what has happened, this is a case that will linger on in the minds of so many people for a long time. For now let us all go home and reflect on the judgment and victory of the rule of law that has been demonstrated in this court today. It is a privilege that we all have been a part of seeing this case from the beginning through to the end.''

Journalist: ''Mr Keith Bradford, you have been given a suspended sentence of twenty four months, you are never likely going to serve this sentence, you were an unfortunate dad who paid a heavy price for not raising up your son when it really mattered to the boy in life, what do you have to say to that?''

Keith Bradford: ''The dilemma I faced began when I set my eyes on Tom and he was exactly my carbon copy if I can put it that way. I instantly knew he was my son, but I never knew who he was, yes you can say that I have not been part of his life when it really mattered and that is the price that I have just paid today, having to stand trial alongside my child. Yes I am ashamed of myself. I am not proud of not reporting Tom's confessional statement to the police, after we returned from USA. I began to pick the pieces from a relationship I never had with my son, I began to bond with him when I realised that my son's case is almost beyond redemption. I do not wish what I have experienced throughout this trial on any living lawyer. I will for ever be grateful to Justice Tremaine Hernandez for tempering justice with mercy on me; otherwise I could have been sent down for life imprisonment.''

Journalist: ''With the awful experience you have just been through, are you going to return to CPS to work as prosecutor?''

Keith Bradford: ''Right now I honestly don't know what to think, going back to my profession is the last thing on my mind. My life is a roller coaster right now, a big part of me feels like taking time out to mourn my late wife Teresa, I let her down. I have let down the only child I have by not bringing him up the way I should and I hope people in similar situation as me thirty years ago will be courteous in the choices they make when it comes to their private family life.''

Chapter 40

The Reminiscence, (Keith Bradford)

If I could turn back the hand of the clock, then I would, there are so many things that I could have done differently. Please don't judge me. A lot has been said about what I have done wrong or what I could have done differently. I may have turned out to be a trained lawyer and attorney but my own childhood background experience was a near miss from being a disaster. I did not grow up with a male figure or role model myself, my dad had walked away on my mum when I was an infant or at least that was the story she told me when I was a child. It was when I was about to go to University of Pennsylvania to study law, that my mother called me to tell me the truth about my paternity. The story that she had previously told me when I turned 10 years old was not the right story; she was trying to shield me away from the bitter truth. The truth is that she never knew who my dad was, she had been gang raped while in college when she got pregnant of me, and she decided to keep the child, raised me all by herself. When she opened the truth up to me, I was devastated and deeply troubled. It disturbed my entire being. I could not put it behind my thought while I studied law at University. I was conceived as a result of a violent attack on my mother. I still feel the pain up till today. I have lived with it all my life. My mother's traumatic experience made her stay away from men as far as relationships were concerned.

My mother struggled on her own to raise me; she was a trained and disciplined secondary school teacher. I was lucky that she was a responsible mother. I watched my mum sometimes do up to two jobs to make ends meet. When I finished my GCSEs I had to work in the kitchen as a porter for about two years to support my mother, I started working at the age of 16 years old; the only thing I could think of for survival was to work. I grew up quicker than I should have. I never enjoyed my childhood like the other children who went clubbing, to discos or cinema to while away their time on weekends. I had to work as a kid to help my mum. I was a child saddled with adult responsibilities like paying bills and rent to help my mother. By the time I graduated I started my law career working as an attorney. The only profession that could have ever attracted me was to be a prosecutor. It is fair to think that I was so keen on seeking justice and upholding the law more than anyone else (maybe because of what happened to my mum).

I am not trying to make excuses for the mistake I made by walking away from Teresa when she needed me the most, what I am saying is that I had problems that were not resolved in my head about my paternity, I was a bitter young man and so when I met Teresa after my degree in USA and we got married I was not a patient man, I had not had a male role model all throughout my life. I was functional at work and in my profession as an attorney but I was dysfunctional as a husband and a dad. Teresa had her own demons that she was dealing with personally in her life; she was dealing with drug abuse. After the birth of our son Tom, she suffered from what I now know to be post-natal traumatic depressive disorder; she needed an understanding husband to be patient with her because her parents were based in the United States at the time and she left her family to settle down with me in the UK when we returned from the US. Teresa needed a man that would be there for her but I was always at work at the CPS, the job of a prosecutor was a very demanding one, after a hard day's work, I would come home and go into the study again to prepare for my court cases the next day. I did not have time for my family as I should. May be I should say I did not really know how to manage or run a home as a dad and husband. I can look back now and at least be logical in my thinking and be fair with apportioning blame to myself, Teresa or even Tom. I was not affected by Teresa's obesity at all, she only added weight after our first son and I did not find anything wrong with that, like some people may attribute the breakdown of our marriage to that, but that was not the case.

I should not have got married at the time I did. I was not ready. Marriage is not about just having a spouse or partner and a child, it is about being ready for the responsibility of combining home and work life and making sure that you balance both successfully. I could not manage my home and work concurrently and this is why my marriage broke down irretrievably. I simply did not know how to, but the deepest hurt that was eating me up inside within my inner man is that my head was screwed up ever since the day my mother told me that the story she initially told me about my father walking away was not the truth and that I actually did not have a dad, that she truly did not know who he was. My surname 'Bradford' was her own father's name because she did not know who my father was. This revelation disturbed me and so I found solace in my career, I worked like no man's business. What was I going to tell my own son about who his grand-dad was, I bet I could not just handle things? I walked away on a two year old son and the price for doing so is the nemesis that caught up with me today.

I should have been there for Teresa and looked after her like a husband should. I should have helped her through her rehabilitation and get her through the pain and sorrow of addiction. Tom was taken into care because Teresa could not cope with looking after him, at least we now know that assuming she was well enough she would not have lost her nursing practicing license or lost custody of her son to social services. Her husband was not with her and that made things worse, I will never forgive myself for doing that, I was a dysfunctional man that was on the run and nowhere to be found. I had a well-paid job as a prosecutor, but I ran away from family responsibilities. I never remarried after Teresa, even up till today. The issue of my unknown paternity remains unresolved.

When I asked you not to judge me, I have my reasons for saying so. This is the first time I have opened up to anyone about what my own mother had told me about my paternity. I can now move on and hopefully let go of my worries, regrets and shortcomings.

It saddens my heart to see my only child end up in prison for a good part of his life. My heart bled when he confessed to me that he truly killed Stephen. I wish I could reverse what he did. I wish I could start again from where I made the wrong choices when Tom was only 2 years old. I wish I could put things right, but it is too late. I will have to wait for 18 years before I could salvage whatever is left of Tom's life. I have to wait for 18 years before I can bond with my son, if it is ever possible.

The question that will never go away in my head is who then is my dad? At least Tom has a dad, he only walked away and now I am back, but mine was never known to my mum and that is something that I would have to continue to live with for the rest of my life. That is why I said that you should not judge me, please don't!
This is my story.

Keith Bradford was a free man but with a lot of lessons learnt. After working for 30 years as state prosecuting attorney, he decided to spend his life savings to establish a trust foundation that he named 'Teresa Trust Foundation' in memory of late Teresa Claxton, Stephen, Matthew and Phoebe. The aim of the foundation was to support women suffering from depression after the birth of a child, it was meant to help women who suffer from prolonged post-natal traumatic disorder, depression or a mild and moderate depressive disorder and people suffering from drug and substance abuse going through rehabilitation. The foundation was also meant to follow up young adults who have served long-term prison sentences and helping them to resettle back into the society by giving them Education, Employment and Training. Keith was passionate with helping women who have experienced rape incidences to go through guardian and counselling in raising up the children who are born into such families.

The Teresa Trust Foundation is also considering helping young men dealing with paternity issues similar to that of Keith Bradford.

Tom spent a total of 18 years behind bars. He benefitted from 'The Teresa Foundation' as he was sent to adult education and later was employed at the age of 48 years of age. His father Keith Bradford became a Magistrate at the age of 61 and was later on appointed as a Judge before he retired.

The End

Epilogue

"The Lawyer's Dilemma" is a debut exposit legal crime fiction on the dilemmas that lawyers, judges encounter during criminal trials. The first trial in the story revealed conflicting expert witness evidence in court trials. The burden of proof is on the prosecution and he who asserts must prove, however the task becomes onerous for the investigation and prosecution team when the lethal weapon used in a murder trial is cyanide or strychnine.

Lorna Marie, in this twisty thriller, with her gripping, giddy style, skilfully narrated the life of a prosecutor who walked away on his marriage leaving an eighteen month old son with a troubled wife battling with heroine abuse and substance misuse. The toddler was taken into social authority care and sadly he grew up to become a notorious criminal. His father who was a prosecutor later found out that his son who was his carbon copy had been involved in murder of his half-brother, Stephen, Keith a prosecutor in a bid to save his son joined the defence team to help in his son's trial. The first trial acquitted Tom due to insufficient evidence, but a re-trial will soon reveal that new admissible evidence emerged pointing to Tom as Stephen's killer.

Powerful, intensive, inspiring, gripping with giddiness as the author exposed difficulties faced by lawyers in court when evidence are conflicting or simply not sufficient to help the prosecution to prove its assertion.

"The Lawyers Dilemma" is a professional twisty thriller on a calculated murder with the use of cyanide poison by the 1st defendant to eliminate his half-brother.
The author held readers in suspense as the story unfold a revealing controversy surrounding the hero characters paternity, Keith Bradford all along, was having to deal with an

unfortunate revelation he was told by his own mother regarding his paternity, the shocking news left an indelible mark that cannot be removed from his life.

Author's Note

"The Lawyer's Dilemma" is a heart-rending story.... with a legal tour de force. Keith a prosecutor walked away from his marriage leaving his eighteen months old son and his wife who battled with depression, low self-esteem, drug addiction and substance misuse. Keith had a robust career. He never remarried after he divorced. However, his ex-wife Teresa remarried after rehabilitation and gave birth to Stephen.

After almost three decades Keith had reached the peak of his career. He was lead prosecuting attorney in a murder trial when he found out that his toddler son whom he had walked out on thirty years ago was the accused person in the murder trial.
I featured plight that some children who are fostered or adopted go through during their time in social care. Tom was a child that never knew his dad when it really mattered. His mother suffered from anxiety, panic attacks in a dark and lonely place. I touched on the consequences of addiction and mental health issues at the centre leading to low self-esteem. Teresa battled with heroin addiction following her post-natal depressive disorder.

Keith was embarrassed when he found out that his only son (who now bore his adoptive surname Blackstone and not Bradford) had become a menace and notorious criminal in the society with a record of all manner of conviction ranging from theft, rape and currently murder. His defence attorney was a strong team arguing that Tom had been fostered by several families before his adoption. The author revealed how underlining problems in childhood could be the cause of behavioural problems. Tom battled with substance misuse like his mother, but it was when he met his half-brother Steve who had travelled to England to study from Pennsylvania where he lived with his grandparents. Tom got jealous of Steve's achievement as an accountant and he conspired to have him

murdered in cold blood. The prosecutors were later to discover that Tom's motive for killing his half-brother Steve is to solely inherit the property and real estate bequeathed to Tom and Steve in the Will and Last Testament of their grand-parents: Phoebe and Matthew who lived in Pennsylvania. The use of invisible weapon in murder trial was brought to light. The difficulties that prosecution and investigation face in proving guilt and the role of expert witness during the trial. During the first trial there were conflicting report in the Consultant pathologist test result and the Forensic medical expert result, these made some of the evidence inadmissible in totality and there was balance of probabilities before the judge, the prosecution team were faced with difficulty in proving their assertion, there was insufficient evidence to render a guilty verdict, however in the re-trial, new evidence emerged from CCTV footage directly linking Tom to the crime. The author revealed difficulties that prosecution face in cases involving the use of poisonous substances like cyanide or strychnine in murder trial investigation. The second trial showcased the use of confessional statement in murder trial and its importance when Tom made a confessional statement to his dad Keith.
Each time I think again of how to end this novel, I find it hard to finish. The consequences of a father's action neglecting his son and mother at a young age and the adverse consequences. The effect of trauma of his own childhood, Keith bottled a lot inside of him, how his own mother was a victim of rape and he had to deal with his mother not knowing who his dad was. Keith had a lot to deal with himself as a person; the trauma of his mother having suffered violent gang rape which led to Keith's conception taunted Keith throughout his life. It was therefore very difficult to Judge Keith with his irrational behaviour when he could not handle or deal with family life by helping his wife. His choice of career could also have been as result of the horrific crime that his mother experienced leading to his own birth. He became obsessed with his career as if to say one day he would find the rapist who defiled his mother, perhaps that would solve his mystery of resolving his paternity problem.

Tom has had a previous convicted for raping the daughter of his adoptive parents. Tom planned to kill Stephen out of jealousy and inferiority complex. The consequences of a couple's separation and divorce and the effect it could have on the children and their development was also highlighted by the author.

This book exists and you are holding it now. The Lawyer's Dilemma is powerfully magnetic and could be heart-breaking. It is affecting and powerful, a tremendous punch with many layers of truth, how sometimes the devil that behoves us is not far-fetched, but unknown to us, comes through our bad habits that we cultivate, exposing ourselves to vulnerability, leading some people to drug abuse and substance misuse were discussed along the story lines, like Teresa picking up bad habits and suffering from post-natal depressive disorder, self-harm and so on. This story is insightful and skill-embedded, it is scotching, gripping and can't put it down while writing it, can't put it down while reading it; you just want to finish it.

Come; let us think of it, the prosecuting team missed out on a vital piece of evidence which enabled the accused person to walk free after the first trial. The CCTV footage was not discovered by the prosecuting team making it difficult to pin the crime to the accused person.

Sadly, Keith a prosecutor who has practiced his profession for 3 decades found himself perverting the course of justice when the offender turned out to be his own son. The issue of his own unresolved paternity made him emotionally weak in resisting the family tie with his own son. He was now ready to bond with Tom but he's left it too late.

If this story has affected you in any way at all, I ask that you please seek counselling. Please don't let it stop within the pages of this text. When Keith was told the truth by his mother regarding his paternity he was distraught. He should have sought the advice of a psychotherapist to help him deal with his worries instead of bottling it all inside his head, he then exploded with anger in his own marriage taking it all out on Teresa and Tom. There are many problems that come and go; they plague on us like a locust. These problems sometimes outweigh us, but let this book comfort you to know that you are not alone in this world; let this book prove to you that we are human, we can err; be it a lawyer, judge or prosecutor young or old, yet we can always do something about our error.

There is a lot that communication can do to save the day. Talking and speaking out helps; we can do something about our emotional instability at a time when family relationships experience separation or divorce, we need counselling on what we need to do when a member of our family or someone we know is experiencing drug misuse and abuse, let us speak out and talk to someone. Don't shy away from counselling if that is what you need, or maybe thorough rehabilitation for addiction to misuse of banned substances.

There is a lesson in this book for everyone. Rest in peace Steven. Thank you to the two lawyers Nigel Stanley and Howard Sullivan, both attorneys stood the first trial and the re-trial. It must have been so difficult for Nigel Stanley prosecuting his colleague Keith was also a prosecutor but had to stand trial of his son. The four investigation team officers were brilliant. Thanks to the CCTV footage and control room team for releasing vital evidence, if not, Tom may not have been re-tried. Thanks to technology.

The two expert witnesses were brilliant: the forensic medical expert and consultant pathologist, the question as to admissibility of some of the conflicting evidence during court trial. An invisible lethal weapon like cyanide or strychnine will always be difficult to prove by any prosecutor or investigation team.

The incessant kidnapping currently plaguing Nigeria needs to be addressed by the government, lawyers, Judges and legislators, there are security challenges in both the Northern and Southern Nigeria. Thank you to prosecuting attorney during Tom's trial who brought in the facts surrounding the kidnapping and abduction of Steve while he was on holiday in Nigeria during his world tour. Would there have been another loss of life if the tourists were not able to hand over the huge amount of money that they were held to ransom for. It is now time for change and time to nib kidnapping in the bud for the safety of both Nigerians and foreign visitors into the country. Kidnapping is the taking away of a person by force, threat, or deceit, with intent to cause him or her to be detained against his or her will. Kidnapping may be done for ransom or for political or other purposes. Abduction is the criminal taking away a person by persuasion, by fraud, or by open force or violence.

I was at the concluding part of my book when the Covid-19 (Corona virus) epidemic began and when I reflected on how Tom poisoned the late Steve with Cyanide in my story it opened my thoughts to various debates and discussions going on about the mystery of Covid-19, an unprecedented deadly virus that took so many lives away from the planet earth, it makes me wonder whether the best way to conclude my note is by adding some on-going debate on the use of biomedical weapon in disguise of a natural virus…it feels strange and don't know what to make of an invisible virus that brought the world to a lock down…like a mystery or could it have been that an attack took the world by surprise? Or was it a plague? Or is it just another re-occurrence like the *Spanish flu pandemic of 1918/19,* over 50 million people died world-wide and a quarter of the British population were affected. The **death** toll was 228,000 in Britain alone. Global mortality rate is not known, but is estimated to have been between 10% to 20% of those who were infected. With the Corona virus pandemic, the impact of this infectious disease was catastrophic as the disease started by attacking humans so rapidly that the spread went quickly more than any country's medical infrastructure delivery system could cope with,

suddenly the world was faced with a state of emergency, an unprecedented and uncertain times as so many people died across the world. Unlike the impact of the use of cyanide on the deceased in *The Lawyer's Dilemma* story, Covid-19 we were made to believe was a virus at the time of the epidemic, according to scientists, in a simplified form Covid-19 prefers to reside in the coldest part of the human body i.e. in the upper respiratory tract in between the upper nasal passages and the nasal cavity in the upper respiratory tract. Once the virus settles, it starts multiplying rapidly and day four onwards it starts to move to the trachea the bronchus and eventually into the lungs. It starts destroying the lung cells and in response to defend the lungs produces hug amount of mucus. Pneumonia follows and breathing becomes difficult and the patient dies of suffocation unless put on a ventilator. It was mysterious.
As the corona virus epidemic affected the whole world and all it's continent, there was one big lesson for developing African countries to learn from the outbreak, and that is for the presiding democratic elected government in those countries to provide and maintain standardised basic medical systems and infrastructure for the country because for over 50 years, citizens of some of these countries have been begging their government to do the needful, but leaders turned deaf ears to the people's cry. They focused on their own pockets for their children and unborn generations. The corona virus outbreak came at time when some medical infrastructure in some of the states in the country had not been put right for the citizens to enjoy, it is a well-known fact that the rich and affluent would often fly out of the country to receive medical treatment in Europe, America, Saudi Arabia instead of improving medical facilities in Nigeria in order to make life bearable and access to medical treatment suitable and affordable for all. During the peak of the corona virus epidemic countries in Europe, the United States, the United Kingdom, Africa and Asia closed their borders making it difficult for Nigerian government official to fly out of the country to receive medical treatment abroad, they were forced to use the hospitals and medical facilities of which some were in a shameful condition, what

made it worse is that the government reserves are empty and fully drained and it was time for both the rich and poor and even the government officials to suffer together the poor medical facility along side poor citizens who have been deprived for over 50 years. It was a moment marked with reality that everyone in Africa had to face the scourge. The big lesson therefore is for African government to learn from the Covid-19 outbreak - that even developed countries with advancement in technology and medical infrastructure managed to contain the epidemic, they could not have accommodated sick patients from abroad under the circumstances, African leaders therefore should use their country resources to develop their medical infrastructure for the common good of their citizens and for themselves too because this is what they have been elected into their political posts to do for their citizens.

'Lornamarie did her research and this book shows it. She keeps the reader in suspense with its twists and turns. I couldn't put it down.' – James O'Brian
"This story is insightful and skill-embedded. It is scorching, gripping, and you just want to finish reading it" – Crime fiction lover.

About the Author

Lorna Marie was born in Islington, London, before leaving for Lagos where she attended Marywood Grammar School and Methodist Girls High School, Lagos, Nigeria. In 1986, she bagged an award as the overall best student in her A-level examination result. Consequently, she gained admission to study Law at the prestigious University of Lagos, popularly known as Unilag.

She obtained her LL.B (Hons) degree with honours at the University of Lagos in 1989. In 1990, Lorna attended the Nigerian Law School, Victoria Island, Lagos, and after completing the bar final examinations was called to bar as a barrister and solicitor of the Supreme Court of Nigeria. The author is a member of the Author's Alliance, headquartered in the United States. She is also a member of the British and Irish Association of Law Librarians (BIALL). Lorna adores preserving the memory of humanity, reviewing library books and managing knowledge, covering a wide range of subjects wherever possible.

Lorna Marie is the writer of: The Judges and Lawyers Companion, How to Write a Good Dissertation, a guide for university undergraduate students, and The Power of Words to The Human Spirit, Soul, Body and Mind: a compendium of great speeches by world leaders and some landmark court judgements. She is the author of The Crime Fiction thriller novel ''The Plea on Oath''. She has inspired the young generation of writers at 'meet the author' events in schools, colleges and libraries. She also co-ordinates a book reading club for children. She is a Chartered Librarian and Information professional. She has a deep sense of humour. Lorna is married with two children.

Lorna Adekaiyaoja is the Winner of the BNLF 2019 Award in recognition for Community Service.

Also available by Lorna Marie
(Nonfiction)
The Judges and Lawyers Companion

How to Write a Good Dissertation:
A Guide for University Undergraduate Students

The Power of Words to the Human Mind, Spirit, Soul and Body: Great Speeches by World Leaders and Some Landmark Court Judgements and Rulings

The Plea on Oath

Author Award

Author Award

Lightning Source UK Ltd.
Milton Keynes UK
UKHW022237130522
402993UK00003B/154

9 781716 921704